Bone Idle in the Charnel House

RHYS HUGHES

BONE IDLE
IN THE
CHARNEL HOUSE

A Collection of Weird Stories

Hippocampus Press

New York

Acknowledgements: See p. 245.

Published by Hippocampus Press
P.O. Box 641, New York, NY 10156.
http://www.hippocampuspress.com

Cover art © 2014 by Mike Dubisch
Cover design by Barbara Briggs Silbert.
Hippocampus Press logo designed by Anastasia Damianakos.

First Edition
1 3 5 7 9 8 6 4 2
ISBN13: 978-1-61498-087-2

Contents

Introduction

I am a "weird" writer but not in the traditional sense. I guess this makes me an odd weird writer, rather than a normal weird writer. Does an extra weirdness ultimately result in more weirdness, or do two weirdnesses multiply together like negative integers to produce a positive? I don't know.

That wasn't a serious question, of course, but it does seem a reasonable idea at this point for me to briefly outline my personal history regarding "weird" fiction and how I see my own role within this remarkable artform; and an artform it truly is, rather than merely a "genre," for the literature of the weird is one of the great cultural triumphs of humanity and I am a humble part of it.

As are all those who read and write in it. As are you.

It was Edgar Allan Poe who first filled me with a deep and abiding love of weird fiction, for although I had read a few H. G. Wells novels before discovering Poe, there was a rich darkness in Poe that instantly overwhelmed my soul in a way that Wells had not. Wells appealed to my intellect; Poe appealed primarily to my emotions but *also* to my intellect, for Poe was a cerebral writer, a bold ideas writer, as much as an atmospheric one—a fact that is often overlooked.

I was fifteen years old and the story that introduced me to Poe was "The Tell-Tale Heart." It was the first time I had encountered a mad (and perhaps unreliable) narrator in fiction, and I felt the rules had suddenly changed, or rather that I was now aware of how much more potential there was in literature than I had previously imagined. So I became an immediate Poe enthusiast and devoured all his work, even descending into obscure basements of libraries to seek out his rarely reprinted works and marginalia. I was a bona fide Poe devotee. I *worshipped* Poe.

It should go without saying that I admired enormously his famous tales, "The Fall of the House of Usher," "The Murders in the Rue Morgue," "The Cask of Amontillado," and all the others most closely associated with his name; but I also found something peculiar happening. I found myself enjoying even more keenly those less renowned stories that may be called his "comedies," though the humour in them tends to be grim and gruesome rather than light-hearted and sunny.

Some of these comedies mirror the serious tales but with distortions that are very unexpected, so that ultimately they can be more disturbing than the thing they reflect. In a few cases the comedies came first, for it is a misconception that comedy always feeds off seriousness and is never archetypal. Not infrequently, brand new ideas are engendered within a comedic context and pass outwards into the world of the serious tale, where they are tamed and standardised.

In "A Predicament," the minute hand that is moving to slice through the neck of Signora Psyche Zenobia, after she manages to get her head stuck in a church clock, is a surprising version of the blade that is descending to rend the breast of the unnamed narrator of "The Pit and the Pendulum." The situations are not dissimilar, but there is more irony in the clock than in the execution device. And it was the *irony* that I responded to. I am an irony addict, and I first learned of my addiction (and possibly even acquired it) thanks to Edgar Allan Poe.

A short list of his more offbeat and ironic tales that made such a deep impression on me might include "The Duc de L'Omelette," "Loss of Breath," "The Man That Was Used Up," "Never Bet the Devil Your Head," "The Angel of the Odd," and the utterly remarkable and vastly underrated "The Thousand and Second Tale of Scheherazade," in which the irony is exquisitely bitter, imaginative, and amusing at the same time, a satire that is simultaneously a sincere science fiction story and an acute and ingenious piece of analytical philosophical fiction.

Poe is a gateway through which many readers pass into the greater landscapes of weird fiction, and the path onto which he discharges them often takes them directly to Lovecraft and from there to modern horror; and so might have been the case with me had I not chanced on Voltaire's *Candide,* a picaresque triumph of a philosophic novel that, in combination with Poe's odder work, served both to confirm and to strengthen my enthusiasm for intolerably ironic comedy.

With no attempt at presenting a naturalistic basis to the action, or even a realistic starting point for his characters to embark from into the most extreme of ludicrous situations, Voltaire showed that vérité is superfluous in certain texts and that ideas can be enough on their own; indeed, that when great ideas are embedded and developed in a richly stylised format the result can be as thrilling as the darkest hallucinations of subtly generated psychological and spiritual terror.

When given a proper chance, the absurd is as delirious as the mystical. This is the lesson I learned from Voltaire. And so I ended up on a path different from that on which the majority of weird fictioneers tread. But I maintain that the paths, while apparently separate, do cross over at numerous points.

Kafka is one of those junctions. Borges and Calvino too.

Discovering the work of those writers was another series of revelations for me. In Kafka I found unarguable verification of something I had long suspected but hadn't been able to clarify adequately for myself—namely, that the delays of civilised life are the factors of an authentic nightmare rather than the minor inconveniences they are usually claimed to be; and that to dismiss the intensity of the frustrating oppressions of everyday existence is to fuel that nightmare.

Nonetheless, Kafka's work is still humorous and his colleagues often reported that he was overcome by laughter and unable to proceed during private readings. One may imagine that it was bitter, dark laughter, but laughter all the same. And the particular ambiences through which his characters move, not always in shadow, are scarcely less spectral than the moods of sensationalist Gothic fiction. Comedy is a serious business and sometimes even more than that: a tragedy.

Borges is a writer I chanced upon by accident, my hand plucking a volume of his stories from a library shelf for no reason other than that I was intrigued by the title, *The Book of Sand.* Borges demonstrated to me that the intellectual side of Poe was alive and well, that it had evolved into a form so pure it glittered; for the mind-games that Borges likes to play with his readers have precise geometrical lines and the smoothest of surfaces. Borges is mathematical and his symmetries are terrible, and yet they can be endured, for they are invigorating too.

Borges is the ultimate, or one of the ultimates, of a kind of fiction that has a name in German: *gedanken*. This category is small but vital and contains stories that have a mathematical or logical problem or puzzle at their core, which is then solved through the unfolding of the plot. They are almost wholly intellectual in substance and intent, and yet I maintain that the emotional satisfaction they can provide is equal to that of the most heart-rending tragedies, acutest comedies, or most soul-stretching visions of mystic grandeur. There can be cerebral catharsis as well as catharsis of the spirit, and the satisfaction provided by *gedanken* is as atavistic as any, for humans are problem solvers by nature. It is our primitive urge.

Calvino, for me, is the great synthesist, blending the concerns of the heart with the wonders of the head; he has a foot in the liquid mirror of rigorous logical ideas where Borges dwells and another in the thicket of human emotions on the far side of fiction, and thus he is easily able to be a realist, fabulist, artificer of awe, tragedian, minstrel, magus, and trickster. To many readers Calvino isn't a familiar deity in the pantheon of orthodox "weird" writers, but he is among those demigods nonetheless and he deserves attention from all disciples of the literature of imagination. There need not be tension between the sects. The destination is the same.

And that destination, that objective, is to explore worlds, ideas, and moods beyond the mundane, the dull, the trivial, and the utilitarian. For myself, the journey is best made in the company of those authors who adore and manipulate the absurd, the paradoxes and contradictions of many different kinds of logic, not merely the logic of everyday events but that of word- and ideas-association too, the lateral thinkers, rubber science researchers, rogue conceptualists and wild thought experimenters, the wizards of wise whimsy. Thus, aside from the authors I have already cited above, I am most forcefully enthused by Queneau, Perec, Pavić, Lem, and Vian.

It is extremely important for me to stress here most strongly that I don't regard the more traditional types of weird fiction to be in any way lesser than the idiosyncratic and more mathematical kind I most deeply enjoy. They are different but based on the same fundamentals. The vagaries of atmospheric chaos in an orthodox ghost story and geometric thought experiments of the *gedanken* are all part of the Family Fantastical. It all goes back to Poe, from whom more than one path emerged, and all those on any of those paths are comrades and fellow travellers.

Bone Idle in the Charnel House

The Swinger

There was a haunted tree in the garden of the hotel. Everyone knew it was a haunted tree, though they treated it as a joke or a mascot, something that didn't need to be taken seriously. Only Uncle Dylan had authentic respect for the old tales, the gnarled legends.

It was the highest cedar among a dozen others, and a curiously straight branch jabbed out near the very top, like the crossbeam of a gallows. The stories insisted that no bird dared perch there; but I saw several ravens in a line on it once, and I waved at them.

One of my habits, waving at birds, an energy-efficient royal wave that must look absurd to anyone else. I have been doing it since I was a child, secretly with much embarrassment, like those people who salute magpies by pretending to scratch their foreheads.

This tree was part of my soul and my dreams.

But I never looked at it properly.

It was with amazement that I realised that the reason why it was higher than its neighbours was simply because it stood on the summit of a grassy mound, a bizarrely symmetrical cone of densely packed soil. The tree was actually fairly short, compacted, stunted.

Uncle Dylan had hung lanterns in the limbs of the other cedars, paper spheres with little candles inside, so that they resembled gigantic oranges that had suddenly appeared where they shouldn't; but the haunted tree he left undecorated in the evenings, a stark silhouette against the starry sky. I didn't believe he had no spare lanterns.

"It's for the sake of the guests," he told me once.

"I'm not fooled by that," I said.

He sighed and shrugged, then turned to wipe clean the beer glasses. A fire of logs snapped and hissed in the grate; the click of cribbage pegs and the plucking of a harp; the creak of the rusty sign outside. These made the music of the place, a false re-enactment of a time that never truly existed, the merry days of yore, of pastoral life.

Uncle Dylan was obsessed with his personal vision of what the ancient times must have been like. In vain I objected to his notions and explained in detail the brutality endured by our remote ancestors. The good yeomen waded in filth; they crouched in squalor; for the most part, they beat each other with sticks. But he wouldn't listen.

Matthew Loveday, a writer and historian, shared similar utopian ideals and mindlessly approved every one of Uncle Dylan's prejudices, agreeing that the hotel had stood on the spot for eight hundred years at least, that a monastery had existed here before it, that primitive men had danced to an unknown god thousands of years earlier around standing stones that must have been carted away by a greedy king.

Like most of our long-term guests, Loveday was from England, and he had come here to sample a past long since covered by concrete in his own land. Uncle Dylan lived up to his expectations perfectly, even playing the old raconteur with greater than usual relish, lighting a pipe stuffed with a foul and oily smuggled tobacco and saying:

"Oh, yes! We have a ghost. A man of letters like yourself. I found him swinging one morning under the tree, dangling on the end of a long rope from the highest branch. And now his spirit wanders the garden wailing. A miserable sod. Does he rattle things? He ransacked the kitchen, looking for a knife with which to cut himself down."

"And did he find one?" Loveday asked, gazing through the window at the haunted tree with a pensive expression.

"No," said Uncle Dylan, abruptly and with a scowl.

"So his ghost is unsatisfied?"

"Yes, yes! And they say he seeks one like himself to give him aid; but I don't know who 'they' are to say such things, so I can't be certain and I can't even ask them to hold their tongues."

"Why should anyone wish to hold their tongue?"

Uncle Dylan thrust out his own pink organ from between his thick lips and clutched it in both hands; that's how large a tongue he had. For a full minute he held it, then let it go; it slithered back into his mouth like a chastised flatworm, and Uncle Dylan's throat pulsated as if it wanted to slide down even deeper than was normal.

"It's not an unpleasant thing to do, that's why."

"I don't suppose it is," said Loveday.

I smiled into my beer. The wind whistled around the house. Indeed, it was getting quite eerie again. The fire in the hearth was dying; the embers glowed faintly in a gale howling down the chimney. As the mischievous Uncle Dylan spouted more of his nonsense, and as Loveday leaned closer to hear it, I couldn't resist an interruption.

"It won't last," I said. "They're all coming down, every last one of the cedars. The entire garden will be concreted over. Then a car park, electric lighting, and satellite television aerial . . ."

Uncle Dylan scowled. It had taken me a year to persuade him that the hotel would be better off without the overgrown wilderness of a garden. Ecologically minded, he had objected to the felling of trees on principle, but yielded after I made him aware of a few facts concerning increased profits. The haunted tree he wanted to be made exempt, of course. Finally I'd persuaded him that it would look so ungainly standing atop its mound all by itself that we really had no choice.

"Times do change," he finally admitted to himself. Loveday, however, didn't seem at all disconcerted by this threat to his beloved past, this end of a heritage right under his very nose. He was in high good humour. His latest novel, he explained, had just been published. It was, he felt sure, his masterpiece, an effort that would finally secure his place in the pantheon of great moderns. He drained his glass.

"Let's drink to my success and to the next one!"

He bought a round for the three of us. I felt uncomfortable sipping the ale of a man I eagerly wanted to disillusion, to drown in disappointment, to send back to England, his tales between his legs. I can't explain why I felt this aversion to the man. An instinct.

"There's a legend about the man who hanged himself," Uncle Dylan said in a very small voice, and I blinked at him.

"Do you have to? I've heard them all many times."

"Not this one, you haven't."

"What do you mean?" in my sharpest tone.

"I've kept it to myself all these years. I *am* allowed to have secrets that you don't. There's no law against that."

"Well, tell us the legend!" gasped Loveday.

He was desperate to know more, to gather every fact, every fiction and speck of rumour, every flake of hearsay about the case. Why it fascinated him so intensely, I couldn't understand.

"It is said that if a man manages to hang himself in that garden *higher* than the top of the haunted tree, he'll earn the right to live in any period of history he desires. Myself, I would go right back to the Middle Ages, to the time of Llewellyn the Great; but though I believe the legend, I just can't think of a way of fulfilling its terms."

Loveday was impressed by this. He drank his beer in slow gulps like a man drinking his own excellent destiny.

"Time travel through hanging," he said at last.

Uncle Dylan nodded. "Apparently."

"How can this be possible? You are talking nonsense!" I interjected, a false but enormous grin on my face. "The man killed himself two decades ago; he's not a legend yet, not a tradition."

Uncle Dylan swivelled his head like an owl, his eyes unmoving, facing me with an infinite weariness, and sighed. "Yes, the legend of the hanged man predates the reality of the event. Why should that be impossible? It's an assumption that a legend follows the truth; it's a distortion of the facts. After all, it's time travel we are debating."

"We're not *debating* anything," I snarled bitterly.

Loveday turned once again to stare through the window at the tree and the mound. He spoke without caring whether we heard or not. "The story is ridiculous, no doubt about it, but that's no argument against it. In fact, it has a ring of truth about it on some level."

A harp player on a nearby table struck a soft chord.

"You are mad, both of you," I said.

Uncle Dylan nodded. "Absolutely. But so are you."

My mood lightened. I laughed and stood and bade them goodnight. It was early, but I had a headache and stiff neck. Better to leave them to their strange games and hobbies, the defective worship of a past glued together from memories of films and novels, where archers in green trousers shot arrows at juggled apples and damsels wore hats as tall as towers, ribbons streaming from them like levitating rivers.

I lay on my hard bed, my skeleton shifting inside me, the storm outside getting worse and creaking anything it could, including the teeth of the howling dog in the rain somewhere who bit the wind valiantly, foolishly, annoyingly until midnight clanged on the church clock in the village, the dull notes whipped away, carried off like pewter plates by hungry pirates, for the coast was once infested with them.

Sleep eluded me, and I felt almost suffocated or crushed by the weight of the cliché I seemed to have become embedded in; the stormy night, a feeling of helplessness in the face of forces supernatural, malign perhaps or just impossible, which is almost as bad.

But at last I had to admit defeat and get up, dress myself, and stand at the tiny warped window of my attic room.

And then came the flash of lightning that confirmed my suspicions I wasn't a real man but an actor in a drama, a cheaply produced horror play or film; for the tree seemed flat, a cardboard cut-out, in the instantaneous glare of the electric discharge; and from the highest branch swung a man, the puppet I knew to be Matthew Loveday.

I remained calmer than perhaps I should have. I stood for a full minute and peered into the darkness, waiting for the next flash before I went into action. I don't understand this delay; I think it was just bafflement or even a strange sort of boredom. Then the thunder boomed and knocked me out of my complacency like a sonic elbow in the ribs. I flinched, turned and ran down the stairs to the hotel's rear door.

The next flash, even brighter and more intense, came while I was still on the stairwell. I smelled it and felt my hairs prickle. I heard heavy feet somewhere, one of the guests or else a strange acoustic trick. Probably not Uncle Dylan, who was such a deep sleeper he was difficult to rouse even at times of emergency. Once when a lorry crashed into the lobby of the hotel in the early hours, after the driver fell asleep at the wheel, Uncle Dylan remained blissfully lost in dreams.

I reached the bottom of the stairs, twisted the door handle, and felt the punch of the wind on my creased brow. I had to lean forward at an absurd angle in order to push myself across the threshold into the garden. The door slammed behind me so loudly that it came off its hinges and clattered to the floor in time with the next roll of thunder. The body was kicking; it wasn't too late to save him.

"Loveday, you fool! What sort of game is this?" I cried.

My useless words of chastisement, a sop to my own feelings of guilt at not hurrying faster to his assistance, were shredded by the wind, mangled into disconnected sounds, grunts, and clicks.

I raced across the sodden lawn to the haunted tree. The long grass was undulating, lapping at my legs as I plunged forward. I was aware that the tree was a likely target for a lightning strike, being the tallest object in the vicinity, but I felt no concern about that.

My desire seemed simply to reach the legs of the dying man, to touch his feet, to console him with my presence. There was no way I could cut him down, for I had forgotten to bring a knife. But I didn't return to the hotel to fetch one. My quest was spiritual.

That sounds ludicrous, callous, deluded, and doubtless my response to this tragedy was all three. But I'm not justifying myself, merely reporting my actions. I felt drunk, not wholly sane; but a part of my mind retained a lucidity that sneered at the rest of me, at my impetuous dash across damp electric tingling shadows to stand under the shoes of a suicide. Already he was kicking with less force, twitching less.

I stumbled to a halt near him. He had used a very long rope and he was lucky that the drop hadn't decapitated him. Perhaps he had somehow let himself down gradually. His feet were six feet above the lawn; to one side stood the mound, and the tree reared up from the rounded apex of that, so he was suspended at a lower point than the base of the trunk. I found this a fascinating paradox; a man who had hanged himself successfully at a level lower than the tree itself. I stood and shook.

Water streamed over my face. Another flash of lightning made crazy shadows of twisted branches and leaves. Then the shadow of the rope no longer hung straight but began gently oscillating from side to side. Weird how I noticed this from the shadow before learning it from the rope itself, almost as if I couldn't bear to regard as real the scene before me; I had to have it filtered through its own silhouettes.

Like a pendulum gathering momentum, the dying body of Loveday on the end of its vicious tether was pushed by the wind in a growing arc. The whoosh of its passage through the air was audible despite the aftershocks of thunder that echoed in the labyrinths of my ears. I retreated a step, as if a blade swung there in place of a flesh body.

"This is a travesty. Please stop!" I howled at nobody.

But I was rightly ignored, not merely by Loveday but by circumstances also. The tree, the storm, the night, the thick atmosphere of viciousness, my own fear in my own bones, everything.

The invisible hands of an adult wind imparted energy to this man, who was a sullen dying child, with as much efficiency as if he were perched on a playground swing and had to be set in motion by an outside force before he could utilise his legs to keep going, to make the arc wider by swinging his heavy limbs back and forth rhythmically.

As the rope tightened to take the strain it began to sing a note, to drone an accompaniment to the thunder's occasional timpani. On stage with this minimal percussive orchestra of nightmare, I watched the metronome that had once been a writer swing wider and wider, his tempo increasing as an unnatural harmony was established between the gusts and his kicking legs that served to propel him continually faster.

I fought a desire to fling myself forward onto him, to clutch at his legs, less to slow him down than to be taken away, to experience the wildness of the ride, to replay with perverted nostalgia the bravest adventures of a childhood spent swinging from trees on ropes.

The pendulum gathered energy, the pitch of the stretched note rasped higher, and the branch sagged but did not snap.

I moved away, common sense prevailing inside me, the consequences of a collision with his rushing body too bruising to contemplate. I shook my head, in admiration or perhaps exasperation.

Now his swing was so wide that his body was horizontal at the end of each arc, and although the stretched tendons in his neck audibly twanged even over the roar of the storm, I knew he still wasn't dead, that in fact he had no intention of permitting himself to die until he was quite ready. The futility of the stunt appalled me, the faith he had placed in a possibly fake legend, in muttered beery words in a dim room.

"Uncle Dylan, this is your fault!" I hissed, as I turned to look back at a dark façade, the hotel without a single lit window, the panes of glass like fossilised eyelids, a cold hive of insane rumours.

Matthew Loveday was now close to achieving the highest ambition of any amateur swinger, the complete loop. It was clear that this had been a part of the scheme all along, his and the wind's.

I fell to my knees in the grass, privileged to be a witness.

Then it happened. Lightning photographed the event, a perfect circle, a wheel with a single half-alive spoke; and gathering momentum, he looped the loop again, and then a third time, until like a motor cranked into life he began spinning at a dizzying rate, the dreadfully fascinating afterimage of his suicide becoming a disc with a solid rim.

The base of the tree began to shift in its setting, rocking slightly every time he passed, working itself loose, almost as if brass screws had jumped free from an engine block, and moist black earth around the roots bubbled and trickled like water down the side of the mound. I started laughing and pointing and reeling, briefly mad, for I guessed exactly what was going to happen. The legend was about to destroy itself.

Matthew Loveday was now whirling at such a ferocious velocity that I supposed he had reinforced his neck somehow, perhaps by swallowing a hollow metal tube. Decapitation would have been assured otherwise. The roots of the tree were almost fully exposed now, and the soil of the mound was crumbling fast around them as the trunk jerked violently from side to side, a rotten tooth wobbling in diseased gums.

Another flash of lightning blinded me. In the darkness that followed a heartbeat later, I heard a dreadful sucking sound.

My vision cleared. The tree was gone. I looked up and saw it rising, a wooden rocket pulled by an inverted man towards the zenith, applauded magisterially by the loudest peal of thunder yet.

Then it vanished between muddy clouds. The rain whipped at my face, as if to punish it for an act of unknown insolence, and I exhaled all the air in my lungs, deflating my body and my mind.

Something fell back, a clod of earth or black stone, and bounced across the lawn like a bomb, but it didn't explode. It tumbled into bushes, but I watched it only from the corner of one eye. My attention was focussed on the closed clouds, those drawn curtains of brown and grey clotted vapour, a veil thick enough to smother as well as conceal.

And then, as I had expected and hoped and dreaded, they parted again to return the tree to its sessile roost, to drop it vertically like a sepia film in reverse into the gaping socket where it had stood. It bored through the mound, a gigantic flechette, and completely vanished into the soft earth. I lurched forward on legs stiffened by the electric current in the air, scaling the crumbling slope with considerable difficulty.

The tree had buried itself. Albino mists drifted limply out of the hole it had made, the pit that led down into the centre of the mound, from which a length of rope also straggled, thick rope with a rough itchy noose at the exposed end. I saw this when I reeled it in.

Then I sat down on the cold steam and laughed.

The tightened noose was empty.

I walked back to the hotel with a lowered head. I felt at that moment that I would never be able to lift it again, that it was safer to proceed through life with my chin on my chest, to prevent any noose being placed around *my* neck, whether by my own hand or through the malice of others. When I passed through the broken doorway, I forgot this fear. The dying storm was moving away, taking madness with it.

There was a shuffling at the top of the stairs, and a figure moved in the overlapping cones of wan light from a candlestick with two branches and two stubs of sputtering tallow jammed into it. "The storm has brought the power lines down," said a sleepy voice. "We have been plunged into the past, but nobody asked for our permission."

"A cliché," I answered him, but without a sneer.

Uncle Dylan was dressed in comical style, with a spotted red nightcap so long it hung down to his waist and striped yellow pyjamas that clashed with it so horribly I was convinced a nasty joke was being played, that the events of the night had been manufactured.

"Is it worth going outside? I'll have to get my slippers."

"Do they have curly toes?" I sighed.

He nodded, and I began tramping up the stairs towards him, partly to ensure he would retreat, for there wasn't enough room for two to pass. I stood before him on the landing and rested one arm on his shoulder and then I told him what had happened, that Loveday was dead, that his body might have come down on a neighbouring property, possibly without his head, which would land somewhere else.

"Can you be certain about any of this?" he retorted.

There was a note of weary aggression in his voice that baffled me, as if he considered me too stubborn to learn an obvious lesson. We regarded each other with shocked hostility for half a minute, then he softened and in the dropped light as one of the candle flames died he said, "Let's fetch beer for ourselves. We deserve it, don't we?"

"First we should look into his room," I replied.

Uncle Dylan shrugged. Matthew Loveday had occupied a space in one of the many haphazard extensions that had been added to the edifice over the years. It was triangular in shape with a warped ceiling and suitable for any dreamer who equated impractical with quaint. The door was shut but unlocked, and we crowded inside and frowned, disapproving inspectors of geometry and clutter, the leavings of a life.

"He used a typewriter, do you believe it? The stubborn fool."

"A romantic," corrected Uncle Dylan.

"There's a sheet of paper in the machine. Step closer."

Uncle Dylan pulled it out, forgetting to operate the release mechanism and tearing the page slightly. It was a letter addressed to him. Licking his lips, he gave it to me and held the sickly flame at an angle, dripping wax onto the bare floorboards with an audible and regular click, like a rain of insects. "I don't like reading," he grumbled.

I recited it softly in the still air of the doomed man's room, in that old and infinitely lonely isosceles of futile dreams. I spoke as if I really was Matthew Loveday, and my voice changed, adopted his accent and pauses, his timorous yet determined tone. Uncle Dylan shut his eyes, swaying and nodding but keeping the candle flame steady.

"I always knew," I began, "that one day I would sit down and write a suicide note, but this isn't it, so don't squeeze sad expressions from your face too hard or you might damage a muscle. There's no need for either of us to feel awkward. Your company was enjoyable enough, but I won't miss it too much because I don't belong in this *time*. The modern world disgusts me, so I've decided to take a gamble on the truth of the legend you told me and hang myself into another age.

"It's a desperate measure, but if it doesn't work I won't notice, and if it does I'll be free, at least as free as anyone has ever been, for it might be the case that freedom itself is an illusion. No matter. I intend to stay alive if I can, but not in this century. I choose to go back to the era that my new novel is set in, the Dark Ages right here at this precise site, just before the founding of the monastery, if that structure ever existed. I want to live for real the daydreams that I have turned into prose.

"My novel was carefully researched, but how can it be accurate when so little is known about that period of history? In fact, it's safer to say that this part of Wales in the seventh century was *outside* history altogether. I know there are absurdities in my book, incorrect patterns and behaviours, catastrophes of detail, solecisms, other errors. I'll correct them if I can. If I do establish myself among the local people without being pitchforked to death I will rewrite my novel, but more faithfully.

"When it is done, I'll waterproof it most carefully, wrap it in layers of skins, and seal it in a box, closing all air holes with resin. Then I'll bury it at the top of the sacred mound and plant a tree there, a cedar, the very tree that has haunted you for so long. Look for the box, open it, and offer what you find to my publisher as a superior second edition. Of course, all this is a long shot, but what's so fine about short shots? I might even end up as a ghost in your hotel, the one that haunted myself . . ."

I finished and allowed the letter to slide out of my hand and glide into the shadows. Uncle Dylan cleared his throat. "He asked about ghosts but never said anything about being haunted himself. Maybe he thought the correct etiquette was to suffer in silence?"

"Not all hauntings are unpleasant," I answered.

"But by his own ghost? Ugh!"

"If he *had* been haunted by himself, that would have given him plenty of encouragement that he did succeed in travelling into the past. It makes a dreadful kind of sense," I conceded.

"What shall we do now? The box?"

"It must have been entangled in the roots of the tree. I saw something fall out of the sky. It's worth a quick search."

We should have waited until morning, of course, but I was too eager to prove or disprove the outrageous conclusion to the entire adventure. Rain and wind had dropped to a minimum, but Uncle Dylan's candle still went out. It didn't matter. On hands and knees I fumbled in the bushes and pulled out the worn box, mud-spattered, decaying.

Curiously warm to the touch it was, and I took it inside before opening it with a chisel. Under layers of mouldy skins a pallid manuscript gleamed at us. I picked it up and it didn't crumble. The ink was faded but legible and the language was modern English.

"You do realise the whole thing could be a hoax?" I said.

"That would be even more far-fetched."

"Yes, I guess so. I think I'll start reading it now, but I haven't read the first version yet. Does it matter, I wonder?"

Uncle Dylan shrugged. He was good at shrugging. A notable shrugger in any situation that required one. He went to pour beer and brought me a full glass of thick black foam, and I sipped. He drank his own glass faster and soon went for a refill, and then another.

He eventually guzzled enough and left me alone. I kept turning pages and moving my moist lips as I read; it seemed more respectful. The tale was enthralling and presumably extremely accurate, a superb evocation of life as it had been back then. The irony was that the publisher eventually rejected it as a replacement for the original.

"An inferior and implausible rewrite," was his judgment. He reprinted the first edition, and I returned from my fruitless trip to London with sighs stuck in my throat like unripe cherries. When I reached the hotel I learned that Uncle Dylan had acquired a new guest.

"Jerome Nightjar," with an unconvincing flourish.

"Will you be staying long?" I asked.

"I hope so. Months," he replied.

"He's very similar to Matthew," Uncle Dylan whispered to me, "and I have given him the triangular room."

He wore casual but smart clothes with a pale blue shirt missing the top buttons. There was a scorch mark around his throat, as if friction had done him a recent disservice. I wondered about the inhabitants who had greeted Matthew Loveday all those centuries ago, who had beheld a similar mark on his neck but who tolerated his presence anyway, even allowing him to plant a tree on the summit of a sacred mound.

"Oh yes! We have a ghost," Uncle Dylan was saying in his usual bluff manner; and I snapped back to the present.

Jerome Nightjar grinned immensely.

A large bird flew past the window. I waved at it.

Bitter in Sour

I had been tired in Bitlis, but this was the first time I had been sour in Tyre. I wandered the streets. Why was I so sour? It had something to do with a woman, but my memory is vague on the details. Too much time has passed. I was looking for her or trying to forget her, I am unsure which, but whether I found or lost her is beyond my conjecture. Even her name eludes me. Whatever the precise nature of my sourness I needed a place to stay. The sea slapped the harbour walls with damp insistence, and through gaps between houses I saw that the lanterns on the little boats had been lit. It was getting late and I wanted to be sour in comfort.

The old port of Tyre is one of the most historic in the Eastern Mediterranean. The richest of the Phoenician cities, it dominated trade in the region for centuries under a succession of powerful rulers with such names as Hiram, Ithobaal, and Princess Alissar. A number of wars and sieges reduced its power, and many of its monuments were destroyed by invaders. It languished until the seventeenth century when Fakhr ad-Din attempted to rebuild the shattered buildings and re-establish the importance of the city. He was only partly successful, and Tyre remained a curious echo of itself until it was finally absorbed into the Lebanese republic. Now it is a pleasant fishing town.

I walked along the Rue Abu Dib and searched for a cheap hotel. The street cafes distracted me with the aromas of coffee, hot khoubiz bread, falafels, and the smoke of nargileh pipes, but I did not pause. I tried the first hotel I encountered and was disappointed to learn it was full. Tyre was hosting a music festival in the hippodrome, and there were many visitors from other parts of the country. I had chosen an unlucky time to be involved with a woman here. Music was one of my

28

greatest loves, but I was too sour because of love to regard the festival with anything but dismay. Coincidentally the Lebanese name for Tyre is Sour. Almost everything changes. But I felt my feelings would not.

I continued my quest for a room to spend the night. Two more hotels turned me away. Night was gathering itself together, a softer night than those I had lived through in Bitlis and other places far north of here, a night that was dark but never truly black, as if the sky were only pretending. It became cooler. The name Safaa entered my head. Was she the girl I was pursuing or fleeing? I turned a corner into a narrower street. I hardly expected to find a hotel down here, but to my muted surprise I chanced to pass a building on which hung a sign announcing itself as the Hotel Sour. This suited my mood perfectly.

I stopped and approached the door. I turned the handle, but the door was locked so I knocked on the wood with my knuckles. I heard a shuffling, and then the door rattled. But it did not open. I called out and received a muffled reply. For a moment I was bewildered, but then I realised the door was bolted from the outside. I had never seen anything like this before. I drew back the bolt and the door swung open to reveal a man carrying a bulging suitcase. "Do you have any vacancies?" he asked, and in my confused state I could only nod dumbly. He reached into his pocket for a fistful of Lebanese lira and passed it to me. I accepted without a word and he pushed past me and vanished down the street.

While I was digesting this unexpected occurrence, another man emerged from the building and asked the same question. I remained silent, and he paid me in a similar manner to the first and hauled his luggage off into the night. Behind my sourness I felt a small trace of amusement. Had I stumbled into the middle of an obscure game? When the third man came out of the entrance I became reconciled to my situation. I was short of money, and if strangers wished to pay me for simply standing in the street I would voice no objection. In the following hour I was paid no less than eighteen times by a variety of men and women who had chosen this unconventional method of entering the city.

Tyre was filling up fast with visitors, and on the cool night air I heard faint notes of music from the festival. It suddenly occurred to me that my present location outside this absurd hotel was as good a place as any to find my mysterious woman. If she entered Tyre through this door an encounter was inevitable. On the other hand, if my desire was to flee from her, at least I would be reminded of my reasons for wanting to avoid her. I always had the option to run. Not once did I pass into the building. The only time I attempted this I nearly collided with a family who bustled me backwards with an enormous trolley full of suitcases. I remained safely on the street, waiting for Safaa, if that was her name.

As the night wore on I grew sleepy as well as rich. While I waited to receive the next visitor I decided to sit on the low doorstep in front of the Hotel Sour. This worn stone ledge extended a little way beyond the door, and so I did not block the entrance. I closed my eyes. I fell asleep within moments, and the movements and sounds of the outside world became part of my fragmented dreams. Then I felt somebody shaking me, not roughly but with moderate contempt. I woke and jumped to my feet. A woman stood before me, but she was not Safaa. I extended my palm for payment, but she placed her hands on her hips and shook her head. "The manager wishes to see you," she said. "Come with me." She was obviously not a guest.

I followed her into the building, and we proceeded down an interminably long corridor from which branched many narrow passages and stairways. This corridor was illuminated at very infrequent intervals by dim lamps, and the pictures hanging on the walls were obscured by thick shadows. The mustiness of the air and the unevenness of the floor suggested the cheapest sort of hostel. At last I perceived a brighter glow ahead, and I realised we were approaching the manager's office. The door was open. He was seated behind a desk and looked up at me with a sigh as I stood on the threshold. The woman turned to leave, and I found myself alone with this fellow who was almost walled in by the vast amounts of paperwork on his desk. He beckoned me closer.

I shuffled forward and regarded him with some trepidation. It was a long time before he spoke. "Sleeping on the job is not acceptable," he intoned. "A large number of visitors slipped past you without paying. I cannot afford to run this operation at a loss. You are dismissed from your post." He stood and made a wide gesture with both hands. "You will never work in this establishment again." I knew what he meant. He was not referring to the Hotel Sour but to the entire outside world. For him the globe on which we all stand and breathe was merely a means of making money. Before I could turn to leave he leaned across the desk and extended his hand. He did not want me to shake it. I knew what he wanted.

I passed him the money I had received since starting this job. He accepted it and pulled off a few notes, handing these back to me. My wages. As I departed he said, "I hate unpleasant scenes. Now I am in a bad mood. I will take a break from my duties and relax for an hour among my sleeping flowers. There is a garden on the roof." I could not tell whether he addressed these words to me or was merely thinking aloud. "I wish to enjoy my garden," he added, a little defensively. I shook my head as I walked back along the dim corridor. How can one enjoy a garden? I have never understood that. A garden is not a pot of coffee or a downhill bicycle ride. With very few exceptions a garden is not a woman. Indeed not.

I reached the end of the corridor. The front door was closed. I turned the handle, but it had been locked from outside. I was trapped in the hotel. Who had slid the bolt at this time of night? I guessed the answer within a few moments. Safaa. It was not I who was pursuing or fleeing her, but she who was fleeing or pursuing me. If fleeing, then she had succeeded in blocking my entry into Tyre, where she was. If pursuing, then she had managed to cage me in this building, available for whatever she planned next. I was at her mercy. There seemed no point in waiting for someone to open the door. I did not wish to spend my meagre wages paying the next doorman. Finding a job to replenish my savings would be impossible.

I decided to seek out the roof garden. There was a chance I might escape by climbing down the exterior of the building, perhaps using a trailing vine as a rope. I began ascending a random stairway. It seemed to have no end. It finally emerged into another corridor. This hotel was a warren of stairways and corridors, a labyrinth. Everywhere abandoned suitcases made my journey more hazardous. Soon I became too tired to continue. I found an empty room and lay down on the bed. When I awoke birds were singing on the inaccessible balcony outside the barred window. I used the telephone on a little table to order breakfast. A miserable man brought me a bowl of unpleasant porridge within the hour. I felt very bitter.

Bitter and sour are not the same emotions. One can imagine recovering from sourness rapidly if given the chance, say with the honey of a pleasant experience. But bitterness corrodes itself deeply into the spirit. It is a wincing of the whole soul. I did not finish my meal but resumed the ascent of an unimaginable number of creaking steps. I carried my bitterness with me. Would I ever reach the roof garden and gaze down upon the city? I doubted it. Many dreadful things had happened to me in the past, but my present situation was the worst. Bored in Bodrum, tripped in Tripoli. Those were trivial in comparison. Even damned in Damascus was nothing, for now I was bitter in Sour.

The Old House Under the Snow

1. Get Your Spade

I won't say Curtis was a mean man, but that's how he wanted to be remembered. His face was gentle and round and inspired only good humour in the people he wanted to annoy or dominate. Not that he was soft, but his basic nature was too pleasant and relaxed to give him the reputation he craved, which was that of a tough adventurer, an outdoors type, rugged and unforgiving.

He worked hard to keep himself in shape, and his expression always betrayed his inner dismay at a life of enforced marches over hills and early-morning baths in icy ponds. His stamina and frugality were contrived. As for myself, I had less than half his love of trekking, camping, and the wilderness in general, but this was enough to ensure I joined one of his expeditions every month.

"Where are we going?" I asked.

"Not far this time. Just up to the crater. The place where it's always winter and the snow is extra fine."

"What's there? Nothing, if I recall."

He tried to fix me with an intimidating stare, failed, and rubbed his eyes. Then he pulled out a folded sheet of paper from his pocket and handed it to me. I opened it and found myself blinking at a map. It was old and the ink had faded, but I recognised the local mountains. There was something else.

"Where did you get this?" I wondered.

Curtis licked his lips and nodded with childish glee. "Bought a cabinet in an antique store from a senile fool last week. It didn't look quite right in any of my rooms, I can't say why, so I kept moving it about and I guess all that vibration activated some hidden springs. A secret compartment popped out and this was inside. It reminded me of the legend and made me think that maybe there's truth in it after all."

I examined the map more closely. "This certainly looks like a house."

"I'm sure it's the Baron's place. He must have sold the cabinet without realising the map was in it. More than a century ago!"

I sighed. In the rather thin folklore of our region the tale of the missing mansion was the most prominent fable. I couldn't account for its popularity, for it lacked plot and moral and was utterly inconclusive. The Baron was an immigrant from somewhere in Central or Eastern Europe, only he wasn't a real aristocrat but a rich merchant with aspirations to a title. He built a large house in the mountains, and the labourers who worked on it were recruited from a lunatic asylum, so that its location would become a sort of secret, for they were bound to disagree on where it was. And so it was finished and nobody had seen it since.

Curtis enjoyed relating the different endings of this myth.

"The madmen built it inside out and it collapsed. Or the Baron was hiding from the devil, who disguised himself as a labourer and remained behind, to greet the new owner when he opened the door, though this doesn't explain why it vanished. Or some sort of experiment went wrong and shrank it to the size of an eyeball. They said the Baron was a magician or scientist."

I tapped the map with a finger. "But here is a more mundane explanation."

"Yes, and it suits our purpose. The crater isn't above the snowline, but the surrounding peaks mean it is always in shade. It must have been empty when the Baron built his house there. Then an avalanche filled the crater and buried it under tons of snow for a hundred years."

I laughed. "That's so simple!"

"The snow won't melt but will just keep getting deeper until the crater is full. We have about thirty feet to dig through. My guess is that the building is in perfect condition down there. And all the stuff in the rooms untouched."

"Do you mean treasure?" I mumbled.

He offered me a wry smile. "The Baron was a wealthy man, and I doubt he deposited his money in a bank. It wasn't the way they did things back then. Maybe there's nothing of any value, but it can't hurt to take a look."

"Worth it for the adventure," I said.

He slapped me on the back. "That's the spirit! Let's gather some equipment. Ropes to climb into the crater and flashlights for our work."

I checked my watch. "It's getting late."

"All the more reason to hurry. Come on, Warren!"

I needed no further encouragement. Within an hour my backpack was full and my hiking boots were laced tightly to my feet. We tramped through the town to the outskirts and found the path which led into the foothills. Nobody we passed gave us a second glance. They were used to seeing us embark on expeditions, but it was an odd hour to be setting off, with the sun already low in the west, and we had no tents. I welcomed the lighter load and I know Curtis did too, though he would never admit it.

The path was strewn with small stones and as we slowly ascended my ankles began to ache from the constant stumbling, but I didn't complain. Soon we turned off and followed the equally rocky bed of a narrow stream. This was a quicker route to the crater. The chill pene-trated my boots but I had got into the rhythm of walking and felt at peace with nature, enjoying the weak warmth on the back of my neck and the smell of the air, which was clean and exhilarating.

I was shocked out of my complacency by a sudden crash from ahead. The note of violence boomed around the mountains in a pro-longed echo. I paused and was nearly overwhelmed with fatigue and doubts.

Curtis kept going. "Just an avalanche. Nothing special."

I nodded and caught him up, the spade on my backpack swinging and slapping my flank as if I was a mule that needed to be goaded.

2. The Sun Went Down

But we went up, higher and higher, until we were truly in the mountains and could permit ourselves a rest without feeling guilt. We sat and shared a flask of coffee and marvelled at the rosy clouds and the darkening sky.

Our progress would become more difficult, but we were fairly close to our destination. One more hour and we would be standing on the rim of the crater. We had both made this journey many times before, but rarely at night and always on the way somewhere else. Although an impressive geographical feature, the crater had previously held scant interest for us, being little more than a deep hole stuffed with snow.

Now we had a different opinion of it. Greed had blessed it.

We resumed our trek, picking our way between boulders and over the trunks of fallen trees. It was exciting, but there was a hollowness in my stomach. I expected to be disappointed, to learn the map was a hoax or that the house had been crushed flat and its supposed treasures ruined. I knew Curtis was dreaming of gold bars, but I thought paper money more likely.

The moon appeared through a rent in the clouds. Nearly full, it was a great assistance to our uncertain feet and the path became less perilous. When we reached the crater and peered over, the snow below glimmered brightly. Our flashlights were surplus to requirements, but we were confronted with our first major problem. The avalanche we had heard earlier had taken place right here.

"More than thirty feet now!" I blurted.

Curtis grunted and pointed at the dark shapes which littered the fresh snow like giant limbs and heads. They were large rocks and parts of trees. Silently we secured our ropes to an overhanging crag and climbed down. Then we wandered among the debris to the exact centre of the crater and unslung our backpacks. According to the map, the mansion was directly below us. But neither of us felt like digging.

The eyes of my companion glinted and his round face broke into a smile. He had picked up his own spade, but now his grip relaxed and it dangled idly from his fingers. He indicated a boulder which had tumbled from a neighbouring peak. It was black and smooth and rested on the snow with an absurd elegance, but on one side there was a wide indentation where a fragment had broken off in the fall.

"I have an idea. Look at the shape of this rock."

"Like an overthrown altar," I commented.

"Not quite. But it might resemble one more closely in a few minutes. Help me turn it so that the depression is facing upward."

"I don't understand," I replied.

He ignored me and began digging under one corner of the boulder, and his heavy breathing was so sincere I felt sorry for him and joined in. I used my spade as a lever, and together we managed to shift the position of the enormous stone. Tiny crystals on its surface sparkled magically as Curtis roamed the surrounding area to collect wood. We piled branches into the depression, and I finally understood his plan. It took several failed attempts with matches before a few of the smaller and drier twigs caught.

But the fire rapidly took hold.

I backed away but Curtis said, "Use the blade of your spade to reflect the heat back onto the boulder. It would be better to start a fire underneath it, but we can't do that."

"Some rocks explode when heated," I pointed out.

He shrugged. "That's the risk."

I watched as he added more branches to the blaze. The crater glowed with the pulsing light as if it were breathing and blushing. Within the orange of the flames appeared other colours, purple and green, but there was no smoke. I grew tired of holding my spade at an awkward angle and lowered it briefly. It grazed the surface of the snow, and I was startled by an angry hiss. Meanwhile the snow around the base of the boulder began to crackle and give off wisps of steam.

Then the rock started to sink.

It dropped through the snow smoothly, and Curtis threw on a final log before it sank out of view. The moon was still bright, but now the crater seemed gloomy and unfriendly. We moved closer and gazed into the shaft. The boulder was already far below us, spitting sparks, and I briefly imagined I was observing a rocket barging into the sky. This optical illusion confused me, and I staggered before regaining my senses. Hot air rose up the shaft and brushed my face and studded my brow with jewels of sweat.

"It's certainly warm enough now."

Curtis turned and strode off. "We'll use one of our ropes to climb after it and keep the other in place to get us out of the crater."

By the time he returned and tied one of the ropes to the trunk of what had been a mighty tree, the boulder had vanished from sight. We scratched our heads. Instead of flames or at least embers, the base of the shaft was occupied by something dark and shaped differently from the rock. But when we listened, the hiss of melting snow was still faintly audible.

"I'll go first," declared Curtis.

I declined to argue, and he took hold of the rope and lowered himself into the shaft. I followed close behind. We must have gone down more than sixty feet when he suddenly announced he had reached the bottom. He described it as a hard surface slanted at a steep angle. Then he added that there was another tunnel in the snow which ran parallel to this incline. All this mystery resolved itself in my mind when he next spoke.

"I'm standing on the roof!"

"The roof of the mansion?" I gasped.

"Of course. The boulder didn't stop here but slid sideways to the edge. It probably tipped over the side and has melted another shaft down to the base of the crater. If we follow the path it has made we can be sure of standing next to the house. Then it's just a question of finding a way inside!"

I panted my agreement and he crawled along the tunnel, still supporting himself with the rope. I touched down on the roof myself and followed his example. A beam of light told me he had switched on his flashlight. This beam shook and wobbled as he reached the next vertical shaft. I sensed the tons of snow above me and controlled my trembling, which had less to do with cold than fear. Then I also reached the edge of the roof.

To my astonishment, Curtis was standing a few feet below me. I wondered aloud if the mansion was really a cottage and legend alone had expanded its size, but from the expression on his face, which was ghostly in the electric light, I realised this wasn't the case. He confirmed it with his next words.

"I'm not standing on the ground."

"What happened?" I asked.

"The boulder has come to rest on an upper balcony. I'm balancing on it right now. Falling snow has extinguished the embers, but it's still hot. I can't stay here much longer. If I can't get into the house I'll have to come back up."

"Is there a window?"

I heard him fumbling among the shadows. "Yes, and it has a handle. Let's hope it opens inwards. I'll give it a try now."

He did, and the resultant creak was like a laugh. Then he vanished and the flashlight went with him. I found myself staring down at the top of the boulder and the ash which filled its indentation. He had entered safely. I hastened to join him.

3. The House Was Empty

The Baron was absent and nobody else was at home. I closed the window behind me and crossed the room to where Curtis stood. The cold was intense and the floor and walls were coated with frost. This was obviously the highest floor of the mansion, and the room was relatively small and bare. It contained a bed, desk, chair, and a few other small items of modest furniture.

But Curtis was excited. "Look at this, Warren!"

He played the beam of his flashlight over a cabinet in the corner. I saw nothing remarkable in its contours and simple decoration.

"I don't understand," I replied.

"It's almost identical to the one I purchased in that antique store. I guess the Baron must have sold some of his possessions before he disappeared. I hope this doesn't mean he was short of money. I'd hate to think this adventure was pointless!"

"Never that," I answered. "Shall we go down?"

He nodded, and we passed through the open door onto a wide

landing. We instinctively knew the house was too large to explore all at once. We desired to find the main rooms and become familiar with those first, and we assumed they were located on the ground floor. We passed a table on which stood a candelabrum holding two candles. Curtis reached into his pocket for matches and lit the wicks. The glow was weak but welcome.

"One hundred years old," he muttered.

We reached the stairway and began our descent. There were brackets set into the wall also holding candles, some mere stubs, and we lit these too on our way. We decided to light every candle we encountered to chase away the perennial night. Because of the frost it was impossible to say whether there were carpets beneath our feet. I was inclined to the belief the stairs were bare. The lower we went, the colder it became.

When we reached the next floor down we took a detour through some of the rooms before returning to the stairway. We followed this procedure for every floor. In the wavering glow of the candles above us I felt I was swimming through an undersea grotto. Certainly I hadn't been this cold since the caving trip I undertook with Curtis a few years previously, a trip which involved diving into pools which had never seen the sun. Stamping my feet did little to warm them. I was numb all over.

After a while, an odd thought occurred to me.

"The layout of this house is regular. The shapes of the rooms and their relative positions are conventional. I was expecting unnatural angles and corridors which go nowhere. After all, it was built by lunatics."

"Yes, but it wasn't designed by them. The Baron designed it and he was mad too. Doubtless his design was mad and they constructed it in a mad way. The two madnesses cancelled each other out. Thus the result is unintentionally normal."

I snorted. "How grotesque!"

We finally reached the ground floor and wandered together into an enormous room. This was what we had dreamed about, a chamber filled with the trappings of wealth. One wall was dominated by a monumental hearth. A marble mantelpiece held ornaments which demanded closer inspection. A grandfather clock, utterly silent now, stood in the middle of the opposite wall. Between them a couple of elegant chairs were arranged at pleasing angles. A chandelier hung from the ceiling and burst into a cluster of tiny suns as the flashlight caught it.

Smirking at each other, we pointed at a table which held two silver goblets and a bottle of wine. Before sampling this vintage we rested ourselves on the chairs. But something wasn't right and we remained tense.

"I'm too weary to search for treasure now."

Curtis didn't argue. "Yes, and it's too cold to relax properly. That wine won't really warm us. How about if we start a fire and get this room warmed up? Then we can sleep for an hour or two and be refreshed for the plundering later. There are some books over there. We'll use the paper to get the blaze going."

I sat rigid, trying not to let my teeth chatter, my hands gripping the frosty arms of my chair. "But the chimney isn't open to the sky."

"Do you think the smoke will come back down? If it does, we'll vacate this room and shut the door tight. I still think it's worth a try. Fetch the books and I'll break up some furniture. Here are the matches. I wonder why the snow didn't fall down the flue and fill the house? I guess there must be a grille at the top of the chimney."

I rose stiffly and approached the bookcase. I had expected volumes of science or magic in a foreign language, but these tomes were ordinary enough, encyclopaedias and works on local history and geography. I tore out the pages and cast them into the fireplace. Curtis searched a cabinet and, after convincing himself it held no money or anything else of value, he flung it to the floor, repeating this action until it shattered.

We crouched before the hearth, warming our hands and faces.

Soon we were able to add the remnants of another cabinet and a table. There was almost no smoke in the fire and I was grateful for this, but the flames contained unexpected colours. Now we were warm enough to try the wine. I had a corkscrew on my pocket knife and managed to work the frozen cork out.

"Wait! Did you hear that? A gurgling sound!"

"It's the wine in the bottle!" laughed Curtis.

I shook my head. "It's coming from the wall above the hearth."

Moving closer, I placed my hands on the wall and quickly drew them away. Then I moved to the side and tried again. I bit my lip nervously.

Curtis had already poured and tasted. "Not bad. Well?"

"Blisters. It's red hot."

"What do you expect? You touched the wall directly above the hearth."

"No, it's spreading. I don't think this is an ordinary fireplace. There seems to be liquid behind it. Probably oil of some kind in a tank. There must be a network of pipes embedded in the brick."

I followed the moving heat into the shadows. I realised it was spreading along the floor and ceiling too. Curtis unbuttoned his jacket.

"What do you think it means?"

"The entire room is a giant radiator. Maybe the whole house."

"So what? The Baron was eccentric."

I stepped to the window and pressed my face against the glass. A sudden crash made me spin around. Curtis was adding more fuel to the fire. I strode over to stop him but then questioned my caution. There seemed no harm in the idea of turning our domestic climate from polar to tropical. I assisted him, and we removed our outer clothes item by item, pausing only to finish the bottle. I offered to search for more wine. One wall was now so hot it glowed dully. I discovered that the warmth really had spread beyond the limits of this room. Out in the hall I found another bottle, this time of brandy, idle on a table.

Curtis had taken my place by the window. He beckoned to me.

"A gap of several inches has opened between the house and the snow outside. If this continues we'll be able to melt our way out of the crater!"

"And expose the secret to everyone," I pointed out.

"We'll claim the treasure first anyway. And you have to admit this is an easier way of getting back out."

I did. While I was doing so there was a powerful lurch.

"What was that?" I cried.

Curtis answered, "I think the house is sinking."

"There must be more snow beneath it. How can this be? Let's extinguish the fire and stop it going any deeper. We'd better hurry!"

"There's nothing to put it out with. And even if we douse the flames the house will remain hot for a long time yet."

I grabbed his arm. "Upstairs quick! We can get out through a window at the top and still be at our original level. It's our best chance."

But I knew this was a forlorn hope, and so did he. The house was sinking faster and more smoothly now, though it groaned and creaked as it gathered speed. In fact, we just stared at each other and didn't move a muscle, apart from those necessary to keep alive and form a pair of very frightened smiles. Then we regained something of our normal composure and sighed softly at our predicament and remarked on how ironic it was.

"I wonder how deep the snow is?" I muttered.

He returned to the window, and there was a snapping noise which I assumed was his foot treading on a piece of broken furniture which had somehow escaped becoming fuel. But it wasn't. He stood for a long time at the glass, rubbing his hands, which were behind his back. I didn't care for this mannerism and told him so, but he ignored me and mumbled something about the amount of oxygen contained in all the cubic space in the house and how long it would last two men and the fire they had to feed.

Finally he looked over his shoulder and answered me.

"It's not snow now. It's ice. The Baron must have constructed his mansion on the surface of a frozen pool. Not a normal frozen pool but one solid all the way through. We're melting our way into it and the ice is doubtlessly sealing itself again above us. If we extinguish the fire we'll eventually cool and slow down and stop and be entombed forever. We have no choice but to keep burning the furniture. It's a one-way ride."

I was incredulous. "To where? The bottom of the lake? What good will that do us? It's death either way."

The mansion shuddered, and I nearly lost my balance.

"The pressure outside is enormous," he said. "It can only get worse. I'm truly sorry for dragging you on this trip. You were my friend."

"I still am!" I spluttered.

His tone became thoughtful, even slightly mystical. "Very well. We both know that the story of the Baron and his missing mansion is the most popular of our local legends. But there are others. I am currently thinking about one in particular. I've always wondered about this crater and what made it. The result of volcanic activity or the wound inflicted by an ancient meteorite? I never imagined it might be the special lake."

I took his meaning and went very pale.

He added, "The one rumoured to be bottomless."

4. The Days Passed

We dropped like a hot boulder in the shape of an altar. But the only indentations were in our hearts. Ice opened below us and clenched above like a sequence of blue-white fists. And we wandered our domain, our prison, collecting fuel and searching for food. We smashed wardrobes and clocks and existed on sherry and spirits. But in a corner of the kitchen where the heat had not yet spread I found a ham and a tin of biscuits preserved in the frost. We ate without pleasure and listened to our own teeth in despair.

At least we had stopped accelerating. The pressure of the ice squeezed the house but the hot oil in its veins expanded it, and this balance was expressed as a shallow breathing of our total environment—the breathing of a man ready for his coffin, though in fact it was we who were buried. We discussed the legend of the bottomless pool. There was nothing to it really, and perhaps that is why it was so terrible. I'm not sure if either of us hoped for anything. We kept ourselves busy.

The air grew stale in time, but we discovered that fresh oxygen could be obtained by going into a spare room, one we had not yet entered, and there were plenty of those. But we rationed these gulps of purity carefully. I think I was most afraid of breaking through the ice into ordinary water and drowning in one of the rooms. But this seemed increasingly unlikely. The legend insisted the lake was completely solid, an infinite ice-cube in nothingness, and that is what I gradually came to believe.

We still looked for treasure, without success.

I was reading one of the Baron's books, tearing out each page as I finished it and casting it to the flames, when Curtis suddenly shouted.

He was standing at the window, a duty we took in turns, and I glanced at him with a mixture of gloom and wild optimism.

"There's something out there. It has gone now."

"What was it?" I asked.

"It might have been a submarine. An early design. We've passed it, so I suppose we'll never know for certain."

Then he burst into tears.

It was the first time I had seen him weep, and I was grateful he had surrendered to the impulse before me, but I couldn't think of a way to comfort him. Words were useless. I decided to rely on the brandy bottle or whatever alcohol came to hand. There was nothing available in this room, so I rose and departed and passed into the hall. Most of the original candles had burned out, but we had found spares and some were monsters, whole legs of wax which could last months. Yet we were conscious of the need to preserve air and we had blown many out, abandoning the majority of the house to shadows.

I returned with a bottle of rum and some interesting news.

"I've discovered a study beyond the kitchens. It contains a telephone! One of the first practical models. The Baron was clearly a man of the moment. I don't mean to sound ridiculous, but what if it still works?"

Curtis had dried his eyes and was manly again, but his cheeks were damp and his efforts to appear in control were mostly wasted.

"I saw no cables leading into the crater," he declared.

"True. But I'm going to try. Nothing else to do today. Come with me. Won't it be a relief just to dial a number?"

He meekly nodded and followed me to the study. The telephone was a contraption fitted inside a cabinet bolted to the wall. It was a primitive device but recognisable enough, with a mouthpiece and dial.

I opened the cabinet doors and stood there awkwardly, trying to operate the mechanism and rehearsing what to say.

"Who are you ringing? The police?"

"My wife in Kamloops. I want her to know first."

Curtis scowled and paced in agitation as I pressed the earpiece to the side of my head and dialled the number. It was answered almost immediately. There was no need for me to talk. I listened with a frown and then replaced the receiver.

"What happened? What did she say?"

"It was a wrong number. I got a man. He said, 'Who? What? Eh! He's not at home. Haha!' Then he hung up."

"Let me try," demanded Curtis.

I shrugged, and he took my place and his fingers were busy with the dial. Though he held the earpiece I distinctly heard the voice at the other end of the line.

"Who? What? Eh! He's not at home. Haha!"

I was bewildered, but Curtis was terrified. The colour drained from his skin. He staggered back and clutched me to steady himself.

"There's something about that voice," he stammered.

"Yes, it does sound peculiar, almost artificial."

Voicing this thought gave me an idea. I groped behind the cabinet for the cable at the back of the telephone. Then I followed it along the wall and through a side door into a short corridor. I turned a sharp bend and entered another room, little more than a recess, bare apart from a table on which sat an antique gramophone. The disc was spinning and the arm which held the needle was raised above it. The cable stopped here. I called back to Curtis to ring a number, any number, and he replied that he would. Hidden relays in the gramophone clicked, and the needle lowered onto the disc. The thin voice came again and then the arm raised itself. It was a trick.

I wandered back to Curtis. "The Baron must have made that recording and invented an automatic device to set it in motion whenever anyone used the telephone. But why? It's an obscure joke. I'm not laughing."

"Nor I. I recognise that voice."

"Impossible. The Baron vanished a century ago."

Curtis had calmed down. He moved away slowly, out of the study and through the kitchens. The gleam of a bottle on a high shelf caught his attention, and he reached for it. He bore his prize back to the chamber which contained the fire. On the way he paused at every window to look out. This had become a habit for both of us. The dark ice slid past. Back in the furnace room, for such had we termed it, we sat in the two remaining chairs and vainly attempted to drink our troubles away. Then he chuckled sourly.

"It was the voice of the man in the antique store."

I blinked. "The senile old fool?"

"None other. I never imagined the Baron might still be alive. We made a big mistake. He never dwelt in this mansion. He built it as a trap, not a habitation. He became a shopkeeper and existed in humble isolation."

"Well, he certainly never attracted any attention."

Curtis nodded. "That was the idea."

"Who was the trap intended for?" I pressed.

"Remember that other ending to the legend? The devil came for him and that's why he disappeared. But in fact the Baron outwitted the devil. He didn't construct his house in a secret location to escape his fate but to entice it. Once his enemy found it and entered and activated the trigger by lighting the fire, the whole edifice would sink into the eternal ice."

"I can't believe the Baron is more than century old."

"Come on, Warren! Is that any stranger than what has happened to us?"

I began to lose my temper. I didn't want superstition to endanger our hopes of survival more than necessary. "It doesn't matter. The devil didn't come."

"Are you sure about that?"

"The house was still on the surface of the lake when we found it."

Curtis cried in perverse triumph, "Precisely! We entered and sprung the trap. And now we are entombed. What does this mean?"

"That one of us is the devil?" I whispered.

He jumped up. "Not you! Coming here was my idea! It's my fault. I always felt there was something wrong with me, even when I was a child, a discomfort with my own being. I had an urge to be mean to people. I was too shy to do it properly, but now I know the reason for the faults in my character. I'm the devil."

I didn't disappoint him by objecting to this.

Instead I stood and strode to the window. It was a way of avoiding further conversation. I expected to see just the tedium and horror of endless ice, but I was confronted with something startling. I made no comment but waited to observe what might happen. I shut my eyes tight and took a dozen deep breaths. Then I opened them again. What I had seen was no illusion. At last I felt ready to share the revelation.

"There's a shape down there. It's getting bigger."

"The bottom?" suggested Curtis.

I shook my head and held tightly to one of the curtains. My shallow breathing was loud in my ears, but it didn't mist the glass. By its very nature a bottomless lake was infinitely deep. I wondered if we might be entering a region of opaque ice, impure and toxic. Not that this made much difference to our situation. I watched as the shape slowly filled my field of vision with blackness. I bit my lip.

The collision was milder than I feared. Every ornament on every surface jumped once, and then there was silence. Even the logs on the fire seemed to stop crackling. I turned and exchanged a long glance with Curtis. He smiled weakly, and I relinquished my hold on the curtain. I began to walk over to him, but before I was halfway to his chair the house gave another lurch. The sound was terrible. I imagined the cellar under our feet had become filled with pigs. But I knew that our stones were sliding over slates.

"What's going on?" whimpered Curtis.

"There's another house below us. We've touched down on its roof. That's the only explanation."

"Be sensible. It would have to be gigantic."

"I'm sure it is. And it has a sloping roof. We're sliding to the edge."

"And after that? Down again!"

I nodded and counted away the minutes. After so much plunging, this lateral movement came as a shock. I think we both felt nauseous. Then the sliding stopped and we resumed our purely vertical motion. But within less than an hour we stopped again. I knew this was the final destination of this particular house. Beneath us now was stone, not ice, and however hot we made the fire our mansion was stuck here. I ran through the room and the hall beyond to a window in the far wall. Curtis protested weakly behind me.

"Let's get some fresh air!" I called back to him.

"What are you doing, Warren?"

I opened our window and reached for the handle of the window beyond. Fortunately both swung inward. I heard the sudden intake of breath of my companion. He had followed me reluctantly and now attempted to restrain me by clutching my arm. I shrugged him off and climbed through the two windows into an enormous room. In design and furnishings it was similar to one of our own bedrooms but it was much bigger. I drank the clean air with delight and howled in celebration.

5. A Vast Palace

Our own house had come to rest on one of its upper balconies. The structure was so large it confounded the senses, but most of the objects it contained had normal dimensions; they were simply more numerous. A few, such as the candles, were scaled up. We lit a pair as thick as big men which stood in a corner. The light they provided was generous and enabled us to understand we didn't wish to remain here. We wanted to explore. We ventured onto the landing and reached an immense staircase.

We repeated the procedure of lighting candles on the way down. The individual steps were large but not unmanageable. This palace had not been created for giants. It had a more complex layout than the Baron's home, and we found ourselves crossing open galleries suspended above the distant ground floor or passing through sequences of unusually shaped cells, some circular or polygonal, a few trapezoid and disturbing. I can't describe the place as deliberately confusing, but it possessed some of the playful malevolence of a labyrinth.

It was unbearably cold. We had become used to working near the mouth of a furnace and the frost that coated every surface was like an unwelcome memory. The voyage to the ground floor was heroic or pathetic, I am unsure which, but we eventually reached the base of the staircase. A thought had occurred to us, and we searched for the kitchens. Here was the obligatory ham and biscuits, but also cheese and bowls of dried fruit. They were more perfectly preserved than their counterparts in the Baron's mansion had been.

Out of habit we bore as much as we could carry to the chamber which contained the fireplace. We gasped on the threshold of this room. It resembled a gutted cathedral. There were chairs and silent clocks and dozens of cabinets but only one fireplace. It was a monster. A man might erect a tent inside it and set up camp. It was so tall the ornaments on its mantelpiece were beyond my reach, but from previous experience I surmised they were porcelain vases and jade animals and framed photographs blurred by age and chemical decay to sepia blooms of pure abstraction. I sat and waited for our food to thaw, knowing it never would.

"I'm much happier here," I remarked.

"The air is fresh. But it's so cold! This isn't our fate."

"I know what you mean," I conceded.

"Eventually this oxygen will go stale too and the food and drink run out. We've only bought a little time coming in here. A few weeks."

I cast an eye at the anticipated bookcase. Curtis interpreted this gesture as permission to fetch a few volumes and pass them to me. I opened one. It was an encyclopaedia but written in a form of English which was almost incomprehensible. I felt too emotional to attempt reading further. With a mixture of resignation and delight I ripped out a handful of pages and ignited them with a match. Then I stood and approached the hearth and cast them in. At this signal, Curtis went to work.

He added the other books and splintered a chair. This was followed by a table and several cabinets. His enthusiasm was contagious and I joined in, but the gurgling above the hearth was slow to begin. A building this size would require a fiercer blaze to heat up sufficiently.

We worked harder, hurling in entire pieces without breaking them up. We even added one of the clocks. It burned away to a skeleton of cogs and springs and loomed upright through the flames like a phantom of the lost cycles of day and night, now dead to us. We no longer bothered to search anything for treasure first.

The palace shuddered, and we felt it begin to melt the ice which encased it. We continued to pile on the fuel. Then the descent commenced. With an eerie crackling, we accelerated into the frozen abyss. It was peculiar and horrible but also something of a relief. We quickly attained a velocity greater than the maximum of the Baron's mansion. Whether this was connected to our greater mass, the outer shape of the palace, or a change in the nature of the ice, I couldn't say. Curtis became cheerful in the presence of the furnace, standing closer to it than I would dare.

"It's my proper environment now."

"It's not yet proven you're the devil," I responded.

He sighed. "How far do you think we'll go? Surely we can't go beyond the centre of the planet? That's the point of greatest gravitational attraction. Whether this lake is bottomless or not, we'll have to come to a stop there. Will it be like hitting an invisible barrier?"

"No. Our momentum will carry us beyond it."

"How far beyond? All the way to the other side? If so, will we be inverted when we come out? How much momentum will we need?"

"There's no other side to infinity," I replied.

This kept him quiet. We returned to work, adding fuel to the inferno. When we were confident we could leave it unattended for a short time, we vacated the room and located the kitchens. We passed through them to the room beyond. We wanted to see if there was a telephone here as well, but the layout was different. It wasn't a study but a storeroom. No telephone but a large selection of tools. Some of these were a great help in breaking up the furniture. We helped ourselves to a pair of axes, a big hammer, and a wheelbarrow. Now we were equipped to rip up floorboards and demolish banisters if necessary.

Our habit so far had been to stay close together, even sleeping in the same room. But with a larger fire to tend, it became more convenient to sleep in shifts and more peaceful for one of us to bed down in the hall or a side room while the other worked. Slowly we grew more independent of each other but without any resentment or bad feelings. What he did when I wasn't around, apart from work and sleep and eat, was unknown to me. I never asked. Nor did he show much curiosity about my own methods of passing time. I began a systematic exploration of the lower levels of the palace. I planned to make a map.

I was reluctant to stray too far from the furnace room for obvious reasons. The fire required a lot of physical toil to keep the building at a sufficient temperature to melt the ice. In the end my project proved impossible. There was simply too much space to chart. But I did make a complete circuit of the cellars. Flinging back a trapdoor, I climbed down into a network of stone cells. I took my flashlight with me, for there were no candles here. Hundreds of bottles of wine in racks mocked our previous lengthy searches in corners of ordinary rooms. Beneath the floor I heard the grinding and hissing of the ice.

It was in this honeycomb of untrodden dust and unlabelled vintages that I first thought I heard a voice ahead of me. I passed into the next cell, expecting to discover that Curtis had preceded me, but it was empty. Now the voice was still ahead, one cell further on. It was faint and unintelligible. I stepped forward again and once more found only emptiness. I decided it was an echo, an acoustical trick which meant its source might be miles distant. I also concluded it was not a human voice but a wall flexing under the enormous outside pressure and acting like a membrane, pumping weird but random sounds into the basement hive.

I returned from this minor exploit with as many bottles as I could carry, one slipping from under my armpit and smashing on the flagstones. I delivered them to Curtis. He had gone back to the storeroom for a pitchfork and was standing next to a mound of chairs, pieces of tables, and all manner of flammable objects. With a fluid motion he forked them into the blaze, pausing only occasionally to wipe the sweat from his brow with a grimy hand. I didn't mention the illusory voice. It was my turn to take over, but he insisted on working a double shift. My protests were ineffectual.

I wandered off again. It occurred to me that if I could find a labor-atory among the innumerable rooms I might be able to make air from ice. I knew there were methods of releasing oxygen from water. The possibility of suffocation was still one of my major concerns despite the vastness of the palace. I entered at least fifty new rooms. My ener-gies were wasted, for suddenly a powerful jolt hurled me to the floor. Then the building started sliding sideways. I knew what was coming. I rose and seated myself in a chair to await the second vertical drop to the next balcony. This amplification of my previous experience was both satisfying and grotesque.

6. A Lost City

This is how it seemed to us as we passed through the windows into the distorted bedroom and from there down the stairway to the ground floor: a metropolis under the ice, enclosed by walls and covered with a roof. The building was so large it couldn't be described as a palace. At the very least it was a collection of palaces fused together. But in truth a capital city was a closer analogy. Enough rooms to house several mil-lion people.

The eccentricities in the design were more pronounced than in the edifice we had just left. The angles and the layout were utterly strange. A multitude of lesser staircases intersected with the main one, curving away like spare horizons. And the candles resembled pillars, the col-umns of an ancient temple. More agile than I, Curtis swarmed up them to light the wicks.

I remember reading a story about a man trapped in a deserted city. He also felt horror at its design, the product of whim rather than func-tion. He described the routes between its cupolas as the paths of an "exiguous and nitid" labyrinth. At the time I imagined a garden maze with woollen hedges. I had taken the book which contained this story on a hiking trip and had no dictionary to reveal the meanings of un-known words. But now I was in a similar situation for real, and alt-hough this new sequence of rooms and corridors could never be defined as exiguous it certainly became nitid, for the wicks in the can-dles were as thick as ropes and flared brightly.

Tiring of the descent, Curtis grasped the banister and swung one leg over. He whooped as he let himself go and slid out of sight. For some reason this action unnerved me. I toppled a giant candle and soaked one of my handkerchiefs in the pool of wax under the wick. Then I squeezed the cloth into a ball, ignited it, and dropped it over the side of the stair-well. It hissed as it streaked down into the pit like an economy comet. I watched as it briefly illuminated each level it passed. Finally I glimpsed the form of Curtis far below. The flames bathed his laughing cheeks a sooty orange. He was travelling at a perilous velocity.

I heard his shrieks as he thundered around each corner, unable to brake. If he wasn't killed by this foolish impulse he would reach the bottom long before me. I debated whether to follow his example. In truth I was scared. I continued to walk down as normal, but I was less proficient at climbing the candle-pillars than Curtis and soon I was groping in thick dusk, the light of the higher levels fading more slowly than the shrieks below but with graver consequences for my progress. At last it was a choice between tripping or sliding. I gripped the banis-ter between my thighs and attempted to control my speed by tensing my muscles. But I was too tired and abandoned the struggle.

I rushed into the cold depths. The friction was welcome, warming me to a comfortable temperature. Curtis had already melted much of the frost from the banister with his own descent, but the polished wood beneath was almost as slippery. After a long while I saw twin-kling stars below. He had reached the bottom and ignited dozens of candles. But I felt no blast of heat. He had not yet started the fire in the grate. For a moment I feared that perhaps this house was different from the others and lacked a fireplace. We were taking the similarities between the buildings for granted, but in fact the hearth was there. Curtis had found another reason for not creating an immediate blaze.

He was engaged in constructing a ramp from tables and cabinets. With the tools he had carried with him he was nailing lengths of wood together. Part of this ramp consisted of rollers made from the circular legs of certain chairs. The ramp led from the base of the gargantuan hearth and out of what we now always called the furnace room. He worked like a demon, cutting and hammering. I helped him, and eventually the end of the ramp terminated some ten feet above the ground, directly under the stairwell. Then we returned to the furnace room and I selected a shelf of books. I examined a few. They were written in a very peculiar English which included a handful of extra letters. We ignited them in the hearth and hastened back to the other end of the ramp.

"This building is so immense I don't think we can warm it up the usual way. We simply can't work that hard."

I nodded. "So the ramp will help us?"

Curtis looked down. He had trodden in the ash of my extinguished handkerchief. "Absolutely. We can climb to higher levels and push items of furniture over the edge. They will land on the ramp and slide into the fire. Whether they smash or not with the impact doesn't matter. This fire will be very hungry."

We set to work, and his system proved remarkably effective. First we knocked out the struts of the banister and cast them on, then we roamed the rooms of the floor one level above the ground. It was no longer necessary to break up wardrobes and beds and carry the pieces back. We simply shoved them out of their corners onto the landing and over the side. Finally the familiar lurching motion came again and we knew we had done enough to earn ourselves a rest. The continuous impacts had damaged the ramp, and Curtis decided to repair it. I took this chance to wander off alone.

I was troubled by voices again. Louder than they had been in the cellars of the previous house, they seemed both mocking and profound. I almost caught the meanings of some of the words. Then I realised they were talking in the language of the books, an evolved or decayed version of my own natural tongue.

I called after them, "Anyone at home?"

But they remained always ahead, out of reach. I felt increasingly reluctant to rejoin Curtis. I preferred the companionship of the voices, malicious as they sometimes seemed. I stopped by one window and watched the ice sliding past. The inertia of such an enormous building was incalculable to one so little schooled in physics as myself, but I guessed it would be more than sufficient to carry us beyond the centre of the planet. I fell into a reverie. I wondered if I had caught a fever. I decided to return to the ramp and enter the furnace room. If I was ill I would welcome the attentions of Curtis despite my growing distaste for his presence. It was a question of priorities.

I was nearly there when the collision happened. I had been wandering in a delirium for a week. I called out to Curtis, and he answered from afar. We were sliding sideways across an unseen roof. Hours later we began the shorter drop to the next balcony. I felt my companion lift me under the arms. I shouted that I didn't want to be hurled onto the ramp. He laughed, and I saw he had removed all his clothes. He was dressed only in oily sweat and grime. A mad stoker.

"Fresh air is what you need. Lean on me and I'll take you across to the next house."

7. A Sunken Nation

I recovered quickly. Curtis had made elaborate preparations for entering a building as large as a small country. Once through the windows he lit the candles in the bedroom with a device he had constructed himself, a taper fixed to the end of a telescopic pole. Out on the plaza of the landing we didn't bother starting down the steps. Curtis attached ropes to the banister and dropped them into the stairwell.

During my fevered absence chasing voices he had discovered storerooms containing not only climbing and mining equipment but explosives and inflammable liquids. We lowered a selection of choice items into the darkness, following like spiders on threads. This house was so vast and the stairwell so deep there was a substantial difference in air pressure between the level of the balcony and the ground.

Despite the frost Curtis still refused to wear clothes. He was playing his new role properly. When we reached the bottom he scurried and leapt like a wild goat. I wondered how long it would be before he trimmed his beard into a point or fork. With his previous experience he constructed a new ramp in astonishingly fast time. The fireplace we had to tend was a cavern as wide and high as the crater we had originally entered that fateful night. The amount of fuel needed to warm this house was staggering.

I flicked through some of the books on the multitude of shelves which stretched for miles to the end of the furnace room. They were written in an alphabet which contained at least sixty letters. Very few words were pronounceable, let alone meaningful. I was called away by Curtis. He had already started a fire in the hearth. He had plans to dynamite part of the stairs and the next highest floor, bringing tons of wood down on the rollers of the ramp. I took cover in the kitchens, searching for food and voices.

I consumed most of a bottle of brandy, calling for the unseen people to stop hiding; but they always eluded me. Far away, like a storm in an adjacent valley, the rumble of an explosion vibrated the floorboards. In a series of trapezoid studies I discovered collections of musical instruments. There were no telephones here, but I found the inlets and outlets of speaking tubes. They connected different sections of the intolerably large house. From one I heard Curtis singing as he worked. I kept silent and didn't reply to him. I tried to estimate the dimensions of the house, but the answers were always ridiculous.

I knew I had to find Curtis before we reached the next balcony. I was lost in a tangle of corridors and galleries. The laughter of my companion was no clue as to which direction to choose, for frequently it emerged from the trumpet of a speaking tube. I took long detours for little or no profit. I came across rooms decorated with wallpaper so freakish it infected my dreams—the yellow of stained cups and mummified eyes, the orange of dying suns and the blushes of executioners. I strummed a lute as I went, attempting to teach myself tunes at the back of my memory.

There were too many unanswerable questions. If the frozen lake was bottomless, how could it be contained within the sphere of our world? How many houses existed in the lake? Who had built them, and would they continue to get bigger indefinitely? I wondered if I would ever lose count of them, forgetting the exact number of balconies, bedrooms, stairs, and hearths. Already there were more clocks in the furnace room than rooms in the original mansion. Such pointless repetition deeply oppressed my sanity.

At last the anticipated lurch came and the house began to slip into the ice. I sat on the floor as it accelerated to a horrible speed. It had taken Curtis a long time to make a hot enough blaze to set this building on its way. Even with my assistance I thought it unlikely we could get the next house moving. This possibility had evidently occurred to him. I finally found him squatting on the apex of a pyramid of broken furniture. His lips were curved in a smile, but his eyes were humourless.

"I used too much dynamite. Brought down more than I expected."

"We're dropping at a fearsome rate."

He maintained his false smile. "There's an inferno in the hearth."

"Do you believe that explosives and accelerants will be enough for the fifth house? It might be the size of a continent!"

"Fifth, did you say? Don't you mean the thirteenth?"

"I don't follow you," I replied.

He peered at me more closely and rubbed his eyes with blistered knuckles. "You've lost count somewhere. This is the twelfth mansion. We're heading toward number thirteen now. If you weren't so young I'd say you had gone a little senile! Maybe it was that fever you caught a while back? I don't get things like that anymore. I'm the devil. My immune system is too strong."

I shrugged. I was convinced the error was his, but I didn't care to argue with a madman. I was mildly amused to note he had trimmed his beard. Curtis always did the most with what he had, but nothing would ever cause him to grow horns and a tail. His face was less round now. He was learning real hardness, the bake of the furnace and constant physical exertion. He fell silent and probed a tooth with his tongue. I saw that two or three of his incisors were chipped. Then I noticed the gash on his neck, probably an effect of the blast. Even the devil should be careful with explosives.

"It doesn't really matter," I said.

He leaned his head to one side. "What doesn't?"

I frowned. I had forgotten the subject of our conversation. Flinching from his earlier remark about senility I countered, "Don't you remember?"

He sighed. "Listen, Warren, I'm really looking forward to reaching the next house, whatever its number. I want to keep going for as long as we can. Do you know why? Because one day we'll reach a mansion so vast it will be as big as the world! If we can't get back to the surface, that will be the next best thing, a perfect substitute. A house with as much surface area as the world but more compact because all that space will be arranged on many levels. Like tectonic plates stacked above each other."

"But we'll never be able to make fires big enough to reach it."

"Not on our own, true."

I answered slowly, "I don't think we are alone here. I believe there are other beings, possibly people, in some of the rooms. There may even be a great many of them. A tribe. A civilisation, hiding or waiting. I don't know if we could enlist their help, but it might be worth a try. We don't have a choice really. If we don't find them our next stop will be our last. Our final destination."

"I don't want that. I want to keep going until we reach a house as big as an entire world. It will be my equivalent of going home."

I nodded, but I suspected his real motives were different from his stated ones. I imagined he wanted to rule a private empire, a personal pandemonium, a replica of hell in the ice. In our position our ambitions were understandably warped, but at least Curtis had a definite wish. My own desires were vague, as if they sought without success to crystallise in a brain of sluggish lava. I turned away, but I didn't embark on another minor expedition yet. I went down into the nearest cellar and crouched with my fingertips on the flagstones, foolishly hoping to feel the presence of the next house as we hurtled towards it.

8. A Brand New World

And Curtis led the way again through the windows into the bedroom. We despaired of reaching the ground floor, even by ropes, and distracted ourselves from thinking about starting the voyage by searching the wardrobes arranged along the wall. They stood like hollow megaliths in the shadows all the way to the remote door which led to the landing, each sixty feet tall and yet only a fraction as high as the ceiling. As we walked past the vibrations of our feet set the wire coathangers inside tinkling, a soft sound like the stilts of insane acrobats wading through lagoons of mercury.

We opened doors indiscriminately. Most were empty or contained a few jackets and trousers, undecayed but useless, for they all had at least three arms and legs. But in the interior of one I discovered another wardrobe and inside this another. We passed through a nest of concealed boxes. Inside the final one I noticed a lever and a key set into the floor. I remarked that this wardrobe resembled a primitive elevator, and Curtis nodded thoughtfully. Then he stooped next to me, grasped the key, and twisted it.

"A clockwork device," he grunted.

"Wind it tight and then I'll pull the lever. Maybe this is what all those clocks are kept for? Spare cogs and springs."

When he had finished I released the brake. We dropped down a hidden shaft, the wardrobe rattling and screeching. I wanted to clasp Curtis for reassurance, but his nudity repulsed me. After a long time we began to slow and finally came to a halt. We stumbled out into the murk at the base of the stairwell, our ears ringing. The portal to the furnace room was less than one hour's walk from here. I don't know which of us was most confused. I had started to believe this was the thirteenth house, but Curtis now insisted it was only the fifth. We had swapped delusions.

"You have a reasonable excuse for your forgetfulness," I said. "Memory is something which evolved for its survival value. Learning from experience is a useful tool. But the devil didn't evolve from anything. He was always the way he is now. I can't defend my own senility in the same way. I'm just a weak mortal."

We entered the furnace room and gasped. At the very limit of the beams of our flashlights the immense cliff of the hearth reared up. The frost on the mantelpiece glittered like perpetual snows on the peaks of a high mountain range. In vain I looked for tigers and smugglers loaded with chests of tea. I mopped my face with my sleeve. I was perspiring despite the low temperature. My fever had not entirely dissipated. Curtis took a few steps forward, paused, and looked back over his shoulder.

"This fireplace will defeat us. However hard we work we'll never fill it. There's no point even trying on our own. I'm not a giant."

"Nor I. There's only one thing we can do."

There was an uneasy silence, then we clasped hands.

"We'll split up. We must promise not to return here until we find some other beings to help us. It might take weeks, months, years."

"Goodbye, Curtis. Best of luck."

"Thanks, Warren. Take care of yourself. Sorry for getting you into this fix in the first place. I took your world away from you. I'll do my best to replace it. You'll be my deputy in pandemonium. I'll make you my successor."

I released his hand. Before I left the furnace room I decided to satisfy my curiosity in one other regard. I set off on the trek towards the region of bookcases. When I reached it my suspicions were confirmed. Every letter in each word in the volumes I inspected was completely different from all the others. They had descended into pure gibberish. I couldn't imagine what creatures might speak such a language. I didn't need to, for either Curtis or I stood a chance of actually encountering them. Until that moment I would do my best not to speculate. There was no point wasting thoughts.

I passed out of the furnace room through an obscure side door. I found myself in a corridor which constantly altered its width from very narrow to very wide and which ran straight for no more than fifty paces at a time before sloping or veering off at an acute angle. My flashlight died. I ran in darkness, bruising my knees and elbows against the walls. There must have been speaking tubes here also, or else the passage itself possessed its own weird acoustical properties, for as the days passed I infrequently heard the voice of Curtis as if the man or devil himself stood behind one of my shoulders.

He was calling out, "Anyone at home?"

At last the corridor spluttered me out into light. I stood on the landing of an upper level. Candles as high as power pylons blazed far above me, the wicks hissing like coal suns. Curtis must have already passed this way. I ascended a short staircase and roamed through a warren of ovoid rooms.

The final one contained an observatory. A powerful reflecting telescope rested on a tripod with legs as thick as girders. I climbed a ladder to the eyepiece and adjusted the focus. The chamber was studded with windows, but none faced out onto the endless ice. The observatory was located near the centre of the building. I studied burning candelabra in unimaginably remote rooms with the interest an astronomer might reserve for nebulae. I swung the telescope and explored other vistas, the distant reaches of carpeted corridors and spiral stairways.

Once I thought I detected a cluster of moving shapes. They vanished before I could be sure of their nature. Equally hopelessly I looked for Curtis.

Abandoning the telescope, I vacated the room and continued my journey. Within a week I heard the voices again. It was still impossible to catch up with them. On a whim I decided to violate the pact I had made with Curtis and return to the furnace room alone. The passages blended into one, and all I could rely on to estimate the distance I walked was the complex unearthly melody I created from the squeaky floorboards I occasionally trod upon, each one a slightly different note, sometimes less than one thousandth of a tone apart. Or so I guessed. And then I discovered a bicycle leaning against a hatstand. My average speed increased dramatically.

The unseen voices returned and grew louder. This time they didn't seem to be hiding from me. I rang my bell, but they were still a journey of several days ahead. I was pedalling a course I had already examined with the telescope, a channel of inner space. The air slowly became warmer around me. I felt sick. My smugness melted with the ice which pressed upon the house. Curtis had done something truly diabolical. I forced myself to dismount and rest, sheltering under a table in a recess of the panelled wall. Beneath the hissing pylons I slept fitfully.

I woke and resumed my race into the cacophony and heat. The sounds of industry were ferocious, an unbearable clatter of hammering and sawing. I bounced down a staircase and crossed an immense carpeted plain. Shadows danced across the threshold of a portal. I braked and came to a halt on the edge of this room. It pulsed with fire. It was the furnace room and it was full. Nightmare figures capered everywhere, cutting up furniture and casting it into the fire. Sometimes they threw in one of their own kind by mistake. And the house was sliding down, building up speed. I knew for sure our inertia was sufficient to carry us beyond the gravitational centre of the planet. And I suddenly understood something Curtis hadn't even suspected.

I felt an arm on my shoulder.

"Speak of the devil," I joked feebly.

"I was wondering when you'd come back. Look at what I've created, Warren! Just like hell now, isn't it? We're on our way to the next house. I've discussed it with my demons, and they all disagree on which number this one is. I've decided to take the average of five and thirteen and call it the ninth."

"You've become a wise ruler," I said.

"Why not? There's no reason for the devil to be obtuse. Come in and I'll introduce you. The next house down will be as big as our world."

"I'll pass on that offer. It's too crowded in here for comfort."

He made no effort to detain me. "Very well. Tell you what, I'll appoint you my envoy to the farthest reaches of my realm. That way you can go off exploring without feeling you have let me down. What do you say?"

I turned and wheeled my bicycle away. As I mounted it the barely concealed rage in my former companion's voice seemed to push me along. I accelerated from the mouth of a domestic tartarus.

Still he boomed after me, "You are a useful servant of the crown of hell. I salute you, my trusted envoy. Who knows what regions and tribes you might come across? May your mission succeed!"

I laughed to myself as I escaped him forever.

I had plans of my own, less grandiose than his but no less surprising. The development of a puncture halfway across a room so large it contained clouds and entire weather patterns did nothing to deter me. I continued on foot. I sheltered from the rain under a glass coffee table as wide as a lake. One by one the candles were extinguished. Lightning relit them and moved behind a range of sofas. My beard grew ragged as I pressed on. I was looking good for my age, but my skin felt thirsty for the sun. The simple pleasures of life on the surface haunted me: autumn leaves, the moon.

There were no more houses below us—I was confident of this fact. This was the last one. I had worked it out carefully.

Each time we touched down on the roof of a building we slid sideways. Part of our motion had been horizontal as well as vertical. This horizontal displacement had added up to many miles. It was something we had mostly overlooked, and yet the consequences were remarkable and exciting.

If a man moves horizontally across the face of the globe he will eventually find himself at the antipodes, on the far side of the world. But he won't fall off because the direction called 'down' is determined by the centre of the planet, the point of greatest gravitational attraction. The deeper into the earth he goes the less horizontal movement he will need to circle this point. This also holds true for houses.

We were falling back up.

We had reached a position opposite the crater in which had stood the Baron's mansion. We had reached a point directly below the far side of the world. The antipodes were above us. Now our inertia would carry us beyond the centre of the earth and back through the ice the way we had come. But we wouldn't collide with any houses as we went because this house had already collected them. The way was clear. We would break through into the crater and the real world. Upside down.

At any rate, this was my theory.

There were problems with it, but I chose not to dwell on those. For instance, Curtis had seriously underestimated the dimensions of this building. From my experience in the observatory I calculated it as already several sizes larger than the planet which contained it. One of life's awkward paradoxes, I guess. Thus it was impossible to imagine what might happen when the house surfaced.

But whatever the result, I felt deep pity for the owner of the antique store who had sold Curtis his cabinet. The devil was bound to want revenge on the man who had tricked him. The fool would be completely defenceless. And yet, if the Baron was really still alive he surely would have employed his magical or scientific powers to disguise himself with the appearance of youth. There was no better way to divert suspicion, even if his desiccated brain did make the occasional mistake.

I had always been very clever, and senility would take some getting used to. Fortunately I had been clever enough to foresee my own senility and take it into account. I had forgotten my own identity and abode, even my original language and desires, but I was still being controlled by a plan I had invented in my youth. I was my own puppet. At least this was the best option remaining to me. I might as well embrace it. The role of devil had already been taken.

I chuckled to myself. Everything had come together very well. I would resolve the inconsistencies at my leisure. Only one difficult task remained to make my satisfaction complete. I would return to the original mansion. Stored at the end of a sequence of diminishing balconies, forgotten by the devil and unsuspected by his minions, beyond innumerable stairways and corridors and rooms, it waited modestly for me to take up my rightful residence at last.

I was going home.

Degrees of Separation

When the cigarette and glass of whisky were finished, all that was left was the knife. Clute turned it slowly in his hands as he sat in front of the mirror. Then he studied his reflection carefully. The face of a man planning revenge stared back at him. It was no different from the other faces he pulled on any random day.

He wanted to kill Bradman because of what Bradman had done. But to use this knife against that vague and terrible enemy would not be easy. Bradman was difficult to reach, living in a mansion protected by a high wall, guarded by huge dogs. Clute read the newspapers. Bradman had even posted armed guards on his grounds.

If Clute made a direct attempt on the life of Bradman he certainly would fail. He had no accomplices, no influence, no money or power. His vengeance would amount to nothing tangible. He had to seek some lateral method of scoring a strike against his adversary. Bradman's family were no less secure than he. What next?

There was Frost, Bradman's closest friend since childhood. Unlike Bradman, Frost travelled without bodyguards and lived in a house with a low wall and only one dog. But Frost was popular and rarely seen alone. How might Clute get close enough for the plunge? Again he probably would fail, his blade remaining thirsty.

Frost often went to the theatre to watch Cosimo perform. Cosimo was an accomplished singer and actor who was intimate with Frost but hardly aware of the existence of the less cultured Bradman. Ending the life of Cosimo would cause a deep wound in Frost, and if Frost was hurt, Bradman would also feel a measure of pain.

This was the answer! Clute reached for the newspaper on an adjacent table and flicked the pages until he found an advertisement for

Cosimo's latest play. The show began at nine the same evening. If Clute turned up early, he might be able to slip backstage and murderously encounter the actor in his own dressing room.

No, it was unlikely he would get past the doormen. They would grow suspicious and perform a search on him. The knife would be uncovered and the police summoned. Then opportunity for revenge against Bradman would become even less likely. Better to forget Cosimo. Clute remembered that Cosimo was connected to Kingsley.

Clute had read about it in the papers. The two men frequently went to restaurants together. In fact, Kingsley taught Cosimo everything there was to know about fine wine and good food. All Clute had to do was book a table in the same place as Kingsley at the same time. Halfway through the meal, the deed could be done.

But what if Clute failed to kill Kingsley outright? Stabbing is not always effective. In a public place such as a restaurant, his time would be limited. If Kingsley recovered from his injuries, Cosimo would not be racked by grief, and so Frost could not be damaged in any way, and thus Bradman would not suffer at all.

Running the fleshy part of his thumb gently along the serrated edge of the blade and smiling slightly, Clute silently listed the restaurants frequented by Kingsley in order of excellence. The best was run by a man called Whitlam. A hole cut in Whitlam's chest would be no less a hole in Kingsley's life, an irreparable hole.

Yes, he would seek out Whitlam, perhaps in one of his kitchens, or better still during one of his frequent trips to the market to buy fresh produce. The glint of steel among the vegetables, the crash of trays of fish preserved in ice, and the chain reaction of vengeance would be set in motion, all the way to Bradman.

The problem with tackling Whitlam was that the man was an expert in the use of blades and always wore a knife or cleaver at his belt, even when shopping in public. Whitlam surely knew how to defend himself and strike back. Clute would be the one left dying among the tomatoes, his life blood a sauce on the cobbles.

Whitlam had once taught cooking at the local college. He had taught Malevich for a year and even announced Malevich as his star pupil. After Malevich abandoned the culinary arts and went into finance, Whitlam did not fail to keep in touch with his protégé. Malevich was perfect for any sudden death, slow-moving, trusting.

The big advantage of killing Malevich was that Clute knew him very well. In fact, they were close friends. It would be simplicity itself to invite him back to this room on some pretext and then commit an act of righteous violence on the fat dupe. Clute nodded once. He picked up the telephone and dialled his number.

Malevich agreed to come within the hour. Clute simply told him that something important needed to transpire between them. He mentioned few details, only that it had something to do with Bradman, a person almost unknown to Malevich. Clute chuckled. He imagined the expressions on the sequence of faces, the transmitted pain.

Shortly before Malevich arrived, Clute suddenly remembered that new neighbours had moved into the apartment directly below him. They were a bothersome couple, extremely sensitive to the slightest noise. Malevich was a bear of a man. He would knock loudly on Clute's door, roar out his greeting, stamp across the floorboards.

Long before Clute could force his knife into Malevich's heart, the neighbours would be hurrying up the stairs to complain. There simply was too little time for the operation to be performed efficiently. Scowling, Clute abandoned his plan. His need for revenge must remain unsatisfied. Bradman had escaped without a scratch!

Or had he? Clute pursed his lips. Malevich had a friend that Clute could certainly assault. This friend would not even struggle or make an appreciable vocal fuss. He was the perfect victim! Bradman might shelter behind walls, dogs, and bodyguards but here was a chink in his armour, a chink that soon would spurt crimson juice.

Clute almost felt pity for the poor defenceless Bradman as he moved quietly across his room to unlatch the door. Now Malevich would not have to knock before confronting the balancing scene of carnage. Returning to his chair and the wise mirror, Clute raised the knife and savagely drew it across his own unforgiven throat.

The Warlord

The warlord lives in a cave in the side of a mountain that rises from the centre of an island that sits in the middle of a lake. The cave is small but so is the mountain and the island, and he is alone there, with no one to obey his orders. On the other hand, his desires are never disputed, his ambitions never objected to. He dreams whatever he wants to dream and no voice opposes him.

But he has no wish to remain on the island for the rest of his life. A genuine warlord seeks always to expand his territories, to control more and more land, rule over greater numbers of people. So he resolves to leave the island. He has no boat to sail to the farther shore of the lake, nor does he have the materials or knowledge to fashion his own. He must find another way.

With pick and shovel he digs away at the soil on the floor of his cave, hacks his way down into the soft rock, and then turns at a sharp angle, tunnelling beneath the bed of the lake at a safe depth. It is hard work, for he has no aid, but he reminds himself that he is an authentic warlord, the toughest of the tough, and if anyone can accomplish the strenuous dirty project, he can.

Progress is slow but steady, and one morning he estimates that he has passed under the entire width of the lake, so he digs upwards. He emerges on the shore in triumph and sees his island in the distance, wreathed in mist, the mountain like the last rotten tooth in the mouth of an old beast new to science. He washes himself in the little wavelets of the lake and feels ecstatic.

This land turns out also to be an island in the centre of another, larger lake, a ring of earth and stones inhabited by two people. They are castaways or perhaps the descendants of castaways, they are unsure which. He discovers them soon after his emergence from the hole. They are not friendly but not hostile either; and it requires little effort on his part to make them his subjects.

His rule is firm but not murderous. He is a warlord, not an insane emperor, a difference of huge importance to his code of honour. They fetch him food while he sits on a fallen coconut tree and daydreams, for thinking vague thoughts is his chief recreational activity. The pick and shovel are his symbols of authority and they lie crossed at his feet, gleaming dully in the noon sun.

Time passes and he grows restless. He is a warlord and his domain is bigger than it ever was, but he wants it to be yet larger. He is acutely aware of the fact that he is not yet a major warlord, and this is something that rankles more and more. The momentous day finally arrives when he announces his intention to leave the island, this atoll of scarce resources and limited horizons.

He gives the pick to one of his subjects and the shovel to the other. Then he stands and shouts orders, supervising the digging of the new tunnel intended to take them beneath this larger lake to the shore beyond. Because he is a stern taskmaster the work proceeds at speed. Nonetheless, it is still a period of twelve months before the tunnel is fully completed and they can emerge.

Yet again, they have failed to reach the mainland, if there actually is one, for this is also an island in an even bigger lake, inhabited by four people, a quartet that even offer resistance to the invasion; but the warlord and his two followers have the advantage of physical strength, for digging tunnels is conducive to making muscles larger and firmer. The four locals are overpowered.

The warlord gives them a choice, the standard choice offered by warlords in all eras and circumstances. They choose to submit rather than die; and they become his latest subjects. So now he rules a society of six individuals. This island is easily able to accommodate and feed seven people in total. The trees are varied and fruits are simple to pick; there are grapevines everywhere.

Life is more enjoyable here than on the two previous islands; and yet it still burns inside him, his ambition, and he longs for more. He is a warlord, he reminds himself, not a chairman of a social group or the treasurer of a charity. Conquest and hegemony are his watchwords. He instructs his new subjects to make digging tools from the hardest available woods; and thus they do.

The new tunnel has six workers digging it and the task proceeds in shifts, so there is never a moment when the picks and shovels are idle. Reeds drenched in oil are used to illuminate the perilous work. The finished tunnel is twice as long as the previous one, but because there are three times as many diggers the result takes less duration in total: eight months instead of twenty-four.

They emerge on the shore of yet another island in the middle of another lake, an atoll with a population of eight people. The seven invaders overpower them in a bloodless struggle and the warlord accepts promises of loyalty from the indigenous inhabitants after they agree to surrender to him. So now the warlord has an army of fourteen warriors and his stature expands accordingly.

Inevitably, he is satisfied for only a short time in his new realm. His subjects must obey his order to dig another tunnel. All fifteen of them eventually emerge on the shore of another island. This tunnel is exactly twice as long as the previous one, but there are more than twice as many workers digging it and the warlord receives a lesson in basic mathematics he never really wanted.

The latest tunnel would have taken forty-eight months to dig with the original pair of subjects; but there are fourteen diggers now, seven times as many hands and muscles, so the project is completed in less than seven months—6.857 months, to be precise. On this island, as expected, there are sixteen inhabitants. Events follow the familiar pattern and the warlord's contingent swells.

Now he has thirty followers; and with their aid the next tunnel, also twice as long as the previous one, takes 6.4 months to dig and brings them to the fifth island out from the central island where the warlord began his campaign. He has ceased to wonder about the curious concentric nature of this arrangement, the islands in lakes that are in islands that are in lakes that are in islands.

Simply the way things happen to be, nothing more than that, and it is not his place to question the quirks of geography. His destiny is to conquer and expand his empire. Keep your mind on that and try not to get distracted, he warns himself. On the new island there is a population of thirty-two individuals, and he soon adds them to his followers, an army both of invaders and workers.

He now has a force of sixty-two people at his beck and call. The next tunnel to the next island is completed in 6.193 months, though with the first two diggers it would have taken 192 months. As for the next tunnel: that is dug by 126 workers over a period of 6.0952 months, and thus an annoying fact becomes apparent to the warlord.

Although his workforce is expanding all the time, the increased rate of tunnel digging is dropping off. There is nothing he can do about this, no matter how much he screams and threatens. It is a simple truth of numbers. The period for digging a new tunnel is tending towards the value of six months. It always takes him slightly longer than a year to invade and absorb two new islands.

He does the calculations on his fingers. He is no longer a young man. When he is old and ailing, weak of eyesight and feeble of limb, he will be unable to enjoy the fruits of his labours. He decides to set a time limit of ten years to the expansion of his empire. After one decade he will stop, settle down, and rule as a man who has finally achieved his dream. He will sit down on history.

You may do the arithmetic for yourself. When the ten-year period was up, he found himself emerging on the twentieth island, a vast ring of land inhabited by no less than 148,576 people. His own army, including himself, was only one fewer than this number. He should have had no problem conquering this island, his ultimate aim.

But the island was already ruled by a warlord, and this new warlord defeated the invaders, capturing the old warlord and joking with him. I am a major warlord, he said, but I can see from the dirt on your knees that you are a miner one. Then the new warlord embarked on his own campaign, his own dream, but it was a reversal of conquest, quite an unexpected ambition for a warlord.

He led his followers, now increased by the invaders who had submitted and joined him to 2,097,151, down through the tunnels that had already been burrowed, heading inwards beneath the lakes and leaving garrisons on each atoll. Thus the new warlord shed followers as the old had collected them, casting off responsibilities.

By vacating his own island entirely he ensured that he would not be alone, as the old warlord had been in the cave in the mountain, when he reached his ultimate destination. He always left half his warriors on each island, and eventually he came to the mountain in the centre of the most central lake, and there were two with him, for that was the highest number of men he wanted to rule.

It had long been his desire to be a smaller warlord, more modest in his vistas and power, no longer deeply immersed in history but merely paddling at the edges, free of having to make momentous decisions, obscure and safe, happy at last, with nights devoid of assassins, mornings lacking usurpers, afternoons and evenings as calm as the waters of the smallest lake of infinite lakes.

And so he took up residence in the cave, this new warlord, one might say the true warlord, and of his two followers, who served him most loyally for the rest of his days, of which there were very many; one of them was the old warlord himself. That was somehow inevitable. As for the other, it might be me. Or even you. Look around and tell me what you see and I will do the same.

Vampiric Gramps

Logic can be a frightening thing. The power of the mind to apply reason to a problem is often the most highly praised talent of humanity; and yet I have learned from vile and grim experience that pure deduction is capable of reducing a man to mewling and shuddering paroxysms of despair. Not so long ago I *was* that man. Indeed, in many ways, I still am. Logic is the origin of my misery, the bane of my soul.

It began with a mildly philosophical discussion about those legendary beings known as vampires. I was talking to my neighbour and friend, Mr Damocles Blinker. He had won fame in his youth as an explorer of weird lands and beliefs, travelling the world and learning arcane secrets from a succession of improbable priests, gurus, and occultists. Of all his meetings the most memorable had been in Moldova.

"I have told you this story many times before," he said as he accepted the glass of brandy from me, "but as you never seem to tire of hearing it, I see no reason not to oblige you again . . ."

"Thank you, Damocles!" I blurted in my enthusiasm.

He grinned. "My pleasure, Burt."

And he proceeded to set the scene, to describe the woodlands north of the town of Iaşi, the lonely road, the impenetrable night, the fierce storm, the frantic search for shelter, the knocking on the oaken door of an unlighted residence, the creaking as it opened . . .

"Ghetu was a genuine vampire, I assure you, an aristocratic avatar of that particular brand of evil," he said.

"Almost a cliché?" I ventured uncertainly.

Damocles nodded. "Yes, my friend. He had the black cloak, the

74

pallid expression, the empty castle; but it wasn't a real castle, more of a fortified manor house. It was deserted and cobwebbed from highest turret to cellar and filled with antiques that he regarded merely as bric-a-brac, clocks and clavichords, velocipedes and phonographs. He informed me that I was his first guest for more than thirty years."

"And he showed you to a spare room in the attic?"

"He did. With a dusty black bed."

"You were his guest for three whole days?"

"Yes. Until the storm abated."

"And he never tried to bite you during your stay?"

"No, Burt. But there's a good reason for that. Ghetu assumed that I too was a vampire, a kindred dark spirit."

"Damocles, why would he think such a thing?"

"The answer to your query is simple, Burt. Please refill my glass with more brandy first. Thanks. In the long central hall of his house, there was an enormous circular mirror hanging on one wall; but in that mirror I had no reflection, and he noticed the fact."

"This occurred shortly after your arrival?"

"Yes, while I was still stained from the rigours of my journey. I passed that mirror only once; during the remainder of my visit I never went back into the central hall. That was lucky."

"But you're not really a vampire, are you?"

Damocles drained his glass before responding; he was a master of the theatrical pause. "No," he said quietly.

"What are you then? The transparent man?"

I waited patiently, but he was unforthcoming, so I prodded him with a deep sigh. He looked up and explained:

"The reason I had no reflection was an optical illusion, nothing more. I doubtless would have been exposed as a fraud had I stood in front of that mirror on the following days. But that first instance convinced Ghetu that I was as undead and vampiric as he. The truth is that it was an example of camouflage rather than invisibility. The stains on my clothing matched to a remarkable degree the patterns of mould on the wall opposite the mirror and in the dim light of the few candles . . ."

"You blended perfectly into the reflected background?"

"Exactly, Burt! Ghetu never realised!"

It was at this precise point that a sudden thought occurred to me. I had heard the story from Damocles' lips many times; it was enjoyable, almost soothing in a peculiar way, but suddenly there was something I wanted to ask that I'd never considered before. I can't frown like ordinary men, nor can I pout or squint, but my apprehension manifested itself in other ways, in a specific movement beyond the ability of most human beings, a gentle undulation unmistakable to my friend.

"You are troubled," he observed. "But why?"

When the ripple had passed and I was calm again, I voiced the thought aloud, my abrupt revelation, the dark epiphany. I said, "Vampires have no reflections in mirrors. If a big mirror is hung on a wall of a room, or if the wall *is* the mirror, then everything present in the room that doesn't show a reflection will be a vampire. That's logic."

Damocles set down his glass and poured himself more brandy; it must have been clear to him that I was too distracted by my own philosophical ponderings to remember my duty as a host and attend to his needs. "Yes, it is," he agreed. "Unassailable and clear."

"That is the famous test for vampires, isn't it? A good vampire hunter will always carry a mirror with him . . ."

"Or with *her*," he replied, somewhat testily. "Don't forget that women work in this field too. I once knew a feisty redhead with green eyes by the name of—" But he noticed my agitation and broke off. He knocked back his drink and his cheeks visibly pulsed.

"I can think of something in that hypothetical room that will *never* be reflected in that conjectural mirror," I said.

"Never, Burt?" he answered.

"Not once. Shall I now tell you what it is?"

He was amenable. "Please do."

I hissed sharply, "The mirror itself!"

Damocles absorbed this information. His intelligence and experience, both considerable, seemed to bend inside his head, furrowing his brow so thickly with lines that for a moment it seemed he had imprisoned himself behind the bars of a horizontal jail.

"But that means . . ." he said thickly, his tongue protruding.

"Yes, my friend. It's true."

"All mirrors are vampires!" he screeched.

He half raised himself out of the chair, fell back with a deflating hiss, and despite my perspicacity I couldn't tell whether it was the cushion or his ego that had compressed. "All."

Pounding the arms of the chair with his fists, he wept.

We sat in silence for minutes.

Finally I added, "Logic can't be argued with. Tomorrow morning I'll remove every mirror from every room in my house. I suggest you do the same. We'll have to spread the word, let other people know. Because of vanity, we have all been harbouring undead parasites among us for many millennia. This situation must cease."

He nodded. I had convinced him; or rather, logic had. Pure logic. Why keep pets when logic purrs around your ankles with such tenacity? For an hour we tried to change the topic, to discuss a few of his other adventures, lighter in tone than his Moldavian exploit, but it was useless. The stain of darkness had seeped into our souls. At last he bade me goodnight and left me alone. The house was lonely again.

Many days passed and then logic came back, its ramifications causing mayhem in unexpected corners of my psyche. I realised that if mirrors are vampires, then all vampires must be mirrors. Or to put this statement into algebraic form: if $M=V$, then $V=M$. Soon enough the implications of this formula substantially increased my dread.

I reasoned as follows: If all vampires are mirrors, whenever I look at a real vampire I should see myself, my own reflection. Anyone might be a vampire, any random individual in the street. If I looked at someone and they *didn't* look like me, in other words if I couldn't see myself reflected in them, then either they were normal humans or else they were vampires who were failing to show my reflection.

And in the latter case, the only logical reason for this failure was that I had no reflection myself. Which would mean that I too was a vampire! In the following months I stared with phenomenal intensity into the faces of everyone I encountered. I went to restaurants, theatre lobbies, taverns, and libraries, every location where I might reasonably be expected to have the opportunity of meeting crowds of people.

But not once did I find one who looked just like me!

And yet they couldn't *all* be normal human beings. The statistical odds against that were incalculable. At least one of them had to be a vampire. I know that vampires form a tiny percentage of the general population; the most oft-quoted figure is less than 1%, but I had stared into the visages of thousands of individuals. The logical conclusion was that I *had* stared at a vampire face to face, but that he or she hadn't displayed my reflection. So there was no way I could deny the truth.

Burt Smith, namely myself, was a vampire . . .

The horrid realisation of my condition depressed me. Was it foolish to hope for a cure? I had no wish to adopt the lifestyle of a bloodsucker, my outer physique and inner parts aren't suitable for vampiric activities, I'm simply not agile enough; I have the maximum flexibility of a grandfather, no more than that. Indeed, I am often called 'Gramps' by my friends as a term of descriptive or metaphoric endearment. So I decided to seek out a surgeon capable of reversing my condition.

I learned that the only surgeon who might be skilled enough to aid me in my quest was Doctor Ricky Tensor . . .

Thanks to the modern miracle of the telephone network I managed to contact his secretary. I carefully explained what I wanted. By this time, I was so terrified of myself that I refused to leave my house. "He must visit *me*," I insisted, but she was disdainful.

"Dr Tensor never makes house calls," she said.

"I simply can't come to his clinic. I have agoraphobia. I have plenty of money. I'll pay double his normal fee."

"Only double?" she sneered.

"Yes, but I will triple that double . . ."

"One moment." She went off to consult the surgeon.

She returned a few minutes later and said, "He has agreed. Please give me your address. Now I must warn you of something: Dr Tensor doesn't have a normal appearance. He is—"

"Disfigured?" I ventured.

"Just so. Horribly. In an explosion."

"That is of no consequence to me. Ten years ago I had an accident and I'm no pretty picture myself," I said.

"Very well. You may expect him in the afternoon."

I replaced the telephone receiver.

Then I set to work turning my dining room into a temporary operating theatre. I cleared all the ornaments off the table, turned on the lamps, and disinfected the walls and floor. I trembled at the thought of what it might take to cut the vampiric element out of me. Maybe I wouldn't survive the procedure. But I had to take that risk.

The condition of being a paranormal parasite couldn't be endured any longer. Already Damocles was beginning to guess the truth. I had stopped answering the door to him when he knocked. I ignored the social calls of all my other friends. Burt Smith, alias Gramps, was a vampire, and it was better for him to shun mortal company.

The hours crawled past like mummified lice.

At last, after an agony of waiting, the surgeon rapped on my door with the secret knock I had specified. I flung it open. Terror and joy competed for the privilege of bursting my mind . . .

The source of the joy was a realisation that I was already cured! I had got better on my own, without the aid of scalpel or medicine. I've always had a very strong immune system. Proof of my cure was the fact that Dr Tensor looked *exactly* like me. He was my double, my reflection. Thus I couldn't be a vampire. That's logic again.

But if he was capable of reflecting my appearance, he must have been a mirror; and if he was a mirror, he must be a vampire. So I shrieked, and the shock of my shriek caused him to shriek too, and we stood there, face to face, shrieking across the cursed threshold of my front door, shrieking like tortured similes in a grammar dungeon.

I closed and opened my eyes, but his appearance didn't change. And it was a perfect replica of my own. A glass tank mounted on wheels, full of a mysterious bubbling liquid; and immersed in that fluid among a nest of tentacles, eyes on stalks and prehensile mouths fixed to the tips of fleshy tendrils, was a gigantic throbbing brain!

Bone Idle in the Charnel House

I dwell in the charnel house as a punishment for my indolence and I may never leave, for it has been sealed with blocks of basalt and gates of iron, and only the cracks in the poorly joined walls permit enough external light to enter to enable me to perceive my dead neighbours and bear witness to their expressions, which are all grim and leering, as befits the skeletons of times past. I am the only living being in this unpleasant place, and I have not even a corpse worm to keep me company; for the last shreds of flesh vanished from the most recent bones more than a century ago, and the tomb was declared full and shut by a man who knew my grandfather and was reopened only so that I might be pushed inside, an incongruous and belated addition. I remember my anguish at hearing the huge stones being cemented together behind me, but I no longer consider my imprisonment to be a harsh fate and indeed I have come to welcome it, and now I judge those who are outside, free under the stars, to be the real victims.

Even when I was young, I was not blessed with the energy and enthusiasm of my peers, who loved physical games and exertion, and I preferred to lie quietly on a couch and dream of nothing in particular. I liked to retire to bed early and rise late, and even the act of eating seemed to induce in me a profound exhaustion that only an hour or more of sleep might partly remedy. My parents were indulgent and never chided me for my condition, imagining that perhaps I suffered from a medical ailment, but no amount of potions or doctors ever succeeded in lessening my fatigue. If anything, the endless experimentation on my metabolism wore out my body and mind even more, so that I seemed to be living in a kind of clammy fog that had congealed around me from the vapours of the foul and useless medicines; but I submitted meekly and never complained. My schooling was intermittent, and it was decided that a profitable career was out of the question and that I should live out my existence on the charity of my family.

This arrangement was satisfactory if not ideal, for my parents and siblings and other relatives were not without resources, and we resided in a comfortable mansion on the lower slopes of the northern hills among the estates of the remaining semi-noble families with whom we shared similar histories and hopes. The atmosphere of my upbringing was one of faded grandeur and crumbling dignity; often I spent my waking hours studying the stained tapestries that hung motionless on the walls of interminable passages like enormous dead tongues, trying to fathom the meaning of the vague scenes they depicted, which poor illumination and the grime of untold years contrived to render unbearably mysterious and poignant. At other times I might persuade a brother or sister to help me walk as far as the vineyards, abandoned and now hopelessly overgrown, where the remains of an ancient tower still shielded its elaborate shadow from slow sun and stars, its flaking stones held together by creepers and the excrement of sombre, perfect owls.

Once I even managed to scale that tower, step by patient step, pausing frequently to rest, sipping from a flask of wine to revive my spirits, until I reached the shattered summit. There was just enough space for one man to stand, and I was able to peer over the sagging walls of adjacent estates to regard the multiplicity of gardens, some tended even worse than our own, all the way to the city proper, where the poor people and artisans lived in high tenements in narrow streets and where the petrified forest of chimneys on the broader roofscape, few smoking in these late summer months, seemed like the pillars of a temple which still awaited, or had lost, a suitable roof. Looking down I also saw that the shadow of my tower lay uneasily on the vines, like the cloak or soul of one of my ancestors draped over the incomprehensible furniture of olden days. Then my anxious parents called me and I absorbed one final view, that of the extensive burial grounds in the south, before commencing the long and exasperating descent back to my couch.

I remained indoors for about a year, preoccupied with sleeping, dreaming, and examining the remaining tapestries, one of which I was now able to interpret properly, for it depicted a scene almost identical to that which had greeted my eyes when I climbed the tower. It showed the city from the same vantage point at a much earlier date, though I was astonished at how few changes had actually taken place in the urban landscape. There were a dozen fewer buildings and a dozen more fields on the far side of the tangle of streets. This picture informed my dreams in the same way the real vista had, so I was no longer able to distinguish between memory and fantasy; but one detail that troubled me greatly was a vision of carts piled high with bodies being wheeled out to the burial grounds. An historical event or a contemporary disaster? I could not say, but my confusion was resolved in a most dramatic manner when my parents and siblings fell violently sick and a horrible dancing death came to visit our house.

It was not plague or any other kind of contagious disease that had alighted on the region, but a drastic case of accidental poisoning. The corn in the granaries was damp and a colourless mould had grown upon it, undetected by the millers and bakers who made all our bread and distributed it to the masses without malice. Beneath these crusts lurked our dooms. The traditional family meal in our mansion always began with bread, a custom shared not only by other semi-nobles but the common people who wished to mimic us. Only the very rich escaped catastrophe, for their dietary habits were more refined and absurd, and they regarded bread as hopelessly unfashionable. The toxins in the mould entered brains and destroyed the cerebral mechanisms necessary for sleep, so that the victims remained permanently awake and unable to rest for even a moment until they expired from exhaustion a week or so later. In theory I should not have been exempt from the curse, for I had also shared the poisoned feast, but I was already protected by my extreme indolence and merely achieved a normal level of wakefulness.

This unprecedented surge of energy allowed me to tend to my relatives, or rather to fail in the attempt, for in truth they were beyond help. I summoned a doctor and he confirmed my fears, stating that an absolute inability to sleep, a condition he called *agrypnia,* was almost never cured by itself, and he knew of no medicines or surgery that might reverse such damage to the brain. After he departed I conducted my own experiments in a desperate effort to save my relatives. I followed them from room to room and pounced upon them in dark corridors, knocking them to the floor and binding them tightly with leather straps, but still their muscles twitched and they pulled strange faces and bawled stranger songs, so that I was compelled to cut the bonds and allow them to convulse the rest of their lives away in freedom. Once I came upon them all dancing together in our largest hall, whirling without music at frightful speed, limbs flailing at grotesque angles, compulsively ticcing and grimacing and blinking, a festivity I could not endure. I fled to another part of the house and a week later I was truly alone.

The cart came for the bodies the following morning, and I walked behind it down the rutted road to the newest charnel house, passing those already full, each shrouded with the stench of decay at varying strengths depending on how old they were, the most ancient smelling of nothing at all. The corpses of my relatives were positioned inside the tomb on empty shelves, and I was informed that I could expect no further ceremonies, for the city was too full of the dead to allow elaborate rites, even for semi-nobles, and the wagons had to hurry back to collect more grim cargoes. So I turned away and walked into the city to purchase supplies which might last me several months before returning to my mansion to contemplate. Solitude was not unwelcome, and I embarked upon a careful exploration of the upper floors of the building, something previously beyond my abilities, but without finding much of interest beside a few tapestries, apparently imported from unknown climes, for they depicted landscapes with no relation at all to those of my own country. Examining *these* in detail was tiring.

Indeed, as the weeks slowly passed in mystery and tedium, I noted that my hours of sleep were slowly increasing and I dreaded, or perhaps welcomed, the possibility I was lapsing back into my former sludge of somnolence. I summoned my doctor again, and he confirmed my diagnosis, his eyes wide as he announced that I was recovering from my illness. The parts of my brain damaged by the mould were repairing themselves, a situation of dreamlike irony, for it meant I would become unbearably sleepy once more. Full indolence and full health for me is one and the same thing. I realised I only had a short time to make preparations for the rest of my life, and so I filled my days of decreasing energy by arranging my affairs with a respected solicitor, entrusting him with a spare key to my mansion. Unable to earn an income through work, my only option was to sell off my family possessions one item at a time, including the tapestries, and to use the money received to pay for food and wine to be delivered directly to my bedside. With rare forethought this was the deal I made.

My solicitor proved reliable enough; and when I took to my bed and fell into my earlier style of life, with feelings of attenuated relief or exasperation, I was faintly amused by the regular visits of burly strangers who came perhaps twice a month to carry out some object, a carved wardrobe or set of plush chairs or a dozen dishes in a box, and to leave a sack of provisions, not excluding wine, in return. Another irony, of trivial significance, soon came to pass, for it so happened one day that the strangers discovered the entrance to the cellar and raided all the vintages concealed within it, which earned me a few score bottles of inferior wine in exchange, but the wages of these men had to be paid and so I did not complain. The mansion gradually became more and more hollow as it was stripped and plundered over the years, and it began to echo in a more forceful and inhuman manner during thunderstorms. The bed beneath me would be the only item left one day, and then even that would be taken, but I had already performed the calculations. There were enough possessions to last me thirty years.

Thus I delayed worrying about my eventual fate, judging three decades to be a span long enough for me to feel secure in my predicament, longer indeed than most men with ordinary careers and normal levels of energy. I considered myself not unlucky. It was shortly after this positive rating of my prospects that three not untall men in not unbrown suits came to my bedside and waited for me to stir. They were faded characters, not as strong as those who removed my possessions but pinched and withered and yet imbued with a residual tenacity, like the mottled creepers looped around the tower in the vineyard. The instant I shifted my position, the nearest spoke to me, addressing me by name and showing a lack of deference that was somehow different from simple insolence. His fingernails were long and dirty, and he used them to scratch his greasy forehead with a sound that resembled the prongs of a fork scraping the bottom of an opaque pickle jar for the last olive. I was dismayed and had to ask him to repeat everything he had just said.

"Of course. We deliver all announcements in triplicate anyway, hence my two assistants. We are from the Bureau of Employment. It has come to our attention that you are not engaged in profitable or even unprofitable labour."

"I am unsuited for work. I live here alone."

"Precisely. You have no family or friends to protect you and are therefore obvious prey for our department. We are here to present you with a compulsory career order. We cannot tolerate even a single shirker in our society."

"I am able to fund my lifestyle."

He cast a piece of paper onto the bed. "That is beside the point. It is a question of ethics and work is essential for moral and psychological reasons, irrespective of whether an income from physical or mental exertion is necessary. We have performed our task and deposited the order with you. Now we will withdraw without bidding you farewell."

I managed languidly to wave a dismissive hand before drifting back into my slumber, and as I lost the power of conscious thought I suspect the conversation was repeated again, minus my own responses, to fulfil the obscure requirement he had mentioned. The document remained unread on my blankets for several days before sliding to the floor when I stumbled out of my soft refuge to visit the latrine, a duty I always postponed as long as feasible. I forgot about it. Still the other men came to remove furniture and chattels, and I listened to them pacing about in the rooms adjacent to mine. They were reluctant to take the tapestries, deeming them unlucky or worthless, I could not decide which, and so I remained free to explore their peculiar vistas with my fuddled but inventive mind. A season passed in mildness and complacency. Then I was aroused to the admittedly modest limits of my awareness by a voice in distress, a young female voice calling my name, imploring me to her side from somewhere in the depths of the wild garden, a curious summons I was loath to ignore, indeed which I could not resist.

With an infinity of little cramps turning my limbs and body into a chequerboard of numbness and sensation, I crawled out of bed and lurched to the window. She was there, far away, a vision of bittersweet beauty, dark ringlets tumbling about her bare shoulders, her dusky breasts and belly latticed by vines. I had little experience of women. She called out to me again and extended her smooth arms in my direction, but my anxious breath steamed up the glass and I could not discern her expression. I staggered from the room and trod the boards of unnaturally long corridors to the front door, which I threw open in feeble impatience, sinking to my haunches on the threshold and waddling forward like a senile ape into the late sunlight. Still the girl called to me. I pushed into the undergrowth and finally found her, but she had dressed herself in a gown and no longer seemed to be troubled by anything, sitting on a tumbled sundial with a confident smile and sardonic eyes. Then she engaged me in conversation and beckoned me to her side, where I kneeled and rested my head in her lap.

We talked about trivial matters, or rather she spoke and I listened, and although her voice was sweet it was oddly strident, as if she were lecturing a man on the horizon or behind a wall, but this excessive volume did not hinder me from falling into a light sleep. It seemed to me that her heartbeat was louder than it ought to be, and this thought was so unsettling that I forced myself awake and lifted my head from her lap. Disengaging from her was as painful as snapping a toenail from an amputated foot; in other words, it hurt only in my imagination, but she aided me by resting the palm of her hand on my forehead and pushing with demure vigour. She no longer seemed keen to talk; and while I was wondering at this sudden change in her attitude and preparing to challenge her on it, she stood up and smoothed her gown. The vines rustled and the three not untall men emerged and greeted her with nods of minor appreciation and I realised I had been tricked and that I had mistaken sounds of construction for the rhythm of her cardiovascular system.

One of the men lightly swung a hammer. "Thank you for being so agreeably easy to entice out of the house. We have boarded up the entrances and now you are unable to return inside. This is a practical measure to encourage you to take employment in the city."

"I do not know how to begin looking."

"We have secured a placement for you in an established firm. You will hurry there as quickly as possible and commence working in a corner of the office we have selected for you. This is the address of the building in question."

At these words one of the other men approached me and pressed something cold into my palm, a device coated with ink that left a glaring red mark on my skin that turned out to be the official symbol of my arranged employer. I looked at it more closely and saw that it consisted of a stick figure chained to a desk. Then the three men vanished back into the conspiratorial vines and the woman stood and glided off behind them, glancing at me only once with an impassive expression. The moment they were all out of sight they began chatting and laughing, oblivious of the suffering they had just caused me, relieved only to have fulfilled their duties for another day, while I sat on the same sundial in the same place as she, vaguely enjoying the lingering warmth of her body on the cool stone, absorbing this faint trace of her presence, but also dissolving it with the heat of my own sleepy flesh, until the sensation was all mine and no longer erotic in the slightest. I recovered slowly, stood, and wandered back to the house, confronted the impassable nailed planks, rested there too and then moved away forever.

Now the estate was in the care of chance and owls, and I attempted to empty my mind and not think about the daunting task that lay ahead—the journey to the city, which would have to be on foot and without funds apart from a gold ring on my little finger. Not that this ring availed me for long, thanks to the discourtesy of the first robber I met on the road, a dozen paces beyond my gate, who simply jumped out at me from an old clogged well, pushed me into the dust, and yanked the item of jewellery from my digit before running off with hungry strides. I was unable to follow. I sat on the side of the well and looked over the edge at the rubble and volcanic ash deep below. The robber clearly lurked in the bucket until he heard a traveller passing, and I briefly considered following his example, taking his place there and living by crime; but knowing full well that a man who can barely walk without falling asleep would be easy enough to overtake in the ensuing chase, I changed my mind and prayed that my work placement would not be *this*. Then I slumbered and dreamed of bones, chains, and stars.

How long my simple journey took, I cannot state with accuracy, for it had no plan but consisted of a series of little walks and big slumbers at irregular intervals along the highway as the buildings on both sides grew taller and closer until I finally reached the alarming city outskirts. Along the way I dined on the fruit of dusty trees and drank the autumn dews, though once a passing rider hurled me down a husk of bread that tasted of saddle leather and ungulate sweat. I scratched away my shirt on brambles as I collected berries from the roadside, and soon I wore a garment of fluttering ribbons that gave me the horrible celebratory appearance of a fool who has lost his festival, a surplus reason for other commuters to mock me. Only the inky symbol on my skin remained pristine, my branding of future employment, my mark of promised drudgery, and this too was an object of derision whenever it was noticed. Through marginal city streets I lumbered, making enquiries and displaying the symbol, only to be directed further and further into the urban tangle. I spent one night in a shop doorway, dreaming with the mannequins in the windows.

At last I entered a region of vast grey structures where men with downcast expressions scurried from one narrow doorway to another. Here I observed a sign which bore the same symbol as that inked on my hand, fixed to the façade of an especially solemn edifice, and I stepped through a portal into a dimness with the odour of glue, a scent which even seemed to slow my blinks, and waited until a hurrying figure knocked into me and offered a receptive glower. I instantly raised my palm, and he studied the mark and jerked a thumb upward. I was expected to climb a flight of stairs, a tribulation indeed, but I nodded my gratitude and proceeded to follow his simple directions as best I might, pausing on every step until I attained the summit, taking strength all the while from recalling my heroic ascent of the tower in my garden; but this new success was merely a prelude to greater dismay, for at the top I perceived a bare corridor at the end of which began another flight of stairs. The truth is that my ultimate destination lay on the highest floor of the tall building and that at least a full morning of climbing now awaited me.

At intervals, the walls of the stairwell were punctured with niches which contained little statues and busts, most on plinths or metal stands, probable representations of former directors and other executives of the company who owned the premises, a firm still unknown to me. The faces of these figures seemed to glare with hard alabaster eyes upon which dust flecks had settled and tiny flies had expired like mismatched pupils. There was madness in those accidental expressions, but I did not increase my pace, because I was unable to, so I continued one painful step at a time until I finally encountered an empty niche. Perhaps it awaited a future statue or else the one it had held was smashed or stolen: none of my business which, I simply saw an opportunity to rest and took it. Into the space I crawled. Many hours later I was roused by the murmur of two indignant voices. "No, that will never do, a very poorly executed piece, it must be replaced," grumbled one, to which the other replied, "It is not even clear who it is supposed to represent!" Then they moved away and I climbed out.

My eventual arrival at the designated office on the highest floor was not greeted with the gratification or relief I had anticipated. I was ushered roughly into a cramped room and forced down into a chair, without chains I am glad to report, but my knees were jammed so firmly under the low desk before me that I was held almost as securely. Then a sequence of squat indistinguishable men came and deposited heavy files all around me, building a barricade of papers that shut out the light from the solitary small window. A green lamp was lit next to my elbow, and I was ordered to rearrange these documents in reverse alphabetical order. Then men departed and I rested my head on the one clear space of the desk, falling asleep instantly and nearly as quickly being reawakened by a powerful jab in the nape of my neck, so that I made a fitful attempt to examine the contents of the first file, but I soon nodded off again, spilling papers to the floor. The jab came once more and I was roused for another minute before lapsing, and so this process continued, and on one particularly painful occasion I summoned enough reserves of willpower to turn and observe that it was a long pole that poked me, held by an unseen tormentor in an adjacent office, but at last I was too weary to stir at all and the jabs were in vain.

I felt myself being roughly shaken by several hands, and amid the whispery collapse of piles of unread papers I beheld the three not untall men, still in not unbrown suits, bending over me, clicking tongues, and making their eyebrows sizzle on the griddle of their frowns.

"This will not do! You have already violated the terms of the placement."

I protested weakly, "The work was too hard."

"Nonsense! It was too easy, that is the real problem. This environment is too soft and it is necessary to condition your muscles, so we have arranged an alternative job. We suggest you try to be more responsible and conscientious from now on!"

Slowly their rage cooled and their faces turned a little paler and the eyebrows stopped cooking and one of the men lifted up my arm and opened my hand and proceeded to rub it with a rag soaked in some pungent chemical. I saw that he was removing the image of the seal from my skin before drying my palm with a separate cloth. Then a different man pressed another seal onto my flesh, also a stick figure but one chained to a cauldron, and I was brusquely escorted out of the building, my feet dragging on the floor as they carried me away and down all the steps and out onto the street. Here they left me and I huddled into myself, bleating at each pedestrian who approached but unclear in my own mind whether I hoped to solicit help or warn them not to trample me underfoot. The shadows of tenements shifted over me as the day progressed, and I was so intimidated by the interlocking patterns they made that I willed myself to stand and amble out of the region, both fleeing and seeking the location of my new placement but so ignorant of where it was I was competent to do neither and indeed my main talent at that moment was an ability to express my hunger through unusually strident stomach music.

Possibly I followed my nose, for there was no trail of crumbs or rivulet of escaped sauce to guide me to the kitchens at which a menial post had been hurriedly reserved for me, but at length I arrived and was welcomed by a blow on the back with a ladle, thankfully empty, from my new employer, a fellow as sweaty and bloated and porcine as might be dreaded. I fell to my knees over a shallow pit full of encrusted saucepans, and a scrubbing brush was hurled contemptuously into this cemetery of dead meals while water was added from a hidden sluice. Soon the pit was awash with brown liquid, and so famished was I that I stooped for a nourishing drink. It was like a thin cold soup made of too many clashing vegetables and meats, but I was nearly grateful and I accepted the following blows on my back with excellent equanimity. At last the assault ceased and a voice bawled, "Clean this as well while you are at it!" The ladle, dented and stained with the juice of my bruises, clattered among the pots, having been thrown over my head. I clasped the brush and commenced scrubbing the nearest pan, which gradually revealed the distorted reflection of my steamy boss, who was lurking behind me, and I continued with this toil until he went away.

This extreme effort left me feeling shaky and befuddled, and I started nodding off, continuously slipping into the pit only to regain my senses and haul myself out. I realised I had lost the brush somewhere in the opaque water. I waded in after it and then I must have simply drifted off to sleep, for suddenly the three not untall men were standing all around and they had grown short beards while waiting for me to rouse myself and notice them. They were disinclined to step into the pit but leaned precipitously over the edge so that their lips were only a few inches from my ears, and then they bawled above the sounds of chopping and boiling:

"Once again you have shirked your simple duties!"

"I am not cut out for this kind of work," I mumbled.

"True, you deserve something tougher. The flabbiness of your morality is extraordinary, but we are going to give you a final chance to prove yourself a useful citizen, one last placement, in an environment where lapses of concentration may even prove fatal."

They grinned together, and I was repulsed to discover that their teeth were as sharp as their fingernails and no more unbrown than their clothes. My arms were held tightly again and the ink mark removed and a new one stamped onto my palm, then I was pulled out of the pit and discarded through a side door into a foul alley which obviously served as a latrine for a great number of people and dogs; yet my mood was even filthier than this, and I resolved to leave this city forever and sleep and dream and starve if need be in a field or glade far from all centres of labour. With absolute determination I plodded onward, refusing to acknowledge any aspect of my dire surroundings other than the ground I walked on. I was waiting for the horizon to become available, my shoulders stooped as if all the cooking utensils of every existent kitchen were balanced there, my eyelids fluttering like the wings of a hummingbird, my heart dully thudding against my chest like a salt-choked sea rising against the bitter wall of a ruined quay, or maybe they were not like that but closer to something else, similes more original or less, or simply like overworked versions of themselves.

How I managed to depart the city without expiring from sleep deprivation, I am at a loss to tell, but leave I did, my fist tightly closed and extended before me, for I cared not to examine the new mark stamped there, and possibly I did sleep a little without stopping, in the manner of those somnambulists who are supposed to sleepwalk out of their homes and have adventures they never know anything about. The horrid clutter of the urban sprawl thinned out around me, the belching chimneys of factories were replaced by twisted trees on hillocks, and the road I trod became rougher and narrower, constantly forking and forcing my stiff legs to make decisions based on pure supposition. The sun went down, but I trudged onwards, for the rhythm controlled me now. I guessed that if I stopped to rest, I would never rise again. My heart would fall asleep in its ribcage cradle forever.

The gathering darkness was less disturbing than I had feared, and in some ways it came as a relief, for I was unable to see more than a few steps ahead. Distance, the concept itself, lost some of its meaning and all its terror. My velocity, already modest, diminished slightly as I passed through a series of cobwebs stretched between trees and broke them with a wispy sigh, but still I continued. How *do* spiders weave webs across a path? I have always wondered this. Do they climb down and crawl across the ground and back up a tree on the other side and then somehow tighten the web on an internal capstan? I attempted to lower my outstretched fist, but the arm it was connected to seemed locked in place. How far behind me was the abominable city? I reached the crest of a low hill and beheld a moonwashed landscape below, forested but studded at irregular intervals with pinnacles of rock and the narrow high cones of extinct volcanoes. An owl watched me from a fungus-swaddled branch.

"What is the secret of surviving without working?" I asked it.

The owl remained silent, as if it knew not, and I pressed not the point, for I am not a man who burns with excessive curiosity. I descended the winding path back into gloom, and now the trunks of the shadowy trees resembled the not unbrown suits of the not untall men and I shuddered with as much force as I dared, and no more, for to squander the last spark of my cellular energy on an inartistic physical spasm seemed too monstrous a self-inflicted punishment to contemplate. I wondered if I should throw myself on the mercy of the first traveller I met coming the other way, but what might I offer in return for being taken in and looked after? Not my labour or wit, nor even my prestige. I could promise no more than to live out my lifespan as a sort of ornament or non-functional item of furniture in a room. Hardly the most irresistible of temptations to any passing wayfarer! As it happened, no other traveller came along and I had the path entirely to myself.

Along it I plodded, alone, confused. So completely had I lost track of time, so interminable had been my nocturnal walk so far, that I felt sure the night must be over. Where was the dawn? Could it be that the sun had indeed risen but that it had changed its colour to black? The rays of such a sun would be planks of solid shadow. There was no method of reckoning the hour. The dense canopy of the surrounding trees hid the moon, and the beating of my heart provided no clue, for I had not kept count of my heartbeats since the commencement of my exploit. I existed in a reality without comprehensible time or space. Despair might well have taken hold of me, but I was saved by a happy accident—my left foot kicking a cluster of mushrooms as it swung forward to take the next step, releasing thousands of spores into the night air, many of which I inhaled and absorbed. They turned out to have rejuvenating properties, and I was temporarily invigorated, and despite the obstructing cobwebs my pace and mood improved.

The path now passed between two pinnacles of rock, and the rustling of leaves was replaced by the creak of cooling limestone. To my surprise I did not eventually emerge back in the forest but continued down a narrow passage bounded on each side by sheer walls. Had I entered a steep valley? I gave up all attempts to study my surroundings in detail: there was no point. And yet I was vaguely aware that the character of the rock was changing. Fissures opened up on both sides, a network of narrow chasms in the bizarre geology of the region. Glints of reflected starlight high above proved that I was passing through an outcrop of embedded crystals. And still I lurched forward with clenched fist. The soles of my feet burned and my knees creaked, but I was a prisoner of rhythm, unable to pause for even a moment.

At long last the sky grew lighter. The pale dawn had been on its way all night: it was here now. A dog barked. The shutters of a window were thrown open. I blinked in astonishment at such sounds in a remote wilderness. Then I realised my mistake. I had entered a new city, and the walls of rock were in fact the buildings of an urban landscape not dissimilar to the one I had fled from! The path had slowly and cunningly turned itself into a street. The extinct volcano ahead of me was actually an opera house or similar monumental structure. I could not weep with frustration because I was given no chance to do so. Pedestrians started to appear in great numbers, carts and velocipedes also, and I was continually jostled. One commuter hurried up behind me and said:

"Beggars and vagabonds are not permitted to reside in Bismal."

"I am just passing through," I said.

"A likely story! Where are you from? Dask? Ezbyx? Farnar?"

Before I could answer, he had turned down a sidestreet and was already a diminishing figure. The traffic increased in volume as I approached the centre of the sprawl. I found myself walking in the exact middle of a wide and extremely busy thoroughfare. Wheels rumbled around me, people shouted curses, horns and other pocket instruments squeaked or honked admonishing crotchets at me. Tuneless, horrible. If I strayed from my course by a few inches to either side I would doubtless be crushed under the heavy circumference of a roaring wheel. Sweat stood out on my forehead and my teeth chattered. Then I beheld, with a mixture of relief and disbelief, a traffic island not far ahead, a low pedestal of black stone. If I could reach the security of its barren shores my life would be protected.

The fact I would become an urban castaway, condemned to starve in a sea of bustle and motion, struck me as no more bitterly ironic than most of the other things that already had happened to me. I had only one true concern as I approached the basalt slab: how to arrest my motion once I reached the sanctuary? To pass over it and continue on the other side seemed a dreadful fate, rather like throwing oneself onto a bed but missing it completely. Then I saw that the traffic island was occupied by a figure. He seemed to be waiting for me, and there was no dismay or fury in his grin. As I tramped nearer, he raised his arms and extended them, his hands like buffers on poles. I collided with his open palms, and he absorbed the impact easily enough, bending his elbows, and thus I lurched to a halt.

My heart did not cease beating, my internal organs ruptured not, and I opened my mouth to thank this stranger for his shock-deadening generosity; but he spoke first, his eyes twinkling, while my outstretched arm speared over his shoulder like an acrobat's pole.

"You are early! I expected you at a much later hour. Well done!"

I blinked. "All night I walked and—"

He placed a finger over my lips. "Hush! There is no need to dramatise your achievement too much. I have already congratulated your dedication and enthusiasm, and that is your full quota of praise for the week. You must learn to live and work without verbal reassurances from me or anyone else. The task itself should be its own reward. That is the motto of our company."

Although his finger remained in place I could not resist blurting out a reply, even though I feared his digit would bisect each word as it jumped from my indexed mouth. "Task? Company? But I am a stranger to this town, a sleepy loner and itinerant."

He frowned, shook his head, and retreated a step. "There is no mistake. The Bureau of Employment never makes such despicable errors. I was informed of your coming here: they sent you and you arrived. The process was simple enough and the conclusion is obvious. You are he."

"I am he?" I muttered.

"The new worker. The shirker on placement. Yes, you!"

"But what *am* I?" I gasped.

He prised open my fist, bent my arm at the elbow, and applied his thumbs to various pressure points along my arm. Abruptly the muscles relaxed and the limb was once more under my control. Then I raised my hand to my gaze and blinked at the ink symbol stamped there. The irony was dreadful. A violent sob racked my frame, and I stumbled.

"A traffic policeman," he said as he steadied me.

"Most unfortunate," I mumbled.

He did not react to this comment with anger but merely offered me a pitying smile and gestured at the flow of humanity around us— the speeding carts, velocipedes, tricycles, galloping horses, runners with sedan chairs, rickshaws, and roller skaters, all intent only on reaching their destinations as soon as possible. Clearly I was supposed to be honoured by the prospect of helping to keep the lunatic flow smooth and ordered: the gears of commerce itself depended upon it! The responsibility was large, far too large for me, and the work itself difficult and dangerous. When I mentioned this fact, he laughed and frowned at the same time and then widened his eyes until he somewhat resembled the owl on the rotten branch I had met in the forest.

"But of course it is dangerous! That is why you were sent to do it. You have fallen asleep on your previous placements and caused difficulties for legitimate employers. To encourage you to mend your ways you have now been given a task in which failure will cause difficulties only for yourself. Do you not understand? The task requires that you stand on this narrow plinth and direct the traffic. If you fall asleep *here* you will tumble onto the road and undoubtedly be crushed to death by one of the heavier vehicles. What better inducement can there be for you to transform yourself on the instant into a responsible and industrious citizen of this land?"

"Surely I will need training? When does the placement begin?"

"Immediately! You will receive your training on the job. I will take up position on the pavement and fire small stones at you from this catapult whenever you do something wrong. I estimate that within a couple of hours you will have grasped the rudiments very well indeed. Then I shall slink away and leave you to it. In the early evening, shortly after the sun goes down, your replacement will come along, for traffic policemen operate in shifts, and you will be free to seek accommodation in one of our hotels. But you must return here at sunrise."

Before I could protest or even gape in astonishment at the hideous working conditions he had described, he turned and scuttled with great skill through the chaotic traffic to the shore of the distant pavement. Once there, he paused and then rotated on the spot until he was facing me. From his vantage on the very edge of the curb he loosed a stone from a catapult, instantly dipping into his pocket for a second projectile. I saw now that the pockets of his jacket were bulging. His aim, despite the moving obstacles, was true, and the first pellet struck my elbow. I winced and jerked my arm up. The second stone forced me to raise my other arm, and thus he taught me how to control traffic, each stone moving my rapidly bruised limbs into a new appropriate configuration. The commuters obeyed my commands but without good grace, cursing me and spitting in my face as they hurtled past. The pile of small stones at my feet grew larger. At last I understood everything about my job and was able to fulfil my role with the accuracy and efficiency, if not the enthusiasm, of a fully trained traffic policeman, and so my tormentor vanished.

A surge of slow panic filled me up on the inside. I was frightfully weary and had no doubts that I would fail to perform my duties to the end of the working day. My signalling arms felt as heavy as those of a colossal statue, and my eyes kept closing. I winced as a tram hurtled past. Surely I would collapse from exhaustion in the next few moments—but which way, to the right or left, would I tumble? Death waited in both streams of traffic. I swayed indecisively. Then I was enveloped in the labyrinthine folds of a peculiar dream. Relaxation. Then much shrieking, bawling, a shower of something sticky and warm. I snapped open my eyelids and was amazed to find myself slumped in the exact middle of the plinth. Evidently I had collapsed vertically, safely, like a deflating concertina. But around me was scattered the wreckage of many frantic lives, broken limbs at unlikely angles, glassy dead orbs staring at tangled machinery. The road was blocked on both sides by debris. The three not untall men in not unbrown suits plucked at me and clucked their tongues while the blood of commuters dripped down my guilty cheeks. "I dozed off for just a moment!" I croaked, and one of the agents grinned without mirth and said with deep sarcasm:

"Awake at last, I see!" Then he nudged his companions and sneered, "For just a moment!"

"Too long this time," replied one of them.

"Failed," observed the third.

I attempted to stand, but the effort was beyond me. "Yes, I fell asleep on my feet and perhaps made some inappropriate arm gestures as I sagged, but I *intended* at no point to give misleading directions to the traffic. So technically I have committed no crime. If anyone is guilty, it is they, the drivers and riders, trusting to the competence of a listless individual on an unpaid work placement. I regret the loss of life, believe me, but it was not my fault. An accident!"

The first man shook his not unround head. "It was negligence."

"No less," agreed the others.

They stooped and picked me up like a stretcher, but only my own bewilderment and despair, and perhaps also my aura, lay on top of me, and I heard my compressed bones snap back into place as they tugged me first one way, then another, between them. I asked not where our destination was. The chief agent trotted along beside me, his not un-large boots striking the not unoccasional blue spark from the cobbles. I took the opportunity to slumber again, and when I awoke I was on the cot of a tiny prison cell and the not untall men were leaving. A different man, a portly fellow, remained and regarded my return to consciousness with a smile of carefully itemised tolerance and sympathy. "I am your lawyer, dear boy. Hope of acquittal, there is none. The judge is a fearsome example of the subspecies, and he is very hard on idlers such as you."

"You resemble the solicitor I entrusted with my mansion keys," I said.

He chuckled at this. "It is the law."

"Lawyers are legally required to look alike? I am amazed!"

He shook his head, stroked his whiskers. "No, no, I meant that the rigours and absurdities of a career spent in the shadow of courtrooms, dusty offices, and murky adjournment chambers, arguing with rivals, shuffling papers, consoling clients, tends to leave a particular mark on a man. I am portly because I eat too much at unwise times, and I daresay the solicitor you referred to had identical habits to mine. But we are wasting time in such aimless discussions. You are due to attend court in less than one half-hour from now. The authorities prefer to process cases of criminal indolence rapidly."

"The deaths were an accident. I am innocent!" I protested.

"You are workshy," he retorted, "and that is enough to condemn you outright. Three chances were given to you, three placements, and you failed them all. Why should society continue to endure your presence? There is no convincing reason for it to do so."

"But *why* is laziness a crime? Until recently it was a harmless condition."

"The law changed during the fiasco of the mass poisoning. Prohibitions against indolence were written while some lesser politicians were suffering from an inability to sleep or even rest for a moment. Everything they did at that time was tinged with nervous energy and an excessive tendency to movement and struggle. Those politicians soon died, but the new laws remained. It is easier to create than repeal laws in this land, and so the Bureau of Employment was established. You have become one of their victims. Whether you plead innocent or guilty in the coming trial is irrelevant. The judge will want to make an example of you. Have you ever been an example before? It is uncomfortable."

I said nothing in response, for I was too overwhelmed with misery and drowsiness. The nocturnal walk between cities followed by my aborted shift controlling traffic had not only drained my reserves of physical energy to the dregs but also sucked up most of my spiritual resilience. That, at least, is how it felt. The cot beneath me was hard and full of vermin, but I abandoned myself to it. At irregular intervals I awoke and my lawyer was always standing utterly immobile in a different part of the cell. Despite the politeness of his expressions, I knew he regarded me with contempt, and when the three not untall men in not unbrown suits returned to drag me upright and prod me through the door, the muscles of his face twitched with grotesque relief, like a carnival mask finally allowed to relax after a lengthy malign fiesta. Along an interminable corridor I stumbled and through another door into an imposing courtroom. The judge wore a wig so long that its tresses filled more than half the chamber, pounding the benches where the other officials sat like surf and yet absorbing and muffling every shout and objection and jeer. Into the dock I was pushed, and I steadied myself by clasping the spikes of the railing before me and breathing deeply.

The judge raised his hammer and pounded the gavel like a chef tenderising meat. His words were like insults boomed at me from under the sea, encased in bursting bubbles. "Parasite . . . shirker . . . slacker . . . rogue and rascal . . . buffoon and traitor . . . lazy loafer . . ."

The list was long and my eyelids were heavy. A sharp pain aroused me to maximum alertness. I noted that both my hands had impaled themselves like mushrooms on the railing spikes, and I began to weep, to bawl and writhe. The judge fitted a long metallic extension to his finger and used it to jab me painfully in the sternum. "But you *shall* be made to work, irrespective of your own feelings on the matter, for the remainder of your life! To imprison such a vile specimen of subhumanity in a normal cell would be offensive not only to all standards of decency but also to those of indecency. Therefore I have chosen a more fitting place of incarceration. Into the charnel house with you! To count the bones!"

The pain that had awoken me now caused me to swoon again, and this bizarre double function led me to wonder if agony is a feminine force, always changing its mind, but then I remembered that I was no misogynist and so decided it was not. As I lapsed into my swoon, the three not untall men chortled and clapped their hands in long-repressed and not unexcessive glee, and I dimly recall them capering in circles around the courtroom and shouting, "The charnel house! The charnel house!" while tripping over the judge's overflowing wig and scratching themselves on his finger extension, which had fallen to the floor and now jabbed upwards at a cruel angle. Then all was black oblivion for me, cool, convenient, transitional. It appears that my hands were pulled off the spikes and bandaged, and I was dragged out of the courthouse and through the city and back along the very road of my nocturnal walk. To the burial grounds south of my former home they took me! Although still alive, I was fated to be imprisoned with generations of dead people, many of whom might even be my own ancestors. It was the worst punishment any judge might ever devise.

Buckets of cold water were hurled in my face and a bottle of smelling salts opened directly under my nose, and I jerked into a semblance of competent awareness. It was early evening and in the crepuscular light that saturated the landscape I beheld my future place of residence, my awful home to be. There are more than sixty charnel houses scattered across the burial grounds; all are slightly different in style, reflecting the historical era in which they were raised, but the atmosphere of despondency and fear is shared equally between them. They emerge from the ground at shallow angles and the visible structure is only a tiny fraction of the whole, for all lead into subterranean crypts and caverns measureless to moles and worms as well as man. The one that loomed before me was less old than most of the others but hardly more salubrious. Still supported by the grip of the employment agents, I found myself blinking at my defence lawyer, who was rummaging in his multitude of pockets for the keys to the gates of iron that dominated one side of the charnel house and prevented casual ingress and egress. Clearly he was also a gatekeeper as well as a legal vulture. He grinned sickly at me.

From one deep pocket came a set of keys that were not the ones he was searching for but which I recognised. The keys to my mansion! I scrutinised the fellow more closely and said, "It *was* you after all! You *are* the same person! You tricked me."

"Not at all," he replied without rancour. "It was merely the law."

Then he produced the correct key, a brass affair half as long as a midget's wife, and inserted it in the ancient lock. It required all his strength before the tumblers clicked and he was able to swing the gate open. The three not untall men pushed me forward and I stumbled over the threshold, collapsing to my knees in the lobby of the hateful edifice, where only a few introductory bones mouldered. The lawyer spoke to the back of my neck, leaning far enough forward so that I felt the moistness of his hypocritical breath but not so far that he risked toppling over the line that divided inside from outside, and I listened to his words with the numbest variety of intellectual dismay.

"Your task is to count bones, every single bone in the entirety of this charnel house, including the subterranean sections, and to reckon the ultimate total. Do you perceive this narrow funnel that penetrates the thickness of the iron gate? It will be your only connection with the outside world. Precisely at noon every other day a cold broth will be poured into the mouth of this funnel. If your own mouth is not in position at that time, you will have to wait two days for the next meal. You must learn to take responsibility for yourself! Count the bones and count them well, with accuracy and devotion. When you believe you have the correct total, shout the answer through the funnel just before the broth is served. Your answer, if successfully received, will be checked against the old records of the death registers. If it turns out to be wrong, your rations will be halved and you shall have to begin again. But if you give the correct answer, you will be released from this charnel house and taken to the next, to count other bones."

"It seems an entirely pointless task to force on me!"

"Yes, it is work!" he growled.

The gate closed behind me, and fresh mortar was trowelled into the gaps between the basalt blocks, to guard against any unlikely attempt to escape through the walls. I was alone in a sealed tomb, but the darkness was not total, for a phosphorescent slime coated the ceiling and pulsed a dim green luminosity over the scattered bones, shreds of decayed clothing, and dusty cobwebs. I crawled on all fours into the unwelcoming sickly murk, seeking the most comfortable place to make my bed. Outside, my tormentors hurried away from the burial grounds and I felt an intense sadness as I understood how forsaken I was. Yet the authorities had *not* forgotten me, and the absurd task entrusted to me had to be treated seriously, for if I miscounted too many times, I would starve to death: that was the unmistakable threat. My eyes fastened on a bone, an anonymous rib, directly ahead of me. "One!" I breathed with effort. Then I turned and spied a fleshless finger pointing at me mockingly. "Two!" I continued weakly.

I paused for a rest, to steady my shaking limbs. Merely counting bones randomly could not be the best way of fulfilling my mission, for I would be certain to count some more than once and fail to count others at all, and the errors probably would *not* cancel each other out. I needed to devise a system, a method that would ease the task as much as possible. But first, to sleep! I curled up among the white sticks of death, those symbols and artefacts of horror that we all carry about inside us, even as we flee the sight of them, and I slumbered fitfully, jerking like a skeleton pulled by wires. The ground was too hard and I was cold and my bandaged hands throbbed painfully. I sat up and decided to resume my counting, but I could not work out the best place to begin. What sort of system would be easiest and most elegant? I recalled from my childhood reading that the human skeleton contains exactly 206 bones. To reassemble all the skeletons and count *them* was surely a viable and clever solution!

If I did that, I would have a far less onerous job, and once the skeletons were totalled, a simple act of multiplication would complete the task. Accordingly, I began fitting the bones into place, treating each long-dead occupant of the charnel house as a large puzzle, a game that was both a pastime and the key to free me from my surroundings, even if such freedom led only to yet another tomb. I knelt among knuckles, femurs, and kneecaps, and my own vertebrae clicked and cracked as I stretched to retrieve pieces of a spine and fit them together. Dimly I realised that the end result would be to populate this empty structure with rough visual echoes of real people, to colonise the dread hollowness with the last vestiges of humanity, so that I would be less lonely, even if more fearful. I might even recognise in one reconstruction the framework of an ancestor, with the pelvis that made possible my eventual birth exposed to a view so bare and penetrating there was nothing obscene left in it at all.

The days and nights, utterly alike, passed slowly, and though I was now an officially approved counter, I forgot to keep a tally of them as they collapsed into the past, flaking into dust like fragile mummies. Some instinct even more basic than hunger—stubbornness for its own sake perhaps—compelled me to squat under the funnel with mouth agape at the appointed times. The cold broth was vile, and I congratulated myself on the fact that I did not have to prepare or serve it, or even look at it, before it oozed down my gullet. It gave me enough strength to keep going, and that is all that mattered. When I had finished the reassembly of my first skeleton, I laughed and danced, and thus exhausted myself to the point of a sleep so profound I missed one mealtime. The broth splashed the cold stones under the funnel, and its consistency was finally available for inspection. At the sight of it, I retched and vomited for an hour, exhausting myself again, though less dramatically, and pledged myself never to miss another delivery. And since that day I never have. I am an ardent, obedient feaster.

As I progressed deeper into the charnel house, leaving a trail of completed skeletons in my wake, I simultaneously ventured into the past, as it were, for the oldest corpses had been deposited at the back of the incredibly long mausoleum. Under the pulsing green glow I saw how our forerunners, the ancients, were of bigger build than ourselves. The bones were larger and thicker, and the restored skeletons revealed how strong, imposing, and healthy they must have been in life. Eventually, I realised, I would be dealing with true giants. Deeper and yet deeper I went into the tomb, far below the ground, where it was warmer and the floor was spiked with stalagmites like backbones of rock. Many of the bones here were encrusted with mineral deposits, making them yet thicker than they already were. It required both my arms and all my strength to manhandle a femur into position. And the skulls were twice as large as my own head, many of them adorned with horns of percolated limestone, dead humans turned into mythical beasts.

I wondered if the bones at the limits of the charnel house would be fossils too large and heavy to move at all. The skeleton I was currently working on was already almost beyond my abilities. Several days of toil were required to fit all the pieces together. At last I slotted the final toebone into the massive foot. Before I could step back to admire my work, something very unexpected happened: the entire skeleton jerked. It remained still for a moment, then jerked again, the jaw opening and closing as if it were attempting to form words. I watched in awe as the bones reddened and the stench of fresh blood came to my nostrils. Then strips of flesh appeared on the bloody bones, wrapping themselves like grotesque bandages around and around, and organs grew in their anatomically correct positions, and muscles and ligaments and cartilage appeared. This was decay in reverse, speeded up absurdly: the skeleton was turning back into a living man, a colossal figure from the distant, mysterious past.

I did not flee, for there was nowhere to run, and I was fascinated, appalled, sewn to the spot like a button to a grotesque cuff. I waited until the process was complete, until the skeleton was fully clothed in skin, until the bare bones had become a naked man, a man that sat up, blinked at his surroundings, and focussed on me. He spoke, but his words were unintelligible and I shook my head. He tried again, adjusting his accent, tone, and stress until I was able to understand him. His speech was very archaic, like characters in the tragedies and comedies of antique playwrights, but I had read those authors in the idle moments of my dreamy youth and I was able to reply, awkwardly, in kind. He frowned at me, then smiled and stood, towering over me, stooped to clutch at a bundle of opaque cobwebs, and wrapped himself in the folds of this ghostly toga. "Why did you summon me back?"

"With respect," I answered meekly, "I did not."

He considered this and finally said, "In that case, I summoned myself. Such cases are not unknown. You provided the opportunity I clearly craved by fitting my skeleton together correctly. I am a magus and my name is Charm Bumble. But who, may I ask, are you?"

I bowed deeply. "The scion of a semi-noble family."

"Your stature is very slight."

"True. But the semi-nobles do play an important part in the culture and economy of the land. We purchase the produce of the peasants and create entertainments for the aristocracy. Although derided, the semi-nobles are a key ingredient in the steaming dish of society."

He wagged a finger. "I did not refer to your stature in the hierarchy of community relationships but to your actual physical size. You are a midget!"

"Compared with yourself, yes. But that is because this is the future."

He blinked. "*Your* future?"

"No, no, that is an unbearable idea. Your future, Sir Magus."

Charm Bumble stroked his pointed beard. "I see. Your observation was merely a polite way of stating that I am from the past. That does explain your diminutive size. The generations shrink as the centuries pass, and that seems to be true for all animals. The bones of extinct beasts grow bigger the deeper they are found in the ground. Once the humble brontosaurus was believed to be the largest land-based creature that ever lived, but in my own time that assumption had been falsified by the discovery of beasts five times larger, and I suspect that your own palaeontologists have unearthed evidence of creatures five times larger than *those*. Am I not right? And the process will continue indefinitely."

"I do not think factors of such magnitude apply to human beings," I ventured.

Charm Bumble clapped his mighty palms. "Ah, but they do! I am proof of the assertion, but if you require a more dramatic demonstration please follow me deeper into this mausoleum. Come! Permit me to lead you to places where the bones are bigger than mine . . ."

I hesitated. "Much bigger?"

He winked. "*Vastly* bigger!" Then he strode off down the littered incline on his powerful legs. I puffed to keep up with him, like a tortoise running after a bicycle, and in this ungainly fashion we penetrated the furthest reaches of the charnel house, where the thighbones were like toppled pines and the ribcages were spacious enough to house entire clans of brigands. Charm Bumble did not slow his pace, and I feared he would walk right through the wall that marked the boundary of the tomb. So I called out a warning and he came to a halt.

"We can go no further. This is where the charnel house ends," I said.

"You are deceived," he replied with a laugh, "for this white obstacle is not a wall at all. There is much further to go yet, believe me!" And he reached out both hands and pushed. The gigantic pelvis toppled and fell with an infinitely dry clatter, exposing the hidden depths of this foul storehouse of the dead, and I shivered as I obediently followed the magus deeper into the guts of the nauseous earth, down into the unholy crannies of the temperamental planet, through the crust into the infernal regions where the magma bubbles and seethes, cooking diamonds and perhaps even souls in convection currents of unimaginable force and duration. Nothing of what surrounded me now was manmade: the walls were living rock, the ceiling also, rough and untouched by hammer or chisel. It was all entirely natural, though it felt unnatural and uncanny in the extreme. And the bones were so large they were difficult to comprehend and appeared merely as oddly shaped geological quirks.

At last Charm Bumble paused on the edge of a crater. The path continued on the far side, but the crater was filled with magma that boiled and hissed. At this point the Earth's liquid mantle had broken through the crust. There was no way to cross the liquid fire, and I turned to retrace my steps; but the magus clamped one massive hand on my shoulder to keep me in place and with the other he gestured at the pit, his fist unclenching and his palm extended to the heat.

"Now I will show you a trick that will put my earlier assertion beyond dispute!"

"There is really no need," I protested.

"Hush, little one! Watch carefully as I command the magma to cool! This is the truth of our planet, the reality of the world that so few know. Behold!"

I beheld and gasped, for the magma suddenly became solid. I knew deep inside myself that this was no localised effect. He had cooled *all* the magma under the ground, the entire roaring core, turning the Earth into a solid sphere for the first time in its immeasurably long history. He smiled at me, but his face was scarlet and beads of sweat stood out on his forehead. Somehow he had absorbed the heat himself, and from the strain of the expression that lay under his smile I knew he would not be able to keep up this effect for long. So I turned back to regard the newly solidified ground, frowning at its colour and the pattern of cracks on its surface.

And then I knew, I understood.

And I screamed and fled!

But I forgot to flee the way I had come. In my blind panic I ran over the cooled magma to the spot where the path continued. No sooner had I crossed than the rock melted again, returned to being liquid fire, for Charm Bumble had made his point and no longer needed to exert himself. Whether he slumped from exhaustion or not, I do not know. I kept running without looking back. Perhaps his low chuckles followed me, or maybe it was only the mocking slurp of the magma as it rolled against the shores of the crater. I stumbled over bones, but my route took me upwards and the skeleton parts grew smaller. I was entering a different charnel house, approaching its locked iron gates from the inside. It is possible that all the charnel houses in the burial grounds are connected to one another. Certainly at least two of them are: the one I was incarcerated in and the one that is now my abode. Yes, I still dwell in the charnel house, but it is not the same one, and though my fate is terrible it is better than yours, who are free outside.

My jailers are astonished and confused. They do not ask me for an explanation, as they have no desire to appear incompetent before me. Doubtless they attribute the discrepancy to a clerical error. Perhaps they have concluded that I successfully counted all the bones in the first charnel house and so was transferred here. But the fact that they remember no such thing must disturb them tremendously. Yet they have grudgingly accepted the situation as it is and have bored a small hole through the iron gates and inserted a feeding funnel, carefully soldering it into place, re-establishing my mealtimes. I have no intention of ever leaving this grim sanctuary. I do pretend to count the bones, but never again will I dare assemble a skeleton. You, who live in open spaces, under clear skies, are far worse off than I. It is not possible for me to see the stars from my confinement. I am grateful. For around the stars feasibly revolve other planets, and I know what lurks at the centre of our own world. Or rather, I know what our planet really *is*. When the magma solidified, the truth was obvious.

Earth is an encrusted skull.

What I Fear Most

'll tell you what I fear most. It's an irrational fear, true enough, and I know that I shouldn't worry about it and that there are many more obvious things to be scared of all around us, and that my particular fear is the sort of fear that only people with too much time to brood could ever possibly have, and that if I was more engaged in everyday events I wouldn't pay it a second thought, I would laugh and forget about it, yet despite this it's still the thing I fear most.

Well, maybe the word *most* is a bit misleading. I suppose that if I tried hard I could envision something worse, a more horrible situation than the one that makes me so frightened. If I put my mind to it and spent ages inventing a grotesque torture of extreme malice, then yes, maybe I would finally admit that this new thing to fear I'd just created was more terrible than my previous worst fear, and feasibly it would then become my new worst fear, replacing the old.

I fear the cold, that's what I fear most, and as I get older I fear the condition and the idea more and more. Winter for me is an ordeal grimmer than it is for the average man of my race, for I'm a northerner and should have the genetic heritage to cope with the cold; but I don't. My parents never hesitated to frolic and caper in the snow: they first met as students while skating on a frozen lake. Presumably my more distant ancestors were equally or more hardy.

But somehow I lost that adaptation at a very young age. Perhaps an illness was responsible for resetting my internal thermostat. The moment the temperature drops below twenty degrees centigrade, my teeth begin to chatter; and this is no figure of speech. But do not assume from this fact that I am a feeble and cosseted individual. On the contrary, I enjoy outdoor activities, and my physical presence is imposing. I merely require that my exercise take place in the sun.

Needless to say, the moment I had a choice in the matter I relocated from the high latitudes of my family home to a tropical land, a resort on the coast where any fluctuation in the agreeable temperature was reliably small. And yet, even here there were occasional cold nights and subsequent suffering; but my problem was mainly solved and I could exist in relative peace and security. And so I judged myself safe and happy and free from the tyranny of winter shivers.

Then it occurred to me that humans are warm-blooded animals who generate internal heat through particular biochemical processes; and that the moment we are dead these processes cease. So I became obsessed with the notion that after death I would be more sensitive to even the smallest changes in temperature, at the mercy of every fraction of a degree centigrade that might fall because of a change in wind direction or the arrival of a flotilla of unexpected clouds.

Although I am a fairly rational individual who knows that dead people have no feelings at all, yet some superstitious part of my subconscious wouldn't permit me a moment's peace once the notion of feeling cold after death had taken hold of me. I resisted the urge to do anything about this worry for many months, until there was finally no option but to take some practical measures.

I went to visit the local undertaker, a man with doleful eyes who listened to my request without expressing a flicker of surprise.

"You want your mortal remains to be left exposed to the sun on the top of a pillar or a rocky outcrop?" he said lugubriously.

"Yes, yes! Assuming such a request is feasible. I have money."

He pulled his long chin and shook his head. "It's not a question of how much you can afford but the requirements of the law."

"It is forbidden to dispose of a corpse in such a fashion?"

"Indeed it is. There are problems of public hygiene. Plus your remains would not remain in place for very long. We do have storms from time to time; how could your loose bones defy the winds? They would be sent rolling through the town like fossilised snakes. I must decline your request."

"But what *are* the available options? I don't want to be buried in the ground, where no sunlight penetrates, nor do I wish to be cremated and my ashes scattered to the winds and blown back to northern climes."

He shrugged. "I really can't help you. Those are the only two choices. To be buried at sea is no longer acceptable. Too many putrefying cadavers are washing up on beaches. The government is very strict on this question. They are suspicious of anything that may cause disease, and the guidelines for undertakers are clear and unarguable. Six feet under or the industrial furnace."

I left his office and went home. I was riddled with despair.

The sun went down. The stars came out.

I continued to ponder, seeking a solution to my problem.

It occurred to me that perhaps I could bribe my neighbours to throw my body in the sea anyway, but what good would that do me? The currents might take me as far as the frozen oceans; the tides could wash me up on some chilly islet which the bitter winds constantly battered. Burial at sea was no solution. But what were the other options? Even if I decided to ignore the law, to commit a crime, my body would always be in danger of exposure to the cold.

The coastal resort where I had made my home was situated on a spit of land that juts out from a region of lagoons and jungle. Beyond the jungle is a range of mountains and on the far side of those ragged peaks is a desert that undulated its dunes for thousands of miles. There are oases in that desert, some inhabited by isolated tribes, most deserted save for the infrequent nomadic visitor; a few lie too far off the trade routes to be even a temporary stop.

I had a good map and I was strong. With precise planning I might be able to reach one of the remotest oases and live out my remaining days there, growing old in the knowledge that no meddlesome authorities would ever come to interfere with me after I had died, to dispose of my remains in a way that risked facilitating what I feared the most. I would rot in peace under palm trees, and my disintegrating matter would enrich the soil and become a part of the trees.

And those trees would rear up from around the lake they guarded and bask in the desert sunshine. Thus did I daydream of an irradiated afterlife, baked into a vast vegetative thirst by the rays of the blazing sun. But then I remembered how chilly it gets in the desert at night, and I knew that every day of warmth would be spoiled by my apprehension of the cruel chills to come; and I would never be able to relax as a dead but sentient man who circulated with gelid sap.

And what if I never even had the chance to decay into fertiliser, but attracted a scavenger with the stench of my carrion? If jackals came to dismember me, pull my yielding limbs free from my trunk, snip with gleaming teeth morsels and hunks of ripe flesh off bones moistened suddenly and unevenly by the thick panting breath of those beasts, then I would no longer be in control of the destiny of my individual parts. Each tiny speck of me might end up anywhere.

No, a desert trek was not for me. I had to find something else.

Then I recalled that one of the mountains among the chain of ragged, ancient peaks wasn't a normal mountain but an active volcano.

My heart swelled with joy at this memory. What if I climbed up to the rim of the crater and threw myself into the lake of bubbling magma at the bottom? Within a few minutes I would be incinerated completely, my atoms mingled with the liquid rock, and convection would carry at least half of me underground, ripple me out into the vastness of the spherical infernos, nested like orbits, that our eggshell terrestrial crust barely contains; and there I would be in paradise.

But even paradise is only a temporary condition. Our sun will die one day in the far future, swell and collapse and go cold, and even if the Earth survives such a cosmic tragedy and remains warm inside through the vigorous radioactive elements in its mantle and core, eventually it too must cool and became solid cold rock. The universe itself is fated to die of hypothermia: the heat death of the universe is by far the cruellest outcome any creator god might devise for it.

There was no escape for me, no solution to my problem. What I fear most is what is inevitable for everything. All warmth is only transient, ephemeral. The truth of reality is coldness. The infinite chill is the only permanence, the sole hard fact in this life of ours. I was doomed, and the best I could hope for was to delay the horrid sentence that the great tyrant Time had passed on me. But a delay of even a trillion years is naught to eternity, less than a fraction of a blink.

A thin voice inside my skull shouted at me. It was the fool who calls himself my imagination. He is both a wise buffoon and an imp of the perverse, and now he urged me to consider an unexpected course of action. I distrust his strategies, but on a few occasions he has proffered useful advice, so I steadied myself and listened to him. He was persistent. Eventually I found myself nodding in agreement, and I went to bed in a calmer frame of mind. My sleep was untroubled.

The following morning, I entered a shipping office and purchased a ticket for my original homeland. The next northward-bound vessel was leaving that same day, and I hurriedly packed and made certain I was aboard it. I took few possessions and no warm clothing at all. During the voyage I paced the deck in my shirt sleeves and counted the lines of latitude we crossed. The temperature began to drop, but I gritted my teeth and resisted the temptation to hide in my cabin.

An emotional and spiritual strength born from limitless desperation permitted me to proceed with my plan, which was nothing less than the acclimatization of my body to the cold. I planned to make myself immune as much as possible to the very thing I feared most, for I had realised there was no other way of triumphing against the cold other than to embrace it. Only by making it so overwhelmingly present that it was unnoticeable might I hope to consider myself warm.

When I reached my homeland, the terminus of the voyage, I set off north into the icy wastes, propelling myself with the aid of skis. When I finally attain the apex of the globe, that region where the night is darkest, deepest, and coldest, I will give myself to the ice, entombing myself until the sun's death melts me free again. For a short spell I will absorb the heat I once craved, but then I will know it for what it is, a loathsome sensation. And I will yearn for eternal winter.

Rediffusion

They came for me just after midnight, those devious inspectors, opening my door with a special key and rushing into my living room before I even had a chance to get out of my chair. I had always imagined I would have plenty of time to hide the television in a cupboard before they entered, but the reality was quite different. I was helpless and they were merciless and they took my machine as evidence.

True, I had ignored no less than three warning letters, but I hadn't felt guilty in the slightest about not buying a licence. Still don't, in fact. At no point in my longish life had I ever entertained the notion of obtaining one. The expense was simply absurd. The best part of a full week's wages just for the minor privilege of viewing one outmoded and rather staid channel among thousands. It didn't seem right.

I was surprised the inspectors had the power to handcuff me, kick me with fake leather boots, and bundle me into the back of a van. Clearly the law had recently been changed in this regard without my knowledge. Was it even a criminal offence to watch television without a licence? The thug sitting in the back of the van assured me it was, then he slapped me in my insolent mouth, breaking a tooth.

The van swayed around bends, accelerated over a bumpy road, slowly climbed a steep hill somewhere. I had the impression we were leaving the city, but when it finally stopped and I was let out, I found myself blinking up at the renowned corporation tower, a building not more than a few miles from my house. Later I learned that the driver had taken a lengthy detour so he might claim higher expenses.

I was pushed up the stone steps and through the gaping portal into the impressive lobby, but my guards didn't let me loiter in this cool spot for more than a few seconds before yanking me down a narrow passage that twisted and coiled like an intestine and ended in a blank wall. A narrow metal ladder speared into the ceiling at this point, and I was told to climb it on my own. I did so unsteadily.

A dozen rungs later, I emerged into a wood-panelled chamber. A hatch beneath my feet closed silently, cutting off my retreat. I was standing in the dock of an improvised courtroom, facing a judge who was nothing more than a gigantic image on a vast plasma screen. Two smaller screens displayed the prosecution and defence lawyers, but the stations were badly tuned and the pictures fragmented.

It seemed I was late for my own trial and that the process was already over, for the judge was midway through his condemnation. "Unspeakably guilty of living as a broadcast parasite," he intoned, "and therefore wisely sentenced to more years in prison than shall be deemed unseemly." It was an odd sentence, both verbally and judicially, and I was too bewildered to utter an objection. I merely wept.

I had expected a warning, possibly a fine, certainly not imprisonment, and a wave of revulsion engulfed me. I staggered out of the dock, tried to locate the exit, sought to elude my fate, to flee. Instantly three new guards jumped out from behind furniture to apprehend me. One drew a futuristic gun out of a silver holster. He aimed it at my head and pulled the trigger; a hidden spring released its energy.

From the barrel of the gun emerged a cardboard bolt of lightning that jabbed me in the centre of my forehead, then bounced harmlessly off. At the same instant, one of the other guards pushed me to the floor while the third placed his mouth next to my ear and cried, "Bzzzzzt!" I realised this was a typical stratagem of the corporation, a cheap prop rather than a real weapon, a low-budget special effect.

"You've been stunned by the ray," said the marksman.

"If you say so," I replied.

"Don't move at all, you're paralysed," he added.

"For how long?" I asked.

"Until we get you into your cell. Don't forget. Sensation will return to your hands, then your legs, then your mind. We'll be watching to make sure you do it in the right order."

I said nothing, figuring that the paralysis was also supposed to extend to my tongue. They carried my stiff body out of the courtroom and down a wide corridor to a door that opened onto a large courtyard. At the centre of the courtyard stood a brick prison. I was amazed to see such a building hidden within the corporation tower. Tiny barred windows perforated the dizzy heights of irregular turrets.

The perspectives didn't seem right, but then I recalled how an ordinary television set can manage to fit imposing mountain ranges and undulating deserts into the width of a screen, and my surprise decayed as rapidly as a neglected cosine wave or bowl of forgotten cherries. The sentry posted at the prison gate shook his head fiercely, as if he sought to restore reception to a misfiring cathode ray tube.

"An awkward customer, resisted arrest, I see."

My bearers nodded and lowered me slowly into his extended muscular arms. "He's rather a crafty one."

"Soon reduce him in size," came the reply.

Then he turned and ran into the prison at a speed I deemed absurd and dangerous down a succession of dim curving corridors, narrowly missing other sentries and prisoners, clearly anxious to demonstrate his unnatural strength and stamina. His heavy feet slapped the flagstones like tsunamis of molten basalt. Despite my official paralysis, I made appreciative noises to humour him. I even sniggered.

Skidding to a halt before an open cell, he brusquely cast me inside and slammed the grey door, then raced back the way he had come. I landed on a low bed, and my subsequent injuries were minor or imaginary, so I stood and flexed life back into my limbs, obeying the recommended sequence to satisfy any secret cameras that might be observing. Then I realised the key to my door was on the inside.

This oversight seemed too bizarre to be plausible, but I took advantage of the opportunity to slip out of my cell and tiptoe along the corridors. At first I was anxious and excited, then it dawned on me that the prison was actually a complex labyrinth and that I was profoundly lost. The laxity of the security measures was merely an illusion. The outer exit must always elude my desperate wanderings.

Two guards with buckets and brushes turned a corner and yelled at me to halt. I panicked and ran, nursing my aching jaw and whimpering.

Then I tripped and sprawled. I heard the slurp of paint and felt the rough caress of bristles. They were painting vertical lines on my clothes, the traditional convict stripes. After they finished, they casually sauntered away and left me alone, but now I was branded.

I remained on my hands and knees and crawled down a side passage to an open door. The space beyond was an ugly forest of legs, a recreation area of some sort, a communal room. I scuttled like a crippled crab to the nearest vacant chair, hauled myself onto it. Now I was part of an audience facing a television screen. The other members of this audience were also prisoners, and we watched in silence.

Cheap soap operas were followed by light news bulletins and domestic shows concerned with cooking, gardening, finance. Cartoons were also in evidence. After an hour, the situation became unbearable, and I whispered this fact to my neighbour. "I have been incarcerated for neglecting to pay my television licence, and yet I'm clearly allowed to enjoy free television in prison. How ironic is that?" I asked.

He rubbed his bleary eyes and replied, "Not very, considering we're all inside for the same crime. Only licence dodgers are permitted to rot in the private dungeons of the corporation. But it seems you are labouring under the delusion that television is provided to prisoners as a privilege or act of compassion. Even here a license is mandatory. Don't you have one? Theft of corporation images is serious."

"You are joking, surely?" I spluttered.

He shook his head. "The inspectors are vigilant and unforgiving. They always punish cheating eyes."

"This news is terrible. What should I do?"

"Buy a licence, of course."

"But I have no money or means of making any!"

"That is not a valid excuse."

"In that case, I won't enter this room again. I'll forsake the pleasures of televised broadcasts and remain in my cell. But as this is my first day, I'm not sure how to get back there."

"All dungeons are identical. Take your pick."

"I thank you for your advice. Please don't reveal the fact I sat here and absorbed one full illegal hour of broadcasting. In future I'll ask my guards for books or magazines instead."

He plucked my sleeve and pulled me back. "Even if you don't watch it, you still need a licence for any working television set on the premises. It's futile for you to attempt to hide."

I shook him free and fled the recreation area, my heart pounding. Then I soothed myself with the thought that I was merely the victim of a subtle jest, an experiment with practical paradox. An imprisoned licence avoider being forced to obtain a licence for a television set provided by the prison authorities. Utterly ridiculous! Yes, it was a jest. There could be no other sensible explanation, none at all.

I soon located an unoccupied cell, possibly even my own, and fell into a troubled sleep on the uncomfortable mattress. When I awoke I saw that an envelope addressed to me had been slid under my door. It contained a warning letter from the corporation. Apparently, the inspectors had been alerted to the fact I didn't have a valid licence. I sat trembling on the edge of the bed, awaiting developments.

They came a few days later, dragged me away, pushed me up a ladder into another courtroom. Again I was found guilty by a flatscreen judge in a digital wig, then prodded, pinched, and buffeted down endless corridors and through a door into a courtyard in the centre of which stood a smaller prison. I laughed unhappily. Prisons within prisons. A new sentry clasped me in his arms, hurried me inside.

This prison was full of broadcast parasites who had defaulted not once but twice, and we were made to feel doubly accursed. I had the impression that the process of relocating me here had somehow reduced my physical size as well as diminished my self-esteem. Body and soul shrunk to fit an implacable credo, the unbending and illogical will of the corporation, the nightmare of rigorous absurdity.

The corridors of my new home were thin and confusing. I stumbled on the communal television room on my second day and stood silently at the entrance, swallowing hard. When I returned to my cell, the expected letter had already been delivered. It accused me of attempting to exist without a licence despite having access to a television. Inspectors would shortly be dispatched to deal with the anomaly. . . .

They came with their usual sarcasm and fists. This prison contained its own virtual courtroom and judge, its own courtyard that was the location of a third prison, to the entrance of which they dragged me. Then another strong sentry and bare cell, another automatic violation of the television licensing laws, another threatening letter. An appalling process had been set in motion. An inward spiral.

The prisons grew progressively smaller, but so did I, so did my guards, and everything shrunk in perfect proportion, like a cannibal who boils his own head in the same pot as the skulls of his victims. One morning I had a visitor who was not an inspector. He identified himself as a corporation lawyer working for the best interests of the convicts. He entered my cell wearing a silk suit and oily smile.

"There is another way," he declared simply.

"Kindly elucidate," I replied.

"Experiments are taking place on living specimens. Any prisoner who volunteers will be spared the indignity of constant arrest, trial, relocation. Your sentences are adding up to something resembling a paragraph, a page, or even a book, of despair. This can be stopped easily enough. You merely need to sign this form."

Without looking, I asked, "And if I do?"

"A series of controls will be fitted into your nervous system— knobs or buttons that can adjust your colour balance, your contrast, audibility, even the particular channel of your thoughts, whenever we desire. Your spinal fluid will be drained and replaced with a metallic solution that will enable you to receive corporation signals."

"And if I decline this generous offer?"

"You will continue to occupy smaller and smaller prisons until you are trapped inside an institution no larger than a single pixel on a screen. That will be the point of no return, the dot of ultimate doom, the final spark of closedown, the singularity of sorrow!"

I chewed my lip. "May I think it over tonight?"

He nodded sourly. "I suppose so, but you must give an answer before the inspectors come for you at noon tomorrow. In the meantime, be aware that the governor of the corporation, Bogie Laird, is visiting this prison in disguise. Nobody knows what form he has chosen, so it's imperative to be humble to every individual you meet."

I blurted impulsively, "Are *you* Bogie Laird?"

He snarled and raised his clenched fists, his silk suit splitting its seams as his muscles expanded. "How dare you be so perspicacious? I predict a traumatic final episode for you . . ."

Then he lurched out of my cell, howling, his suit rapidly disintegrating as he went, leaving me in an acute state of agitation. But I recovered soon enough and emulated his example, vacating my cubicle and going for one of my usual random strolls. Down one passage I heard a bland vibration, a refreshing change from the ceaseless babble of televised entertainment, and I felt compelled to investigate.

In a tiny room that stank of stale tobacco smoke and was slippery with spilled tea, a brace of off-duty guards sat around a prisoner who had been recently modified. Standing rigidly to attention, eyes popping with static, lips humming a monotone, the volunteer grimaced while one of the jaded guards slapped and shook him, restoring coherent reflections to his pupils for just a few moments at a time.

I wanted to jump forward, make my indignant presence felt, sweep an admonishing finger across every bored face. I wanted to express my fury in a mighty shout. "So this is how you spend your free time? Surfing dead channels within the hopeless eyes of a prisoner! But do any of you have a valid licence to watch him? The corporation will be informed if you don't and inspectors will be activated!"

But before I could make the leap, it occurred to me that the prisoner in question might be none other than Bogie Laird in a new disguise, and the more I pondered this possibility the more convincing it became, so I lost my nerve and slipped away before I was noticed. My one chance to mock the system had been lost; my final opportunity to use irony as a retaliatory weapon had faded and dissolved.

Naturally enough, after this incident I was reluctant to submit myself for treatment, and so the hideous cycle of arrest, trial, and incarceration in diminishing prisons continued. After many years I reached the smallest of them all, a mere dot. I was trapped inside a single pixel on the screen of a television I presumed was unlicensed, a machine whose owner must soon be visited by the inevitable inspectors.

Instead of eschewing the recreational facilities of my enforced abode, I wasted half my free time sitting in front of the communal television. Still without a licence, I was also without fear. Arrest entailed no motion at all, for there was nowhere even smaller to send me. It was therefore possible to ignore all warning letters. On some level, the lowest imaginable, I had finally cheated the authorities.

But the entertainment on offer left much to be desired. Every channel displayed the same unchanging image, a room full of people who sat with their backs to me. They were dressed in grey clothes and their bald heads glistened in the glare of an unspecified light source as they watched with grim reverence something beyond the screen. I studied them intently and thought about them during my walks.

Recursion can be a terrible thing, and one day I found a service ladder to the roof and climbed onto the tiles, my hands rouged with rust from the corroded rungs. There was no safe descent to the courtyard below. On all sides reared the walls of the next-smallest prison, and above those loomed the higher walls of the third smallest prison, and over those leered the still taller walls of the fourth smallest . . .

And so on, all the way back to the almost forgotten beginning. Prisons within courtyards, courtyards within prisons, prisons within the courtyard of the corporation tower. The concave surface of *that* impossible building appeared unimaginably remote now, as unattainable as the inner shell of the universe, and the lights of its windows burned like artificial quasars at the perimeter of a synthetic reality.

The spectacle was unbearable, so I looked directly upwards instead. At the furthest limit of a cylinder so immense and imposing it contained all the misery I could ever conceive for myself, I beheld a glass screen with blurred faces on the other side that were mostly fixed to the fronts of bald heads. Then I knew this truth. If I am part of a fictional drama and not a factual documentary, I might not go mad.

Casimir the Converter

I am a missionary: my fervour and zeal are excessive. The stout wooden staff I carry in my right hand is scarred along its length with notches that represent the numerous pairs of tough boots worn out on my travels. The blue suitcase in my left hand contains spare clothes, a lantern, my camera, a flute, bread and apples, some books. But I keep my money and passport in a wallet that hangs from my neck and is concealed by my shirt. Thus I cultivate the quaint semblance of the outmoded vagabond while strolling the world in search of converts.

I do my true work only at night, and indeed it would be impossible to perform it in the glare of day. The folk I seek are hardly those one might expect a holy man to invest his hopes in. On the contrary, the miserable wretches I deal with are no longer human and commonly are considered utterly beyond redemption. Such beings *cannot* be converted, according to orthodox opinion. But my success rate will speak for itself. Hundreds have allowed themselves to be persuaded by the cool logic of my words, by the promise of future bliss.

This is how I proceed. I rap my knuckles on tombs, let fall the rusty doorknockers of ancient castles, call out in glades of thick forests, swing my lantern at the mouths of caves . . . Always I am greeted in an identical manner, with fury, disbelief, hunger. The truth is that vampires are timid and suspicious in the extreme; the baleful stare and sinister grin convince nobody who understands they are the surface features of a mask. Even the independent dance of the creature's bloated shadow on the nearest wall is an act requiring extreme control.

Yes, vampires are actors, all of them. Aware of how they are portrayed in books and films—glamorous, powerful, and hypnotic—they strive to play the role for real. I encourage and cajole, and wait for the game to end, for the wings to fold. When I speak, it is with the authority of one with long experience among the undead hordes. I do not patronise, I refuse to pass judgement, I never threaten or curse. My voice remains rich and resonant, and I make it clear from my stance that I am prepared to defend myself if necessary, but it never has been.

When they are ready, I tell them my story.

My name is Casimir Ntolo Eya'a and my original home is the country of Gabon, a distant land where still the jungle thrives. I was raised on the shores of the sea in a village that had waded into the surf on stilts. A net lowered from a window would suffice to catch many fish and crabs. Life should have been easy, but when the men had money it was spent on beer and gambling, and then the arguments began. As a child I sought to escape the fights and boasting by hiding in the forest. I always went alone and so learned to keep myself company.

An agile climber, I was able to travel quickly through the trees above the tangled undergrowth, safe from the more dangerous animals, my grip always firm on the branches. From this vantage I might spy on my village and the ocean beyond, the spouting whales near the horizon, the ships that occasionally passed, and it seemed to me that I could never appreciate my birthplace properly until I was away from it. This realisation was a minor prophecy of my calling in life, my fate as a wanderer, but at the time such deeper understanding was absent.

On one of my forays I travelled further than before, filled with terror and ecstasy, under the swollen crimson moon, and I discovered a natural amphitheatre ringed with thorny trees so thickly grown together that entry to the space was impossible at ground level. At the centre of this clearing was a formation of upright stones. I knew the legends of my land, I even knew its official history. Nothing in my knowledge accounted for such a structure, and I took upon myself the duty of defining it. First I realised it was essential to spend a night there.

Dropping from an overhanging branch, I entered the circle and slept on the soft grass. The howls of beasts did not alarm me, for my sanctuary was utterly secure. I slept and was bathed by the moon until my soul was clean or sticky, I am unsure which. In the morning I examined with touch every stone, but still could not decide if the formation was an accident of random nature or a deliberate act of men. Almost perversely I decided that the details were unimportant, that it was a temple in spite of every doubt, that I was destined to restore its status.

I returned to the village to discover a tragedy. One among many, my father had been killed in a drunken brawl, his body dumped in the waves. My mother was pale, remote, perhaps resigned. From that moment I hated all men. We existed in silence for weeks, then came more beer, violence, death. My restraint vanished and I confronted the culprits. I was mocked, beaten, defiled. As I ran across the beach a fishing spear thudded into the sand behind, impaling the heel of my footprint. And I wished for darkness to devour my enemies and the land.

That is how the amphitheatre and its scattering of stones became my new home. I gathered fruit, hunted monkeys and birds, fished in the waves far south of the village, and dreamed of my life to come. I would wander the world with the message of my cult. But first I had to invent or rediscover the workings of the faith I intended to spread. This onerous task required hours of concentration. Questions needed to be formed and answered. In the humming dusk I meditated on the possible god to whom the formation was dedicated. He had no shape yet.

If the temple truly was a temple, had it been erected by the Fang tribe who replaced the original pygmies a hundred decades before, or was it older than that? There was no way of satisfying my curiosity. The bite of an insect gave me a fever. Raving and thirsty I lay, and so acute were my dreams that I did not regret the pain. The imaginary pantheon of gods and spirits that paraded before my half-open eyes had an unearthly colour and bittersweet intensity, and I laughed aloud at this very amusing, disturbing dance of animal and plant hybrids.

But I knew I was expected to choose one as supreme, as the true god of the temple. There was a figure distinct from the others, a being whose angles did not meet, who did not obey the rules of perspective taught me in the little schoolroom I had attended. Almost at once I selected him and the others melted away, continuing to dance into nothingness, some with a chiding backward glance at me. I did not ask the remaining god for his mercy, for a creed, for redemption. I asked or demanded only permission to proselytise, to win new converts.

He gave this gladly, whimsically, with an impossible nod of his head, and I heard his words as if from behind a door. "Casimir, though I do not exist, and never have, and never will, please do not forsake me so quickly as the last mortal to worship me. . . ."

There was no pleading in his tone, only in the laugh that followed. I gave my word. Then my fever broke and soft vegetation undulated in a cool breeze around my prone body. I had all I required to begin my work. I stood weakly and ate enough fruit to clear my head, to calm my nerves. I concentrated on rebuilding my physical strength and refining my hatred into something horribly pure. In my mind the route of my life was fully mapped. But even a journey into the heart of darkness must begin with a single step, one bloody footprint.

It was time to leave, and I wanted to take on my voyage a souvenir of the temple. Let me confide a secret. Years earlier, an item of luggage washed up near my village. I found it before dawn, kept it secret, broke the lock. Thus the belongings of a romantic traveller, a passenger on a foreign ship, became mine. A camera wrapped in towels acquired an almost holy aura for me, and I kept it hidden from my fellows. Now it was right to employ one sacred object in the service of another. I photographed the formation of stones from above, from the trees.

I developed that photograph when I eventually reached Libreville and kept it in my wallet. But my first destination after vacating my refuge was Mayumba, a town between three hills where lagoon oysters are noted for piquancy, and sultry but melancholy music was once an inevitable aspect of twilight. I had ample funds to rest and move on. The suitcase the adult Casimir carries is the same blue one washed up on the beach. It contained undamaged money in envelopes. I took a *taxi-brousse* to the capital along terrible roads, under pounding rain.

In Libreville my hatred of all men grew stronger, my faith also, but I did not yet preach the contrived word or authentic artifice of the god now called, for no particular reason, Segrob, a name as magically harmless or hazardous as the pattern of his stones. I lived simply. I achieved manhood rapidly, formulated my plans with care, completed my education as best I might, watched and despised the inhabitants. In a brothel in the Montagne Sainte district, I learned how women were hardly better than men, but my gestures of amazement were feeble.

Despite my relative wealth, the process of acquiring a passport was a protracted one. I worked as a minor clerk in a shipping office to increase the plausibility of my existence, also to avoid depleting my savings. Still the drunken violence continued around me. I haunted crumbling colonial libraries. One book claimed that Gabon had marked the southern limit of the exploratory urge of the Norsemen, an explanation for the origin of my temple I trusted not. The years passed in obscurity and my childish hatred evolved into a mature misanthropy.

And then I made a solemn promise to myself, a misanthropic promise to a misanthropic man, a promise I still intend to keep, indeed a promise I am now on the verge of fulfilling.

Before too long I will tell you what it is.

From Libreville I next voyaged to my country's former coloniser, France, where I made my first converts in certain catacombs under the mazy city of Paris. Normal missionaries seek lost souls in healthy bodies, but such work held no appeal for me. My strategy was to preach the liberating and untrue fact of Segrob only to the undead, as I continue to preach it; and in Paris, that nest of Maupassant and Lautréamont, beneath the boulevards, I fully understood how truly simple my task would be. Freedom they crave even more than rich pulsing blood. . . .

Paris was the beginning of my career, a baptism of my aspirations and the betrothal of my dreams to reality. I explored France, crossed the high passes into Switzerland, shivered nights away beneath the frowns of cold mountains. The undead lurked everywhere, so it seemed; I found them in Italy, Slovenia, Hungary, in every nation of the European continent. Not one vampire declined the ritual of conversion to the worship of Segrob, a ceremony so effortless it could be performed by a child or an imbecile. At once the parasitic slaves were set free.

In the north of Scandinavia, in Finnmark, on an island in a bleak lake, I discovered a clan of vampires who still adhered to the old religion of the north, who professed a belief in Valhalla and Yggdrasil. They rowed their little coracles to the mainland, sucked the veins of reindeer, but dared not approach the nearest settlement for human blood because the ringing of a blacksmith's anvil made them weak with fear. Yet it was not the anvil that inspired such alarm but the evocation of the hammer striking it, for Thor's Hammer was the symbol of their faith.

And that observation brings me to the most salient point of my arrival among every new community of bloodsuckers. All vampires are slaves to the faith they professed when alive or at least to the religion that saturated the culture in which they grew up, faiths represented by symbols that may be found everywhere. To be terrified of such a simple shape as a cross, a crescent, a hammer, must be debilitating in the extreme. And so it is. My power lies therein. As for those vampires who insist they lived as atheists, the situation is worse, as I shall explain.

That is the story I tell my potential converts. I have delivered it so often that rarely is a fact misplaced. What I say to them *next* depends on what reaction I receive. If it seems I am to be lunged at, I quickly lift my staff to demonstrate a sharp end hardened over a low Gabonese fire that easily can penetrate a ribcage and transfix an unbeating heart. As I said earlier, I have never had to use it for that. More commonly, I am politely asked to prove that the worship of Segrob will be less demanding, constrictive, and demoralising than their own religion.

And it always is, of course. So I laugh uproariously.

Guarding my laugh are my teeth, so unlike the teeth of my converts, a cage of bites opened to allow my mirth to escape. Liberation, always that ideal in my bones, in my essence.

I ask them to divulge what their religion is.

When I have an answer, I tell them what they need to know. I reveal the facts. I have a simple list memorised, a list of religious symbols, and from this list I make a choice. Every religion has its disadvantages for a vampire. I remind them of this.

Consider the unfair power of symbols. . . .

⇒ All Christian vampires are deterred by a cross. Such vampires are no better than cretins, utter failures in business, science, engineering, even in domestic affairs, hampered by their inability to perform basic arithmetic due to an aversion to the addition sign. The cross is omnipresent. Struts, nets, the masts of ships, every grid reference on a map, every scarecrow with arms outstretched, every lattice, every gunsight. Fear of the cross is fear of the interstices of the world.

⇒ The Muslim vampire cannot endure the light of a certain moon, the sight of a curved stick, a scimitar, banana, crooked finger, a bent back or fishing rod when a fish has taken bait, or a wave in profile, the camber of a road. For those forms are crescents.

⇒ The Buddhist vampire fears the wheel, the lotus.

⇒ The Hindu vampire, the lotus also. And whatever resembles a lotus, so they cannot tolerate the idea of a night of passion with a woman. Thus the female vampires who profess that faith are frightened, shrivelled, and ultimately destroyed by themselves.

⇒ For the Sikh vampire the presence of a sword or knife or closed loop is anathema. He must flee from them, his rotting turban unwinding. Every circle is his bane, every cutting edge.

⇒ Stars invoke a disabling horror in vampires of the Jewish and Bahá'í persuasions, six pointed stars for the former, nine for the latter. But as the atmosphere of the world we stand on refracts the light that passes through it, stars with six or nine, or as many points as might be desired or feared, glitter every night in a clear sky. For those who are Bahá'í the situation is truly hellish, for they regard *all* religious symbols as holy. There is almost nothing that does not agonise them.

⇒ Taoist vampires falter when confronted with equal amounts of black and white, cold and hot, active and passive. The mere passing of the days and nights is a chessboard on which their profound grief and despair play against each other, both triumphing.

⇒ The vampire who professes Jainism must avoid all representations of the hand, including the hand itself.

⇒ Shinto vampires cannot bear to view a gate.

⇒ It might be argued that Zoroastrian vampires are slightly freer than many others, for a winged disc does not often present itself to the casual onlooker, but fire is their other symbol. Besides, it is a dying faith and its adherents and vampires are few.

⇒ The atheist vampire has chosen doubt itself or disbelief as his faith. Perhaps science has become his religion. The symbols that he must avoid are even more prevalent than variations of any religious sign. For him, the question mark, atom, shrug, blankness, negative, vacuum, minus sign, all hints of progress, every artefact of technology, the critic and the cynic are abominations. Every chemical reaction, every mechanical principle, every law of physics, burns him like acid. . . .

So inevitable are all those forms, so clearly do they exist in nature and in the artificial world of civilisation, so common to every experience, that any being that must shun them must avoid all activity, hide away, cower, burrow, tremble, forsake reality.

It turns out that vampires are prisoners.

Prisoners of the shapes that exist without effort in every place.

So I make them this covenant. . . .

When they demand to know why they should convert, I tell them that under the law of Segrob they will be granted both peace and power, that loyalty to my god will unleash their frustrated appetites, that they will at last be capable of feeding among men, and on men, without the worry of the simplest geometric deterrents.

How can this be? How might this work?

Because the symbol of Segrob is complex, unlikely, chaotic, random, and almost certainly will never be repeated in any situation anywhere at any time. It is far too intricate.

The symbol of Segrob is the pattern of stones in his temple, a pattern with no symmetry, no balance, perhaps no deliberation at all, perhaps not even a distribution governed by any reasonable law of chance. No victim can ever contort fingers into *his* symbol to ward off the bite. No necklace will suspend the sign, no earring.

The pattern that represents my imaginary god is not intuitive. Whoever believes in it becomes implacable.

When they hear this, the answer is always the same. "Convert us! We yearn, nay lust, to be converted!"

I nod once, lay my suitcase on the ground, open it, extract my flute. I am not skilled on the instrument, but that is irrelevant. The ritual consists of a shrill series of arbitrary notes, one note for one stone, a new sequence each time. I wave the flute over the head of the kneeling vampire. Then it is accomplished. He is now reborn.

As a devotee of Segrob, a nonexistent god . . .

Replacing my flute, I stand up straight and smile.

At this juncture my senses are more alert than before. I know what is coming, and it is rarely pleasant.

"With every factor considered carefully," they say, rubbing their hands or stroking their chins, "it seems only proper you should offer yourself as a sacrifice, as a meal, for we have not tasted human blood for long ages, and if you decline then you can be easily forced. True, you had a pointed staff to protect yourself, but you laid it aside to open your suitcase, and by your own admission we are safe from the showing of rapidly improvised religious signs. Step closer, please."

Despite the gentleness in their voices, it is always they who take that single fateful step. I have unbuttoned my shirt, my wallet is open. I draw out the photograph that is my memento of my sanctuary. In the soft light of my lantern the image is crisp.

"Behold the symbol of Segrob, the only one in existence!"

They recoil in excruciating pain.

Every eventuality was worked out long ago. . . .

They are aware of this. From behind the long pale deformed hands that shield their appalled faces they cry:

"How do you know all that you know?"

I smile thinly and answer:

"The suitcase I carry, deposited on that beach in my youth, contained books, not published volumes but personal diaries, which I studied with great avidity. They were written by one of the most famous of your kind and so I learned your troubles. He was fleeing uselessly from the shapes that tormented him everywhere. I will not divulge his Carpathian name. What I desire is revenge on all mankind, and that is why I have made you free—to slake my anger for me."

They digest the news slowly, as if the gore of an entire species is already clotted at their feet, ready to be lapped. Then they ask, "What of you? Will you continue to convert?"

Not this time. The end has come already.

I shake my head, surprised by my own sudden tiredness. "I have done enough. I intend to return home, to live my life in solitude, knowing that the human race is being bitten into extinction as I sit and saturate myself in the ambient peace of my jungle. That is the limit of my ambition. *You* will do the job of converting other vampires, and the word of Segrob will spread among your kind like a virus."

"Converted vampires converting others? A good idea. But one day, we will come for you too. When you are unaware, when you are asleep in the stillness you crave, we will pounce."

I laugh and turn to depart. "You are very wrong."

On a beach I finally burn the books that taught me everything I needed to know. Those secret journals that permitted me even in my youth to plan a global revenge, to empower demons, are now smoke and flame inside the charred suitcase, which has become its own pyre. I saved only these blank pages that I tore out for later use.

I have returned to the continent of my birth and death with an outward show of tranquillity, but my heart is hugely satisfied and beats ferociously as I turn my eyes from the growing fire toward the horizon beyond which stands my jungle, my amphitheatre.

I will write this account within the temple, when my work is done, not before. But it is done now, or being done on my behalf. If you are reading this, you are not human. Unless . . .

Yes, the other worshipper of Segrob is the one rogue factor that disturbs my victory, upsets my plans, for was it not my god himself who asked me not to behave like him? I will continue to live as if I never had heard of that mysterious former devotee, that rival or heretic whose reality is no greater than the fever in which I was told of him. But what if he tries to occupy my refuge in the forest, among the pattern of stones that protects me from the vampires that finally have no more victims other than us? I anticipate a sordid power struggle.

Because of its unique shape, my temple is the only place in the entire world safe from the undead devotees of Segrob. I do not want to share it with another man, nor to have it wrested from me. Then it occurs to me that the other worshipper might be a woman, that we could live together, raise children, rebuild the human race, breed warriors who might set forth with the symbol of Segrob to exterminate the vampires as now they will make conventional mankind extinct. Then the globe will be mine and a fairer society can arise and prosper.

I linger over this fantasy, calculate, enjoy, expand, and finally reject its ramifications. If I permitted that scenario to happen I would not be a true misanthrope, merely a narcissist or megalomaniac. No, I will follow my original plan and live and die alone.

The last mortal man in a world of vampires.

That is my promise to myself.

Smuggling Old Nick
to Newfoundland

I t was one of those taverns that only appear in old pictures hung on the walls of ancient taverns. It was too impossible to be quaint. Nonetheless there I sat with a tankard of ale and my stockinged feet warming before a fire in a gigantic hearth. The door creaked open so unexpectedly that we all acted as if we had expected it, and a man stepped inside with his beard and glower. Very imposing he tried to be and almost successful he was. He blinked for many minutes, and his eyebrows bristled like porcupine quills stuck in a dog's nose. Then he spoke to the entire gathering:

"How can there be a tavern here? The map indicates only moor and bog for miles around!"

"A secret tavern is what it is," answered Loophole the barman from behind his counter, "and sworn to silence are all those who stumble upon it by accident. But I may make an exception in your case and permit you to babble about it, for I perceive by your garb and bearing that you are a preacher."

"What difference does that make?" frowned the newcomer.

Loophole shrugged. "A man must always be what he is. And so a preacher should preach, otherwise an extra crumb of confusion is brushed off the tablecloth of unnecessary chaos onto the dirty floor we call the world." He blushed slightly and added, "I wanted to be a poet but I was too eager to serve mankind, so I became a barman instead."

"I will sermonise about this place," said the preacher.

Sitting quietly like a fireguard in front of the hot flickers, I groaned inwardly at this inept dialogue, judging it too contrived to be anything other than sordidly realistic. I knew what the preacher did not, that Loophole had given him the gift of life, for if no vow of silence from a newcomer was forthcoming the alternative was usually a fatal sinking in the nearest bog. Loophole was a kind villain, a man who once consulted an encyclopaedia to learn the name of the most painless poison and, not finding it, employed the heavy tome itself as a substitute weapon, bludgeoning his victim to death in a cloud of academic dust. Half hoop, half void, him.

"Not a poetic sermon, though," continued the preacher, "for I despise poetry as sensuous and immoral, a seductive music for depraved ears. I preach in the dry style only."

"Your repression is exceptional," observed Loophole.

The preacher snorted at this and then took a deep breath. He foolishly assumed he had the undivided attention of the entire company, but in truth the patrons of the tavern had already lost interest and were returning to their own concerns. Loophole had spared him, after all, and so he had become merely another fixture of the place, hardly more significant than the warped candles spitting in the empty wine bottles on the rough tables. I was the closest fellow to him and a lone witness to the speech he made. Even Loophole was engaged with more important business, fishing in a huge jar of vinegar for the pickled onions and cashews he served on a little dish with every mug of ale.

"There is much evil here," the preacher began, as he rolled his eyes to the heaven that lay somewhere beyond the low sooty ceiling, "and in truth no worse den of iniquity have I encountered this year. Taverns are vile and the things they contain are guaranteed to warp the soul. Beer is evil, tobacco also; and as for cribbage, dominoes, dice, and other gambling games, it is best not to speak! You are all wicked men and loose women. Verily, the devil is abroad this night!"

My composure was finally rattled at his last words, and I lowered my feet from the stool they rested on, sitting erect and rubbing my chin, the stubble rasping my callused palms like the short wires of a metal brush. I positioned myself so that I was facing him at an angle more conducive to conversation and I asked:

"How do you know that?"

His bushy eyebrows rose steeply. "What do you mean?"

"The part about the devil being abroad . . . How are you aware of his recent movements?"

"I follow you not," he stammered.

Reducing my voice to a whisper I said, "The devil loves to travel abroad, but he lacks a passport. Without a passport there is no chance of obtaining a visa for those countries that require one. Clearly he must find other ways of crossing borders. He often relies on my services, for I am a smuggler and will put him ashore on lonely beaches at night for a fee."

"This news surprises me greatly!" he cried.

I studied my fingernails and noticed the grains of sand beneath them, particles from a thousand different coves and bays. "The last time he appeared, he asked me to take him to Newfoundland, and so I did."

"Really quite remarkable! I am aghast."

"My fees are reasonable. I charge a fixed rate of ten euros for every degree of latitude and another ten for every degree of longitude crossed. Travelling to one of the cardinal points of the compass is thus cheaper than heading northwest, northeast, southwest, or southeast. I can deduce from your expression that you wish to hire me for an illegal border crossing of your own. Am I correct?"

He hunched his shoulders and became a far less impressive figure, a boyish mound of coal, his facial features settling like timid migrants into the mock-industrial landscape of his head. Loophole brought beers for us unbidden. In the thick foam of both creamy heads he had etched a pair of horns. His fingers were matted with salad. I permitted the cucumber vapours to soothe my arid eyeballs and waited for him to saunter back to his counter before pressing the preacher for more information. "Where do you want to go?"

"Belgium."

"Why there?"

He pouted. "The flatness, the proximity, the laxity. My voice can do good work in such a place."

"Very well." I stood to leave. "Follow me."

I led him out of the tavern through the little-used rear entrance. He was outraged by this and mumbled words of rue to himself and to the threshold and jambs, some of which I caught: "More vice and vileness! My guide is a back door man!"

Despite his misgivings, we clattered along a boardwalk perched over the mud flats that stretched to the horizon. This place was entirely uninhabited by mortals, partly because of a persistent rumour that it was a sacred burial ground for golems. I tended to laugh at such speculations, but not very loudly, not audibly at all in fact, and I always looked over my shoulder as I did so, in gloopy fear and squelchy loathing. The boardwalk lurched down to my sloop, which I pointed out to my companion as we approached, but his attention was on other matters.

"You have forgotten your shoes!" he hissed.

"One of my prerogatives," I answered.

"Stockings are immoral, suspenders also, to say nothing of garters. And as for basques . . ."

I misunderstood him. "We are going to Belgium, not Navarra. Climb aboard my vessel, if you please."

He pleased. I joined him and cast off the mooring line before raising the lateen sail. The sloop moved down the waterway. To this day I still do not know whether it was once a river that had been straightened into a canal or a canal that had decayed into a river. We drifted down it towards the sea. For most of the voyage we preserved an uneasy but curiously delectable silence, but the moment we were out of sight of land he appeared to soften. "You have not asked my name," he sadly reflected.

"Very well. What is it?"

He shifted his weight at the bottom of the boat while the sail flapped in a sudden breeze. "Introductio Gaspar."

"It is too late now. You are merely 'The Preacher.'"

He accepted this with poor grace but was distracted by a region of bubbles off the starboard side of the vessel. Something was lurking there just below the surface. I eyed it cautiously and said, "Pray it is not the Spiderpus."

"That prayer is technically difficult for me. Are you referring to a supernatural monster?"

"Of sorts. Consider the following scenario . . . A spider has eight legs but no arms, an octopus has eight arms but no legs. Individually they are too specialised to be a danger to mankind, but working together they are a serious threat to our continued dominance of the planet. The Spiderpus is a giant octopus mounted on the back of an enormous spider. Eight arms *and* eight legs! Nothing is beyond such a beast. It can run, jump, climb, juggle, knit, cook, fence, control oscilloscopes, launch rockets . . ."

The preacher was now willing to pray for us, but by the time I had explained what a Spiderpus was it had gone. Life is like that. And so he decided to raise an objection instead. "A spider lives on land, an octopus in water. How can they collaborate effectively?"

"Eight arms, eight legs," I reminded him. "Anything is possible."

He frowned. "I perceive the circumference of a circular argument . . ."

I changed the subject quickly. "All my passengers are also supernatural creatures. The devil is my main client, but I have smuggled all kinds of vampire, werewolf, zombie, and ghoul across a variety of oceans. I once even ferried Charon to the Isle of Wight. You are a mortal man, but I have decided to make an exception in your case."

"The barman in that tavern set a precedent?"

I nodded. A few hours later the Belgian coast came into view, a stretch of lonely shore between Ostend and Blankenberge. I noticed another sloop approaching the same spot at an oblique angle. I have forgotten to mention that I am not the only smuggler working in my particular field. I have a dozen rivals. To my delight I recognised the passenger in the other vessel. He was returning early from Newfoundland. I waved and he mimicked my gesture in that nonchalant manner of his.

"How I would love to give *him* a good talking to!" cried the preacher as he squinted into the distance.

I licked my lips. "Living men are not allowed to do that. But in this circumstance . . . . If three exceptions are made to a rule, a new rule is created. That is the law. I will introduce you when we reach the beach. You are a fortunate fellow, or a very unfortunate one, I know not which!"

The preacher was nervous. "But only two exceptions have been made for me so far . . ."

"*That* is the third exception," I said.

I left him on the sand with his arch-enemy. The last words he said to me before he jumped out of the sloop into the tiny waves were, "I read somewhere that spiders can breathe through their knees. Is this true?"

I shrugged and did my best to forget about him. I am ashamed to admit that I failed in my efforts. He began disputing with the devil on sundry topics. The devil is too fashionable to be given a dressing-down, but the preacher would not give up. They were still there, standing in the poses of philosophers or gibbons, long after I had returned to sea. The devil can breathe through his knees. And his elbows. It takes thousands of years of practice, but he has plenty of time to spare. I can only breathe through three orifices. I need a new pair of stockings. And a corset. Occasionally I smuggle rum, tobacco, and figs as well as imaginary beings. To make ends meet.

Shelling the Toad

The minstrel had the manners of a corpse.

I don't mean he was impolite. On the contrary, a dead body is stiff and thus formal at all times, at least before it decays. That was the exact problem with this man, not a lack of grace. When he entered the breakfast room, he nodded to all in turn, but the style of his greeting was rigid.

Then the muscles of his face began twitching, and I wondered if the storm of the previous night had charged him with electricity. He crackled as he walked, not as if he trod the earth of his own grave but with obvious pain, stepping on the shed scales of an enormous crystallised serpent.

This metaphor was suggested to me by the sequins sewn along both sides of his boots. They flashed as he moved towards the buffet, probably reflecting the wedding rings on fingers belonging to male hands that were resting, under tablecloths, on the naked knees of women not married to them. I didn't crouch to look: if I was wrong, my own adventure would be less justified.

"His moustache is badly tuned," said Gisella.

I wiped my lips with a napkin. "A pretentious observation," I answered, "but a lyrical one." The napkin crumpled in my fist.

"What's that on his back?"

Turning to look, I said, "The weight of a fantastic responsibility. The fate of being picturesque. Could you bear that burden?"

"No, I think it's a shell."

We were in a region of Europe that still tolerated smoking in public places. I watched Gisella extract a black cigarette from her handbag and hold it between her fingers, but she didn't do anything else with it.

"Like a turtle, you mean?"

"I need another cup of coffee. I'll go over and ask him."

"Why do that? Don't do it."

She stood and I reached out to restrain her, but she shrugged me off with one of her small laughs. I never wanted to control Gisella, though the temptation to disappoint her was frequently strong. I'm sure I managed that without trying. With genuine relish, I finished my plate of *sajtos pogácsa* and drained my own cup. Then I frowned. Something new and almost horrible had adjusted the atmosphere of the room. Whatever it was, it was nearly a sound.

We were always the first couple down for breakfast: otherwise the tomatoes and peppers of the buffet vanished within minutes of the doors being opened. We had learned the necessity of a brave dawn assault, Gisella and I, in many ways so much more precious than an equivalent chorus.

I didn't look at Gisella now. I thought about my wife instead, my real wife, and her despicable habits, her timidity. Then I remembered I was supposed to be analysing the difference in the ambient mood of my surroundings. Perhaps I was reluctant to begin the task properly, a defensive reflex. The obvious solution often sounds psychologically astute. That's a paradox, and in this case a lie. The answer was vague and disturbing but not reluctant.

I noticed the manager of the hotel crossing the far side of the room, and so I beckoned to him. I didn't really expect him to respond to the gesture in any way, no more than a cat might. His eagerness to obey startled me. With a twinge of despair, I realised I had nothing to say to him. Then he was by my side and I muttered, "Do you happen to know the forecast for today?"

He narrowed his eyes and checked his watch. "We don't discuss politics in public here." His thick lips were bloodless.

"No, the weather. Has there been a significant drop in barometric pressure? My ears feel a bit strange. They are ringing."

His face cleared. "Ah, it's the music." And leaning forward so that his long dangling necktie cast a shadow on my plate, he added, "Sometimes it takes effort and time before it registers on your mind."

This answer was peculiar, and I swivelled my head.

The minstrel was squatting in the corner. Gisella was standing above him, a full cup of coffee in one hand, her other hand outstretched, as if imploring, frozen like a statue, her fingers spread apart. And in the uncertain light it appeared to me there was greenish webbing between them.

The manager shook his head slowly, walked away.

Then I understood that the breakfast room was brimming with melody, with an odd tune that was ancient, earthy, and very human, but also alien, demoralising, incomprehensible. I am no musicologist. I know very little about scales, keys, and modes, yet I had a feeling that this music had deviated so radically from orthodox standards it had split in two, forked across millennia in both directions. It was the song of our oldest ancestors but also the anthem of the remote future; the vibrating notes interfering with my thought processes.

I scraped my chair leg on the floor. "Gisella!"

She ignored me. But of her own free will she turned with geological velocity and returned to our table, riding the solar wind of the music that radiated from the instrument the minstrel plucked and strummed.

"The back of a lute, that's what it was," she told me.

"What? What are you saying?"

"The shell. It isn't a shell at all, but the reverse side of the lute he wore on a strap over his shoulder. Local minstrels carry their lutes on their backs. I didn't get a chance to speak to him, but I can tell."

Gisella, the linguist, my illicit lover, speaker of many languages, crooner of sumptuous words in improbable tongues: never any need to doubt her on matters of ethnographic detail. She had been my mistress for only two years, and in that time a new war had come and gone in these lands.

"He looks like a toad," I remarked at last, when it was over.

"That's the first song," she said.

Both of us had been under a lot of stress for a very long time. The way we behaved wasn't especially sane or even reasonable, but it was difficult to have an objective view of anything we did. We knew we were slightly mad, but we didn't know why, and at such times the solution was always to travel. Why we never ventured outside the borders of Europe is still a mystery to me.

But there is plenty of Africa and Asia in Europe; in certain isolated parts of a few countries the customs and culture are as foreign as any can be. Narrow valleys where fleeing Crusader knights settled to breed and ossify, their glum descendants wearing chainmail and carrying broadswords as recently as fifty years ago; caves in cliffs where hermits peep out at stars arranged in constellations older than those the Hellenes gave us; mountaintops from which the syllables of epic verse and heathen prayers are declaimed and altar fires smoulder.

And now we were in a patch of old Hungarian values that was no longer in Hungary itself but in Serbia. Borders had been moved like ropes pegged to stakes, and peoples had been forced to skip over them.

We were hiking the less populous parts of Vojvodina, a province rarely visited by travellers or tourists. Generally flat with wide horizons, a land with its secrets all seemingly laid out, it nonetheless contained a few places that couldn't be seen until one was inside them, tiny valleys brooding between hills so low they were no more than nonchalant shrugs of the geology's shoulders. Following rivers without names, hiking through wildflowers, we explored ruins, relics, and memories not our own in a smoky succession of myth-saturated settlements.

Gisella brought up the subject of the minstrel as we passed an abandoned inn on our way to find the source of yet another stream. The music of the water seemed to emanate from the building itself as the little river skirted it, and it was easy for us to imagine the inn was thriving and full again, that the sagging beams were reliable and merely quaint, the windows agleam with thick glass, the crooked chimney dribbling smoke from the communal fireplace.

For in such structures, in the old days, wandering musicians would come and go and play for whoever happened to be staying.

"His lute had holes cut into it," she said, as I stopped to listen.

"Who do you mean?" I was baffled.

"The minstrel at the hotel."

"Ah, yes. Do you think he is the last of his kind?"

Gisella brushed the hair from her eyes. She couldn't know the answer to this any more than I might; but the question had affected her deeply. Perhaps he was the final gasp of a tradition stretching back millennia, and we had been witnesses to this concluding chapter of his art. History rarely has a habit of loudly rustling the pages when it turns them over, so we were honoured.

"Almost certainly," she replied at last. "I don't know why."

"Every melody and man has its echo."

"No, I didn't mean I don't know why anyone should ever be the last of their kind; I meant I don't know why I felt I had such a strong feeling of something lost, an artform about to be consigned to oblivion, when I heard him play. I didn't really like the music much; but I'm convinced that was because the world has left behind what he does, not because I am insensitive."

"A living fossil. Impossible to empathise with."

"Could be," sighed Gisella.

"An anachronism," I persisted, blinking.

"The holes made every chord sound strange, bitten off," she said. We passed within touching distance of the inn's walls, and she reached out and introduced her fingertips to the lacquered wood. "Dead."

"But still audible. Ghosts, in other words, phantom songs."

"Feasibly. But not quite—"

"Not quite what? Not quite the ghosts of real songs, of human music? Then his notes must logically be alien, demonic."

"Last night you said you felt connected to at least a part of it in some minor way at least; so it can't be anti-human."

"Unless there is alien blood in everyone. After all, our ancestors might have been demons or ghosts, anything at all."

She said nothing in reply. Neither of us believed such things, in spirits or any other supernatural manifestation, but they remained useful metaphors. And yet they can still be troubling, those metaphors, as difficult as the real thing. The truth is that we were struggling to express how we felt about a performance that had resembled no other in our experience; it had redefined for me the meaning of 'music.' I wasn't sure I welcomed this, or even understood it.

"I don't know if he cut the holes himself or if the instrument was supposed to look like that. What do you think, Elzéard?"

"My knowledge on the subject is scanty. There was that peculiar lute in that mountain village in Corsica, do you recall?"

"It was a cittern, and the holes were painted dots."

"I can offer no other examples."

She laughed. "Nor should you be able to."

We continued in silence. Our destination lay somewhere ahead, but we would only know what it was when we reached it. Then Gisella held up her hand, the one that had touched the wall of the inn, and the illusion she had webbed fingers was as strong as it had been at breakfast. Sunlight filtered through the greenish membranes, and as she shielded her face the tinted light bathed her features unpleasantly. I felt I was viewing her underwater; that she was some kind of river sprite just emerged to dine on dragonflies and other insectile ephemera.

I blinked, and the impression was dispelled. The webbing was nothing more than a distant heat haze observed between her spread digits; that was obvious now. But the toad had entered the hollow stone of my mind, lodged itself there ready to be discovered, alive, centuries after my death.

"Does it ever seem plausible to you," I began mildly, "that some of us didn't evolve from apes but from other creatures?"

Gisella laughed. "Bears, wolves, and cats. Perhaps."

"Also lizards and amphibians?"

"You are thinking about the minstrel again. Do you know what the manager of the hotel told me? There's an old superstition, Hungarian in origin, that persists in these parts, namely that if a toad enters a house someone in that house is fated to die shortly. A guest toad is always a bad omen."

"A variation on the bird of death. Once, when I was small, a sparrow became trapped in our kitchen. We returned from a family holiday to find it there. My father opened a window to let it out, and my mother said that its presence augured a loss. I still can't imagine how it got inside. My grandfather died soon after, and I doubt I'll ever be able to break the connection I made."

"Phobias are created that way."

I shook my head. "I feel no fear. Just resignation. We can't evade our dooms and should be grateful for any warning."

"I would prefer not to know when my time is up."

"A question of taste, no more."

"What creature did *you* evolve from, Elzéard?"

I laughed. What else could I do?

We approached a deserted settlement and knew this was our turning point, a place to give structure to our meanderings, to turn them into a definite journey on the map, to fix the randomness of our day and set it into the form of a mission. The river passed through the centre of the settlement. There was a broken waterwheel, a dozen stepping stones, mostly submerged. Dust constantly fell from walls of eroded plaster, spiralling back up in the minimal wind.

The houses of the village were like the audience listening to a minstrel at a respectful, and therefore safe, distance. The minstrel must have been the inn, there in the mist, beyond the fields and fields and more fields of wild flowers, alone and imperious and full of holes, resonant, peculiar, and possibly full of toads, or at least sounding like a toad, a grotesquely enlarged example. And this audience of senile homes, empty, melancholic, joined the chorus.

We reached the village square and our ears ached.

The shutters and doors of the abandoned village didn't creak as they flapped slowly in the wind. They croaked instead.

The following day we decided to make one more trip and then move on to another region. I had pinpointed our exact position on the map. We were an equal distance from the borders of Croatia, Hungary, and Romania, and some vortex of clashing energies, historical, cultural, or ethnic, was disturbing our peace, twisting the spines of our unease into fantastic shapes. In our room before descending, we laced our boots with the determination of mountaineers, though the landscape remained as flat as ever.

Gisella studied herself in the mirror.

"Is my beauty yours? Do you think you own it?"

I turned to look, but not directly. I studied her reflection. "Your beauty isn't mine, but I don't even think it's your own."

A poor answer, but she smiled as she brushed her hair.

I leaned forward, shook the map, made it rattle. "Where shall we go today? We have already been west, north, east . . ."

"South it must be, in that case. Away from Hungary."

"Very good." I folded the map.

We didn't go down for breakfast this time. I couldn't face the possibility of another musical performance with my food; and even if the minstrel wasn't there, some essence of his strange melodies remained, like the film of vaporised fat that varnishes every surface after a man has spontaneously combusted. The manager saw us stealthily depart, and he raised a languid arm in a sardonic gesture as we hastened past the glass doors of the dining room; or maybe his salute was sincere and it was everything else that was warped.

We left the hotel and strode away from it as if it were a congealing dinner. There was unusual force in our legs today; something had energised us, filled us with power and yearning, the migratory impulse. The path took us through more meadows full of bright blooms on absurdly long stalks, abandoned fields full of rusting scythe blades and crumbled hovels.

On the horizon a wall of distant trees danced in the haze.

"Those are untouched forests," I said.

"Untouched by what?" Gisella goaded me.

I couldn't answer. Everything felt unbalanced, my legs virile, my tongue heavy and formless, like a mouthful of mercury. I had no deeper desire than to enter the trance of the true wanderer, the rhythm of the nomad, of our ancestors, the archetypal man. Locked into a sense of well-being in which time loses half or more of its meaning, the habitual walker flows through the landscape seemingly without effort. That was my goal, my hope.

And so we marched south, and butterflies danced with one another in duels of colour, and we imagined we felt, or really felt, the tiny cooling breezes of their wings, frantic and languid at the same time.

The forest came to meet us, but slowly, very slowly.

Wars had threaded its depths for dozens of centuries, had hidden archers and snipers, concealed bear pits festooned with sharpened stakes; and yet it stood dense and wise, innocent of woodsman's axe or charcoal burners' pyres. A sea of dark green lapping an occasional island glade.

We didn't pause for our first rest until we reached the front rank of trunks, the vanguard of the magnificent, troublesome verdure, a row of pillars that held up a green sky. We drank from our flasks and pushed on, crossed that threshold, stepped from a world of grass, flowers, ferns, where we were the giants, into one where I felt smaller than I had since I was a child.

It was like entering a portable night.

The hours became rhythmic, weaving like the sine waves of low-frequency sonar signals between the mossy boles.

We sat on a fallen trunk and consumed some of our rations, smoked cheese rolled up in a tight spiral, bread blasted with poppyseed grapeshot, strips of red and orange peppers, olives in a waxy bag.

Gisella blinked. "How far have we come?"

Her words seemed to snap me out of a mesmeric fugue, and I gazed around in dismay. "The sun is still low in the sky."

The thin beams slanted diagonally through the trees like the searchlights of technically proficient dryads, glimmering with motes. Fungi on trunks gleamed; a branch broke somewhere with a whip crack.

"So not far?" she whispered.

I nodded, spat crumbs. "Just a short way."

"But the sun is lower than it was when we set out; and it's lower on the far side of the sky. I think it must be setting."

"Impossible." I reached for an external pocket of my rucksack, unzipped it, and groped inside for my wristwatch. When I retrieved it and studied the position of the hands, I felt compelled to do the traditional thing and shake it a few times before taking a second look. Then I pouted.

"The day is over already."

"I don't understand. Where did the time go?"

We had both walked ourselves into a state of sleep, but a sleep that required no pause in motion. Somnambulists, we had lost ourselves in the pathless deeps of an extremely ancient and complex forest.

"We ought to go back immediately, Elzéard," she said.

I agreed, and we retraced our steps.

But it was a futile endeavour. We had too far to go and not enough time. It was possible to walk for almost an hour after the sun went down; then dusk took away the final tint and abandoned us to true night and an obstacle course of black and grey silhouettes that looked menacing.

In the next relatively large clearing we paused to acknowledge defeat. Now we would have to spend the night here, bivouac amid the sylvan colossi, and keep our spirits calm by sharing anecdotes and memories and quips. Fortunately I had packed a tarpaulin in my rucksack for emergencies.

We used it to construct a temporary shelter on the rim of the glade, tying it to the branches of a tree so that it hung down like a tent. Then we crawled inside and I fumbled in my pockets for matches . . .

There was a lumpy shape in the shelter with us.

I assumed it was a small boulder. I found my sheath knife but no matches. I heard Gisella begin to move away from me. Then she recoiled with such a swift jerk into me that I dropped the knife automatically. I clutched her tight. Before I could ask her what was wrong, she hissed:

"It's alive. Whatever it is. A living thing. A creature."

The boulder stirred a little.

Then it hopped. And a shivery sound came from it.

I said, "Wait a moment. Please wait."

And I resumed my search for the matches, found them, fumbled to take out and strike one with an agonising rasp.

A cone of light illuminated the little interior.

The thing had four short limbs and a long stiff tail and a hard carapace like an armadillo. But it hopped grotesquely.

The match went out. Gisella pressed hard into me.

"Another," she commanded.

I struck a second match. The creature was leaving the tent. Then I surprised myself by lunging forward and grabbing the tail in one hand. I didn't pull it back but twisted my wrist, and the monster flipped over.

As the match charred the fingertips of my other hand I saw that I was holding a lute by the neck; that the limbs were the feet and hands of a human being; that the face glaring out at me from behind the thin strings was the minstrel's, the minstrel with the manners of a corpse; that he and his instrument combined was the toad. I swallowed with difficulty, and the match died.

By the time I had struck a third, he was gone. We listened to him hopping to the far side of the clearing and jumping into the undergrowth. Gisella clutched me and I clutched her and we rocked each other for comfort as the dreadful hours of the night passed with cruel hesitation.

But the toad did not return. And eventually the morning came.

Gisella said, "We have survived."

I shook my head. "One of us is fated to die. That was the superstition, you said. If a toad comes into a house, one of the occupants must die. We erected our house *around* the sleeping toad, but I don't think that technicality will save us. A toad shared our house last night, Gisella."

"It was a shelter, not a house," she objected.

"There's no difference really."

"Why let foolish folk tales trouble you?"

"It was you who told me about this one. I wouldn't have known."

"We must find our way out of the forest."

"I don't want to die, not yet."

"Elzéard, you won't die if you take good care of yourself."

"It is better to be safe, Gisella."

"If the superstition is true and one of us must die, it could be me. And if I die, then it won't be you. Cheer up."

"Yes, if it is you, it can't be me. That's right."

The handle of the sheath knife was hard and cold under my knee. I took it and my grip was sure. I once accidentally disturbed an owl in the morning, and it took flight with a look of furious disbelief. I saw the same look in her big eyes. I knew how gullible I was, how frightened I could be. It was a tough lesson, and it left me sobbing, gasping for breath afterwards.

I washed the blade and the tarpaulin in a tiny stream, packed them away. I reflected on how it is possible to cheat destiny by helping it; that a self-fulfilling prophecy is still a prophecy. I left her body with its perfect manners for the wild beasts, the real animals with natural bodies that mostly do not hop. Then I strode boldly out of this land and back to my wife.

The Hydrothermal Reich

What joy there is when we recall times of misery! Because they exist not in the present but far away, moving deeper into the past, like prisoners in a sealed train, each hour closer to the horizon at our rear. And once over the edge of memory they will be gone forever, perhaps unloaded at a camp where they will be stripped of all significance and gassed. I dream of myself in my prime and I am always whole, good. But the deeds visited upon us are mere specks, dwindling towards annihilation. And whenever new misfortunes come to me, I dispatch them the same way. My locomotives run on time, for days turn the wheels.

I am a boorish man, rarely at ease with elaborate metaphors, unless they can be bartered or threatened. Age has altered me. Not to soften my perception on matters of taste or conduct, rather to make me tolerant of abstract sentiment. I have spent tons of gold, much of it stolen, though my talent with legitimate accounts cannot be doubted. I was always aware of the importance of luxury, despite the modest opportunity for enjoying material distractions during my vocation. I worked harder than anyone in the bunker. Speer, no slouch himself, called me a workhorse, a hint that I should be boiled alive for glue.

He left early, the way he had arrived, in a battered *Storch* plane. The women thought he was wonderful, but I knew him as an opportunist and traitor. I once asked him to persuade the Führer to let me fly south, to the Berghof. His personal influence was profound and he promised to try. I waited at the foot of the fifty cold steps at the deepest level of the bunker, but he emerged from his final meeting without news. I envied his emotional power over our leader. I manipulated Hitler's mind through the controlled release of his written orders, but his heart still remained a peculiar mystery. Not so to Speer.

It is obvious our leader regarded him as a surrogate son, the successful architect he had himself aspired to be, back in his Viennese youth. My own son was also a deserter, a priest, and a teacher. Of all the creators of the New Order, it was I who was most responsible for assaulting the Church, for pulling down the cross on the altar and replacing it with the spear of Wotan. So the ordination of my child was a severe shock. Yet we anticipate acts of rebellion from the young. I admired Speer almost as much as I hated him, purely for practical reasons. Later in Nuremberg he became an epitome of cynicism, denouncing the Führer to save his balding scalp. He failed us, but he was only one of my options.

The twilight weeks of the bunker were suffused with wine and ghosts and testaments. Hanna Reitsch and Ritter von Greim had brought in a case of good champagne, despite being shot down over the Tiergarten, and this fuelled a dozen parties before the capitulation. The phantoms, even more heady, took the form of Wenck's rescue army, which only truly existed on paper, and of Heinrici's troops, who were retreating to the west, hoping to be captured by American, not Russian, forces. The testaments were all dramatic, none more so than Goebbel's Appendix to the Führer's Political Will, but I continued with serious work. Transmissions received from the unoccupied regions became frantic.

An aerial suspended from a single balloon above the Chancellery was our sole link with the crumbling Reich. I occupied the radio and sent my schemes radiating through the filthy atmosphere. Göring, most obscene of my rivals, and now Himmler, with whom I had forged a shaky alliance, had betrayed the Führer. The way was clear to secure dominance over Dönitz's rump government. I had to leave quickly, but only with an escort. Hitler ranted at the actions of his former deputies, his face swelling like the white bosom of a Bavarian maiden. Not once did he bite a carpet. That is facile propaganda, a fitted lie.

One of Goebbel's men, Heinz Lorenz, had brought the announcement of Himmler's treachery, and I stood with him in the passage outside the room where the Führer attempted to regain his composure. Lorenz was suspicious of me, but we exchanged a few confidences. If Hitler decided to commit suicide, he claimed, then Goebbels would also kill himself. I barely concealed my delight at this prospect, for it removed another rival to my succession. That cripple was forever working to weaken my grip over the making of policy. Like Göring, Speer, and Ley, he resented my unobtrusive power. It annoyed him that I had no public face. The *Brown Eminence,* he termed me, an insult I found ludicrous.

When the Führer stepped out into the corridor, he was calm and most of his natural colour had returned. Lorenz hurried away, while I lowered my head to our leader's moist lips to catch the fateful mumble. Hitler's eyes were beautiful, but his saliva was glacial and inhuman. I shuddered as the wax in my ear froze and shattered. The new orders were vague and romantic, as always, allowing me to refashion them in the style I chose, and I took them, myself, and my chilled lobe back to the radio room. More news came to depress the bunker. We had thirty hours at most to rehearse the ultimate scene of our tragedy.

The Soviets were already nearing the Potsdamerplatz, having blinded the remaining *Volkssturm* units with vast arclamps. Boys and grandfathers weeping tears of light. I understand why Artur Axmann deserted his squad of youngsters at the Pichelsdorf Bridge. The Hitler Youth leader felt no remorse for that, and saw no bright shapes on his eyelids when he slept. He was another enemy of mine, but we arranged a truce for these critical times. The Führer decided on impulse to marry Eva Braun, so Goebbels was asked to snatch a qualified magistrate from the squinting *Volkssturm*. He returned with Walter Wagner, who published the banns orally and was sent back to die after the other rites.

Himmler's chief liaison officer, Hermann Fegelein, was dragged up to the Chancellery garden and shot as a substitute for the Reichsführer SS, who was sitting safely in Rechlin. The chicken farmer had been useful to me, and we had made mutual efforts to endure each other's company, but he was a bourgeois pervert. For all my spending excesses I was never such a decadent. He had a second home and mistress at Berchtesgaden, and in the attic a collection of furniture fabricated from human parts. His special lair, as his mistress gleefully declared.

Chairs, sofas, with real legs, books bound in *Rückenhaut*, the flesh of the back, from the Dachau Press. My son visited once and became upset.

The roar of artillery never quite managed to penetrate to the lowest level of the bunker, but I felt the slow vibrations. Extra copies were made of Hitler's Will and entrusted to Johannmeier, Zander, and Lorenz, who hoped to break through Russian lines and deliver them to the Reich's very last intact army, under Field Marshal Schörner in the Bohemian Mountains. It turned out to be a successful adventure, though unnecessary. By the time they had traversed the Tiergarten and Charlottenburg, Dönitz had already decided to capitulate. The Third Reich lasted less than a week after the Führer's death. But that is none of my business. Saving my neck was more relevant then, as it may be again.

In my mind's nose, I can still smell the precious petrol carried by Erich Kempka, the Führer's chauffeur, from the Chancellery garage to the exit of the bunker. This was for the funeral of Hitler and his bride, so much fuel that when Goebbels took his own wife up to greet a bullet, the remaining allowance was too low to adequately char their corpses. Hitler bade farewell to his staff and retired to bed. There was an absurd party with a broken gramophone, a festivity I declined to attend and which was terminated by complaints from the Führer's room. I was busy most of that night, gathering my belongings. General Weidling had failed to hold back the Soviets beyond Potsdamerplatz.

With the ruin of our major defence, further military resistance was a waste of optimism. Only ideologically might we continue, to escape and plot for the future. Schörner in Bohemia could caper as he pleased with his grenades. I was for planning the Fourth Reich in disguise, safe at a desk in the democratic west. The Allies would never recognise the Dönitz government as legitimate, but Hitler still believed his death might help this and shot himself in the mouth, an applicable target. His wife took poison. The interval was decent before Goebbels and myself checked. Then SS Sturmbannführer Linge carried the bodies in grey blankets. Outside, they were rested in a hole and ignited.

We saluted the flames until Russian shells forced us to retreat. As I turned for a last look, a direct hit scattered the pyre, hurling teeth and ribs into the air. The next night, Goebbels followed his master into an identical oblivion. Before that, he sent General Krebs to negotiate a safe passage with Chuikov. The results were extremely disappointing. The Soviets demanded unconditional surrender. We would not be joining Dönitz quietly in Flensburg. The Red Army was a block away at most, firing into buildings at point-blank range, reducing them to gravel, milling this to ash under the tracks of T-34 tanks, welded from scrap by farmers in the Urals. But I felt no need to weep for concrete.

Goebbels had other ideas. He was deeply distressed by the magnitude of the material destruction. He was Gauleiter of Berlin, responsible for each brick and tram cable. A city can work its way under a man's skin. I may not remark on that. However, I know that Berlin worked its way under my fingernails as I left the bunker to join my companions in the shelter of the Chancellery. I had never loved Speer's pompous designs and nodded in satisfaction as the marble tumbled. Obergruppenführer Heinrich Müller lit a cheroot from the general conflagration and outlined the schematics of the breakout over a ragged map.

His project was to descend into the subway at the station below the Wilhemsplatz and grope north to the Friedrichstrasse Bahnhof, then cross the River Spree and fan out through the Russian lines beyond the Theater am Schiffbauerdamm, as it used to be known. The drop into total darkness with only a dozen electric torches to guide several hundred bureaucrats, soldiers, and secretaries, most of whom were unused to walking a distance longer than one end of an office to another, was damply memorable. There was always the alarming possibility of encountering Red Army shocktroops in the icy tunnel, but we were armed. Kempka and Axmann were my shields. Buffoons for buffers, I might say.

It is supposedly common knowledge that when we finally emerged, the majority of us were captured or killed. My little group followed a tank, from Weidling's dwindling stock of Panzers, but it was split by a shell. I fell from the bridge where the Invalidenstrasse rises over the tracks. Rumour has it that I employed my cyanide capsule. I did not. I staggered at random, my mind filling with silence. My eardrums were damaged. I did not imagine what had happened to my companions. Kempka and Axmann lived, as it happened, and later testified against me, but at least they always claimed I was dead. That helped. I wiped my eyes with the hem of my coat, but they remained spheres of acid.

I reached a street of intact buildings with smashed windows. It was weirdly calm, an illusion. The glass sparkled on the cobbles like Jewish stars, clotted yellow under a sky which was also a battlefield, of light and shade, flickering with the reflected glare of arclamps, gala rush of shells, sooty horizon infernos. Hell is happiness for a salamander. Here was a shop where naked mannequins, far too many of them for one display, huddled together, limbs at tortured angles. Behind them, a ruptured pipe leaked gas. The irony of fashion! One day we may have a Sobibor seasonal line. Casual attire, slave labour.

I continued my peregrination. I had somehow managed to slip through a dozen Russian circles. Sporadic resistance occurred down alleyways and in garrets, but there was no more organisation. The tenacious *Volkssturm* were now cells of National Socialism, perhaps even ready to turn on one another, if our equally stubborn enemies would give them a chance, as must happen when any extreme network is deprived of its linchpin, its spider. I speak in convoluted figures because I was shocked out of prosaicism. A Red Army shell bounces on the inner wall of my cranium in my sleep. Even now, when I own a different shape.

The rattle of automatic pistols was an audio fog in my ruined ears. I had wandered into Charlottenburg, the western reaches of the city. The Schloss frowned like a massive forehead at the end of Mierendorffstrasse, and I wondered whether I was the object of its disapproval. It was holed only on one edge, but the famous statue of Friedrich Wilhelm in the main courtyard, the other side from where I stood, was still sunk in the murk of the Tegler See, for safekeeping. Turning aside, because this landmark was too obvious, I limped toward more deserted shops, mixed with charred housing. Burning timbers. Corpses in the gutter, on lampposts. Trams and buses overturned and weeping rust.

A dull oscillation from the east shook the cobbles and my knees. In my cosmos of quiet, I seemed to feel the rush of totally black water far below. I realised that some of our engineers had detonated explosives in the Landwehrkanal, flooding the subways where the remaining survivors of the Kreuzberg district sheltered from the Russians. I regretted the loss of hundreds of Berliners in this attempt to buy an hour of time from Red Army shocktroops. I imagined the terror as they were swept away, finding air pockets against the roof of the tunnel only when they fully expelled the contents of their own lungs and bellies, but unable to breathe these screams as bubbles more than once.

I am capable of sympathy, provided it can be treated like any other necessary expense. The techniques of creative accounting are also useful when trading in emotional resources. I offered enough pity, no more. The drains in the road ahead spat crimson steam. I did not rest but hastened toward the Olympic Stadium. My precise motions are unknown. A few images remain in my memory. I only became really clear, more lucid than a glass grenade, after uttering my first words since I had cursed my combustive separation from Axmann. An encounter. Shadowy figures down a backstreet, laughing, dancing. Not with girls.

Four Russian soldiers were kicking a man on the ground. They lifted sticks and fists of rubble, but these were just for show. The boots were the functionaries of the assault. The victim offered no defiance. He was obviously infected with cynicism, if not cholera. How I roared! A German submitting to inferior soles, eight in total. I heard my own voice in my high cheekbones, not my ears. My rebuke was strange, directed not at the game but its style of play. Amateurs! This did not stall them. Only when I also called them cheats and swindlers were they persuaded to turn. And ruefully they nodded in agreement.

They continued to kick, but without aim, and now these motions were fitted into steps, walking, running towards me. I drew my pistol and shot the nearest through the head. A hole like a spare nostril, quite neat, a lesson to the clumsy gougings of the plunging shells. The others did not pause or swerve, but their sudden frowns had much of the acrobat's shame at failing a trick, missing the trapeze. I dropped a second. He clutched his breast like a man ready to serenade his own wife, a fidelity of pain which amused me. As the range lessened, my accuracy worsened. Paradox of parallax. I reloaded, fired blind.

The third was punctured in the knee but kept running with his good leg, as if he could leave his limp behind like a raped whore. The moment his damaged limb had no more slack to give, he tripped onto the point of his own knife. I had not noticed this weapon, but certainly his belt had lent something sharp to his hand. The last soldier was almost upon me. My trigger jammed and so I was saved, for I remembered my pocket and the capsule inside it. The oddity of combat is one feature which redeems it. Disturbing and often helpful. I held up the pill until it caught all the colours of the flickering skyline.

The sugar coating crackled between my finger and thumb as I offered him the gift. He accepted it furiously, snatching the intriguing object, nesting it on his palm, closing his hand, unwitting and ungrateful. Such wars breed reflexive greed. Then he punched me with this new fist. Teeth broke on knuckles, capsule ruptured in grasp. My mouth grinned stupidly, a model shark, an alpine range. First he sucked his fingers, then licked the whole hand, digesting potential bruises. I had planned this doom not with my mind, but with the public will, the very force that once allowed me to miscast their votes and hopes.

Cyanide is a fast agent, but like one of those Weimar cabarets full of senile comedians, it insists on rehearsing the same farcical routines before it is dissolved. I did not linger to applaud the contortions. The urgent business was at the side of my new friend, even now struggling to his feet. I dragged him up, slapped bootprints from his coat, hugged the shame out of his shoulders, neglected to offer his relief my name. I did not want him to develop faith in the wisdom and justice of coincidences. But here was a man easy to underestimate. A closer look. Oily hair, lips too thick. But with the bluest eyes.

An entire face can lie, and I waited for confirmation of his status. There are many valid reasons for an unusual appearance which have little to do with character. Our people are not always perfect. I kept my trust in his gaze. Tanned and shivering, coldly burned, he might have recently retreated from days in the Südtirol, fighting backward over the highest passes, under the poking sun, with Kesselring's starving troops. Finally he uttered a long groan, and the vowels of this complex exhalation had a suspicious lilt. I became defensive again, lonely too, and nodded at the ground, at his metallic briefcase.

He blinked. "I know you. The worst."

My ears were still cooling as I retorted: "Please define your terms more carefully. It is not adequate to say *worst*. That is a conceptually poor accusation. Ponder the charge of cruelty. There are many variations on this important theme. I defer to others in each category. First there is base brutality, the habit of the uninspired thug, the discharged duty of Stahlecker and Blobel, the *Einsatzgruppen* bullies, a simple bullet in the nape of a neck. Any pleasure at death other than job satisfaction is wasted time. Those pet atrocities have no sensual or metaphysical basis. Thus I distance myself from them."

"Your own gratification was erotic?"

"That is also naive. I left it to Streicher and Koch to develop the onanistic potential of torture. I am disinclined to believe they came up with anything new. There was even a type of sexual sadism which remained psychologically virginal, for the men who indulged in it were squeamish. I was never perverted in that sense. Himmler regularly offered me one of his exhibits as a gift, but I always refused. What use have I for chairs with real human legs? The notion is genuinely distasteful. More accurate to label me an ideological creep."

His smile was thin. "Consider it done."

"Then you are wrong again. Do not follow all my suggestions. Mental fanaticism was never a purity for me. My methods were too sober to rival those of Goebbels or Ley. They owed allegiance to martial destiny, but I had no serious plans for further fatalistic resistance. No, my ambitions are indebted to my patience. Already future paperwork is shuffling in my dreams. I must cost and fund a fourth attempt, an economic Reich without ammunition, perhaps even without butter, but with numbers, transactions, handshakes, and above all offices!"

"You tell me this? Am I so expendable?"

"I am fascinated by your accent. When I rescued you, I assumed your grime, the shadows, were to blame. Now I see you are dark under those. I am curious. What is in the case?"

"My name is Albert Parra. I am from Paraguay. I worked in a camp. A surgeon, a *specialist*. I will show you my instruments. Not here. We must seek cover. That building is clean."

His comments relaxed me, and I followed. My professional familiarity with the footnotes of our colonial history ensured I anticipated much of what he might tell me. There were German settlements in the jungle, the tropical swamps, founded half a century before by disenchanted patriots. One of Bernhard Förster's cultural exploits. In my capacity as secretary and manipulator of the state's wildest schemes, I had tried to contact these lost towns, to recruit fresh blood and hate for the final months, prodigal sons basted in ape fevers and practical nostalgia. No time to check the progress of this desperate option. The reports still waited on my desk unread, if they had not been reduced to ash. But clearly there had been some success.

Inside, I said: "This is a printer's shop."

He rested his briefcase on a table. "My camp was Oberweiler II. The order for its destruction came through only last week. We liquidated the remaining prisoners, burned the machinery, dismantled the towers, coiled up the electric fence. We fled alone, in random directions. I swapped my real uniform for that of a dead Hitler Youth. A tighter fit but safer. I could not bear to lose my tools."

"You lie without reason. There was no such place."

He worked the catches, opened the lid. The sparkle of hooks, little saws, needles was just another fallen constellation, apocryphal sign of an indoor zodiac, in a land where the stars were deliberately misread by government astrologers. This city was shrieking with low-level twinkles. Comets born in cellars: the tails of magnesium flares and flamethrowers. Beams of searchlights forced through shattered façade and shredded roof. Tracer fire conjuring profiles of snipers out of thin hope or thick air. Tumours in a skull are felt as lights. Berlin was the brain of the Reich, and these flashes were symptoms of a cancer of the dream. Too late for a cure, but this doctor was confident.

"It is not my design to humour you. Oberweiler II existed. A centre for the most astonishing biological research. The records are gone, the results must soon be forgotten, but our procedures may be rediscovered a century hence. The grafts, the transplants. Our inheritors will take the credit. For that I pity them, not myself."

"Impossible. The name is still unfamiliar."

He touched my face from a distance with a long arm. One hinge of my jaw had locked tight. He leaned forward faster than his whisper, so that I was mesmerised by the sincerity of his eyes rather than alarmed by the irony in his words. "Now you must lisp. But you saved my life. I owe you a favour. I can fix your teeth."

"A painkiller will suffice. Time is short."

"Probably too late to flee the city with any chance of success. You lurked behind the scenes, but you are not unknown. I recognised you. The Russians have your name on a list. Try to picture your trial. The damage to your teeth has already altered your appearance. Give me permission to finish the task. I really can do it, change your face, here and now. The transformation will be hilarious."

I answered in the negative, but an exploding shell in the adjacent street killed my words. He clutched my collar. "What was that you said? Was it yes? Did you say *yes*?"

I nodded. Panic, sudden horror of shrapnel, a gut reaction. Or else the promise of evading persecution, a seductive idea even to the part of me which craved martyrdom. My success usually relied on suppressing that officially sanctioned urge. He helped me to a bench. I was still sitting up when his needle entered my throat. He sighed. A full minute to inject the syrup in the syringe, working without blinking, like a watchmaker. A great deal of pain, but lower, in my chest. Every ache seemed to migrate there, from teeth and eyes. Even from him. The rest of my body, my skin, felt like paper, signed documents.

He boasted: "I invented this anaesthetic myself. The production of toxic gas meant shortages of chemicals for clinics. But at Oberweiler II it mattered less. We were able to extract cyanide and methanol and most of our other medicine from the tabun and sarin. Army trucks diverted it from the front, down rural roads, through villages of women and babies, while bombs churned meadows into afterbirths! Behind your back. And you knew everything. Consider that!"

I was too weary even to misunderstand. I had lost interest in local mythology, rumours of my omniscience. A flat object struck my head, the surface of the bench as I collapsed. Still the lights, outer and inner, did not dim. I wanted to congratulate his resourcefulness, but too many vibrations prevented me. Not detonations: rasping, drilling, boring. My nostrils filled with bone dust. My tormenter, my saviour, appeared to be capering around the room. His speed was sickening. I was watching a fly magnified to enormous size, climbing walls, settling at my side, goggles cut into innumerable facets, sucking or filling me with detachable iron and crystal mouths, tubes, valves.

He flicked my ears. "It is done. These too."

When I recovered enough to speak, I confirmed my feelings of health and renewal, the usual patient banalities. But my head had little of the world inside it. Overdose of imagination had sealed it tight against the ambient *Zeitgeist,* the truths of environment and rage. I could not quite move or ache. In this limbo between the waking of my tongue and mind, he was reckless and vengeful. Later I admired the suave horror of his grin, the cursory wipe of blade on cuff, the casual shutting of his briefcase. The surgery was finished, but he had nowhere to wash his hands. He paced around haughtily, dripping with me.

"The inks came in useful. Some men enjoy the odours of new books. I prefer those of old printer's shops. No mirrors here, but I will offer a description. Pocket slave. Sweat gleams like venom on ebony muscle. Neat work. Not one speck of white left."

"What do you mean? Where is my original skin?"

He lifted his goggles, and the bottled blue tears flooded his sunken cheeks. "A dare. See for yourself."

A monumental effort. Resting my chin on my chest, I focussed on the swarthy torso, the arms which lashed from it, pounding stomach and hips, equally dark, with stained fists. Not bruised. And my legs and feet, the colour of shadow and puddle, the umbra of awnings in the Tiergarten, ash of leaves on autumn bonfires, freckles, shafts of hammers, an abbey beer or peasant loaf. A night, dusky, grubby. Filth. Disease and vermin. Apes and failures. The livers of drunks.

"What have you done? Tattoos?"

"Yes, I have turned you black. Not just that. A dwarf. Feel between your legs. *Black Jewish Dwarf!*"

In the silence between my pulsed screams, he added: "Several inches can be removed from each femur and the remaining stubs fused together. I perfected the technique at my camp. More than that. A new, mosaic skull, fabricated from the men you killed outside. The circumcision was a witty afterthought. A triumph of comic timing. No need now even to change your name. The ultimate metamorphosis."

"Why? But why? These measures are too extreme. Transplantation from communists? Mutilation of manhood? Nigrification? Why go so far? I asked for none of this. A different citizen I wanted to be, another human. Not a freak. Is the process reversible?"

He wagged a finger. "I sincerely hope not. It is beyond my talents. Live with it, love yourself. Do not slander your new skull. My attackers were not what they seemed, not part of the invasion. Quite the opposite. They were *Hiwis*, Red Army defectors, Soviet volunteers in the service of Germany, active collaborators. Veterans of the Kaminsky Brigade, drafted into the Russian Liberation Army under General Vlasov, employed to fight their own people. Uniforms stripped of Soviet insignia but with armbands which you did not read. *Im Dienst der deutschen Wehrmacht.* Another error you made: a personal assumption. I am not fighting for you. I am opposed to Hitler. Which is why they were so desperate to rid the dying Reich of me. You rescued the wrong victim."

"Tell me the truth. Why are you here?"

"There are Jewish colonies in Paraguay too, you know. Perhaps other desperate recruitments took place parallel to yours. They did. No German guards at our camp. We ran Oberweiler II. It was established on the whims of your Führer. He wanted somewhere to send dissidents within his party. Traitors. The piano-wire gallows at Plötzensee were too mild to serve as a special fate. I guess that was the one thing he never told you. Jewish guards, torturers, fanatics. Do you really want to know why? Comparison. He loved that. He had to prove that the German was superior in *every* way to the Jew. In art, science, athletics. He staged secret competitions in all spheres. Even in genocide."

"A joke. Ha! An extermination camp within the Reich run by Jews!

It is a grotesque idea, unthinkable! You have a diseased intellect. Germans at the mercy of Jews! Shut in cells behind wire! Absurd! Why do you mock me so? A Jew! Ridiculous! And did you win? Were you better at organising torture? More efficient at evil?"

"Yes, we surpassed you. We treated our captives to more horror than anything your side managed. We outperformed the Aryan even at this final solution game. The competition was a failure for you. I was matched with Mengele. His results were nothing compared with mine! But do you think I have taken revenge on you? I believe what I said. I owe you my life. The surgery was an act of kindness."

"How will I explain this appearance to the invaders? A black Jewish dwarf is likely to arouse as many suspicions as a Reich Marshal. I shall be executed without even my arrogance."

"Not true. There are other blacks in Berlin. You never got round to dealing with them. Captive French auxiliaries, a few leftover immigrants from the Weimar jazz age, kept alive to work on propaganda films, lavish costume dramas. Act as if you have escaped from a studio. Claim you were locked in a cage. Tell them you were an extra in Von Baky's *Münchausen,* but that your scenes were cut."

He spat this last word with a vicious leer. Then he turned and left the shop. There was a bicycle waiting for him outside. He must have been riding it when he was set upon by the *Hiwis.* He still held his briefcase in one hand as he mounted it, something hollow white in the other, not a helmet, but a head, probably mine.

"If it proves too difficult to pedal with both these prizes, I must abandon the skull on the railway tracks. I am trying for Kurfürstendamm and the Zoo. Where else in Berlin may I feel at home? I hope some of the animals are still alive. Paraguay is far away, and I am close. To death, disgust, notoriety. But I refuse all these fates. My advice: if you also survive, choose a different career."

I did not watch him depart. I willed my strength to return. A sound of boots outside, irregular rhythms. It is said that Russians dislike to climb stairs. A foolish tale for a matching time. I eased myself off the bench, crawled to the rear of the building. There were steps to the next level. I kept going until I reached the attic. The windows were smashed, but the warped air refracted the view like glass. I balanced on the edge and gazed across and down. Craters and smoke, like bowls of broth, bones of old men and boys stacked on the rim. Some defenders still frustrating the remorseless advance. Gunfire, howls. Then horizontal lightning. Blue bolts spurting across a courtyard.

At first I assumed a natural thunderstorm had been shot down to the ground with its attendant clouds, sparking neon death agonies in plaster dust. But it was an electric weapon, one of the few working experimental devices set up in Berlin in time. It licked a tank. Stench of ozone. The Soviets had lost many vehicles to *Panzerfaust* bazookas and had sought to shield them with sandbags. This tank popped rivets, poured melted tracks over cobbles. A sudden glitter as the sandbags burst, grains fusing into glass ingots. Then the lightning died. The gun had overheated. Always we put too much faith in secret weapons: rockets, heavy water, the reign of ice, the Sangraal, the windcannon, the hollow Earth, flying saucers, the ghost king, Swiss banks, polygamy.

Red flags on other roofs waved in the light of false dawn. I raised my arms in surrender, but no rifle was aimed at me, only laughter. They beckoned for me to jump across. More laughter when I declined. I waited to be captured at their leisure. They sent for an interpreter. He shook his head, declaring my German to be poor. Prejudice of appearance. But I repeated the story my doctor had given me. An actor in films. Not until I babbled a dozen meaningless words did he relax and smile. I had eased his suspicions, relieved his bewilderment. He offered me food and wine, looted from some government cache.

Arrangements were made to introduce me to another black actor found roaming the streets. I fretted at this, but the promise came to nothing. I was passed to a different unit. The assumption I was a French prisoner of war, a Senegalese or Chadian auxiliary, led to my removal from Berlin in an open truck. We drove south. There were many stops, many exchanges. A chaos of language. Troops of various lands blocked the road. Ukrainian nationalists marching west to surrender to the British. Slovenes, Croats, and Italian partisans. Displaced armies, lost youth. I was pushed aboard a train, trundled high into hills.

My destination remained elusive. I still have not reached it. In an elegant port city, perhaps Trieste, I was herded onto a ship. Below deck it was warm and miserable. My face burned on the lamps as I was buffeted against the bulwarks by waves and men. A cargo of refugees: bilge. I was too sceptical to enjoy the abominable histories of my new comrades. Some told original tales of abuse. Most were just variations on the themes of barrel, bayonet, shell, and noose. One fool had trained dogs to bite only double agents. It was tedious. At night, before the lights went out, the begging began. Pencils to write letters to mothers, lovers, and nuns. We docked for days at a mysterious location.

Someone said it was Marseille. We were not allowed to leave the hold. More guards descended to harass us. I pretended to be an imbecile, a ruse that worked well, earning me easy contempt and substitute papers for my figmental identity. Within a week I was in Paris. I starved for a month under sundry monuments, and for a year in a rented garret. Because I was now subhuman, such pangs were correct. My continued use of my real name earned me a reputation as a jester. Glacial faces melted with tears of acid laughter. I ranted on the steps of Montmartre. There were firing squads and women with shaved heads in the boulevards. There was a little paid work. The sewers, the graves.

My bogus experience in films led to offers in minor roles. I acted for Clouzot and Grémillon. I auditioned for Marcel Carné. A set designer introduced me to the managerial side of the business, the offices behind the camera, where I was more comfortable. I pushed pens again. I kept my ears open for subterranean news. My investigations were mostly useless. I began to doubt my past. What if I had been the accidental target of a different experimental weapon in my Berlin scramble—hallucinogenic dust puffed over Weidendammer Bridge? I knew Mohnke's Brigade had possessed such equipment, giant bellows stuffed with powdered mushrooms grown in the dung of doomed Polish cavalry charges.

The few available rumours had jagged edges. I fitted them together to form an indistinct picture. Others had attempted to proceed with the founding of the Fourth Reich. A meeting of bankers in Strasbourg. Some of Schacht's men. Plenty of stolen gold and fine art at their disposal. I itched to involve myself in their endeavours, but my manifest racial and genetic poverty was an insurmountable barrier. I could not contact my former associates. My life was in danger when I tried to introduce myself. Perfect mastery of German language and history did not avail me of their patience. Because of my colour and stature, these virtues were ignored, denied. Even had they accepted the truth, they would have excluded me from their programme.

The surgery had interfered with the running of my biological clock. My metabolism was very slow. I aged at a reduced rate. Perhaps it was an effect of the transplants. More of the future widened before me. I travelled. Morell, the Führer's physician, had fled to Ethiopia to tend the Emperor Haile Selassie—an incredible irony considering what our Axis partners, the Italians, had done to that ancient kingdom. I avoided him when I passed through. I almost bought a ticket to Paraguay. How amusing to meet my torturer on his home territory! I hoped to apply for a job at Oberweiler II, which possibly still existed, broken into many parts at numerous locations, stored safe for times of reassembly when its example proved too glamorous not to mimic.

But any welcome waiting for me in the jungles might be too inhuman, too inappropriate. The risk of blundering into Förster's descendants was high. Only if I could contact the Jew before I left would I feel obliged to make the trip. I had no idea what had happened to him. My enquiries came to nothing. There was no information on Albert Parra or his camp. I learned only that the Zoo had received many direct hits. A hippopotamus found floating in its pool, the fins of an unexploded shell protruding from its side. Strangely, in the ape-house, Pongo, the largest gorilla in European captivity, had died from two deep stab wounds in the chest. My conclusions and life: mutilated.

These difficulties encouraged me to believe I was still the victim of revenge. The most painful aspect of the moral lesson of my condition was its transparency. As a black Jewish dwarf, I was finally supposed to understand how it felt to be on the wrong side of the racial, cultural, and ethical divide. But I had only contempt for the simplicity of this degradation. It was childishly symmetrical. I did not allow myself to suffer under such a neat trick. My adaptability is remarkable. To ease the torment, cheat my enemy, nullify the requital, I simply turned my back, with its reduced spine, on National Socialism. I recanted all my previously cherished concepts.

It was gloriously simple. I dismissed the *Rassenkunde* as irrelevant and illogical. Strength through Joy became a meaningless quip. I sniggered at the Aryan jaw, the blond fringe. I did not buy tickets for operas by Wagner or Bungert, nor read the *Nibelungenlied* right to the end. I did not invest in South African mines. I bought only a German radio. Other survivors lacked my advantages. Speer anguished endlessly over our sins, at least in public, but I ignored them. I could not be guilty, because I truly *was* a changed man. More than that: I had never been my prior self. My mirror was in the continuous habit of disowning that phantom. I still wished the Fourth Reich all the best luck, but I no longer desired to be part of its success or failure.

I increasingly came to judge the latter more likely as I monitored its progress from afar, not as an obsession but a hobby. The plan was to control Europe economically. The flaw in the formula was the parasitical nature of hypocrisy. It feeds on its agents. It demands they frequently behave as they claim to maintain the pretence. With sufficient practice the act becomes easy, finally easier than the hidden agenda. And as the mirage wins genuine adherents and the ulterior motive is filtered down through generations, the original spirit is lost. The absence of mortal terror in financial dealings, the democratic framework which must be erected to support them, betrays our blood and legends. A pacifist Reich is a contradiction in terms.

There could be no doubt Germany was reclaiming its pride and status as a serious nation, but that is not the same as belated victory for our Reich. I persisted with my personal reconstruction. I started to unlearn German phrases. I searched for the polar opposite of the vocation of the Führer. Having recorded many of his casual conversations with party officials, I knew his preferences in this regard. He had a phobia of the sea. He once admitted to Rundstedt that he was a coward on water. His mission had been to spread death on land. Thus I resolved to make the ocean my new occupation, and not only that, but its *life*. I worked hard, saved money. I emigrated to America, enrolled at college. Within a decade I was a respected oceanographer.

Even in the academic world there are offices and documents. Not all my time was spent sitting behind a desk, though undoubtedly that is the prime location for my brand of rump and talent. I embraced the practical side of my career. I enjoyed standing at the rails of a research vessel, vomiting into the waves and watching the fish share my capitalist meals. There was the taste of salt in the air but not in the food. I won grants to investigate turbidite layers along those margins where abyssal plains and continental shelves battle for definition of the scenery. I chose my crews and bathyspheres for their durability and obedience. Nobody argued with my decisions or questioned my authority, because they were liberals and I was a living icon of that cult.

In a city such as Berlin, the sunsets are always humiliated by the rosy grandeur of marble monuments and maiden cheeks. Out on the ocean no such distractions exist. The transition from afternoon to dusk had a mystical effect on me. I felt empathy with the eels and decapods which rose to the surface to bask in the emerging starlight. I left portholes open on both sides to ease the passage of flying fish through the hull. As I polished the sonar with my sleeve, I felt an ancient peace. I began to appreciate the beauty of dolphins and other structurally *effeminate* creatures. I genuinely cared for their health and happiness. I might even have started to sing to them, for I believed I had truly become an exact negative of my previous self. But then came a discovery which reverted me to my former condition. Not one of mine, but it brought all the old feelings rushing back.

Black Smokers. Hydrothermal vents. New chains of life. Ecosystems with no reliance on solar energy. A volcanic loop, the architecture of brimstone and misplaced geological youth. Heated in the magmatic bowels of the planet, having percolated through fissures in the oceanic crust, cold honest seawater returns as scalding fountains of dissolved minerals feeding colonies of alien fauna. Usually associated with mid-ocean ridge systems, the newest part of the seafloor, volcanic and free of sediment, beds for pillow lavas, the vents themselves rise like gigantic chimneys, belching digestible elements, supporting microbes adapted to converting this soup directly into energy through chemosynthesis. And dependent on these germs, larger creatures. Mussels, anemones, vestimentiferan worms, galatheid crabs, bivalve clams and shrimps. Unlike my people, they never had a place in the sun. No need for one!

The first vent was discovered by the submarine of a rival academy, but I was not jealous. I was more emotional than that. I strove hard to become an expert on this phenomenon. New vents were found, but all shared the same curious property. If the chimney was obstructed for any reason, the chain of life collapsed. The animals were extinguished. I trembled as I considered this fact. Colonies of creatures, many still undescribed by science—including six dozen new genera, fifteen new families, one new order, a new class, and a new phylum—packed like trade unionists in the Reichstag lobby, or like housewives in the Lustgarten, acting as if they had a right to life. Pretending to communicate, to comprise a community, but really polluting the purity of the abyssal currents. And all chilled out of existence by a simple blockage in a pipe!

My reformation had been only temporary, a necessary penance to open my eyes to the facts of force and power. The more I learned, the greater my divine ignorance grew. I gradually willed myself back to boorishness. I can scarcely describe my ecstatic disgust when it emerged that many of these exotic animals, these parasites and scroungers, lurking in eternal darkness and timidity, had evolved reciprocally beneficial relationships with the chemoautotrophic bacteria, harbouring them within their bodies, deriving nutrition directly from them in return for physical protection. A blatant challenge and gross insult to the tooth-and-claw honour of the upper world! Seabed communism! And thriving on the slopes of the twisted chimneys of a fairytale industry. Appalling! I could not bear to imagine it. But it stirred me, inspired me.

The true point of the Reich was not about the supremacy of Germany. I see that now. Nor was it about the dominance of one particular culture or creed or race. It was grander and simpler than that. It was about the deification of violence. Inequality was its key. It does not matter who is the oppressor, who the victim, so long as there *are* oppressors and victims. Our defeat was a demonstration of our own principle. The smashing of National Socialism was willed by the Reich, even if we did not appreciate it at the time. We merely swapped roles with our enemies, allowing them to implement the beauty for us. We were right after all, and our detractors were forced to prove it. They did so, but only now do I hear the call to rejoice.

And yet we have not quite won. Not yet. The ideals of pacifism and democracy still fester. No use striking the iron while it is hot, for it will eventually cool, over generations. Plunge a hot iron into blood instead! Then red vapours will plug every nose and the stench of the Reich overpower all sweet perfumes. How can we best do this? That is the crucial question. Certainly not by rebuilding what we had. Camps, gas, pits. These are too obvious. They require the blessing of a state, and a state is too ungainly an object to conceal from view, to move from place to place. Much better to create a portable Reich, or a Reich too silent to know. And this task is simple when the real traitors of our previous attempt are exposed and uprooted from the growth. Who were they? Not men nor morals, but arithmetic abstracts.

The numbers! *They* were the weakness in the structure of our dream, of all our dreams. While our Reichs were sequential they were fragile. First, Second, Third! While they were numbered, there could only be one at a time. And with only one on the planet, it was easy for weaklings to unite and defuse it. I foresee the same sad destiny for all subsequent Reichs. The Fourth? Even if it had a military agenda, it would fail in identical fashion. Fifth, Sixth? Equally useless. Equally! How that word stabs my heart. And the heart is the answer, the true end of the quest. The numbers have failed us. Even unto the Infinite Reich! Numbers must be abandoned. All future Reichs will be run *concurrently*. They shall be given other names, names that allow a dozen, a hundred, a billion Reichs to operate simultaneously.

What does this modern world need more desperately in its past than Hitler and his nightmare? Our degradations form a service ceiling of monstrosity. Whatever sin a man commits, he may always compare himself favourably with us. He is never as bad as we were. We are a reference point of unacceptability. No wrong can go beyond us. We arch over all perversions. And yet this is false reasoning. Because we span the cruelties, they belong to us. They are in our domain, beneath our skies. They are not lesser than us, but our stem cells, the ongoing life of the Reich. Every man who beats his wife, every boss who sacks his staff, every boy who aims a catapult at a dog, every child who hurts a mother in a birth has a Reich in his heart. And we all own hearts. And what do they pump? Not tears!

Let us acknowledge this fact. Let us celebrate and expand it! Bully your lovers, mistreat your neighbours, abuse your position. Every cell which divides in a fit young body is an avatar of violence. Every star which explodes! The whole universe demands a Reich. Only liars deny it, the men who call themselves pacifists. Fools like Speer who wanted a conscience to exchange for mercy. Only the numbers weaken it. But in the composite Reich to come, the Reich of Reichs, the parts are crueller, more beautiful, than the sum. You must become Führer of your own domain of hurt. By spreading ourselves we can endure anything. We will be inviolable! *Little Hitler* is no longer an insult, but an admission of the wisdom and power of miniaturisation.

Without my surgery, I should not have realised any of this. I would have remained loyal to the numbers. I was compelled to think laterally. So it is true that my surgeon did not take revenge upon me. He offered a gift. He forced me to consider the superiority of Reichs with proper names and power. More imaginative names. We can still win. My Reich *will* win. I tell my assistants that I am ordering a new type of bathysphere. They will allow themselves to be fooled when they see it. I shall lie to them through my smiling mouth. And they will swallow these lies without spitting anything in my face. This bathysphere will have no windows, no hatch, no sensors. Its justice and edges are rough. It will sink fast. I will prepare the report in my usual style, doodling in the margins, recalling times of misery and feeling joy.

At last I am ready to begin my own rule. My little final solution. A modest sacrifice to the divinity of violence, but a satisfying one. Even under the sea there is no refuge for vermin, cowards, mutants. Even when a lesser man is of a different species he will not be spared. But I ask you: Who do shrimps most resemble? Is the affinity not obvious?

The vile way in which they crowd together, scrabbling at the rock. The outrageous *interest* they generate among those with whom they share their environment. It is hardly a subtle metaphor. On the contrary, it is too blatant. And yet my crew suspect nothing unwholesome. They are naive, easy dupes. I blame the specialisation of modern education. It teaches facts out of relation with the need to struggle in this world. There is no context. But I have my private Reich. Now claim yours.

I have already toyed with the idea of sewing tiny badges onto their shells to advertise their abhorrent status. A brown triangle or star, to match my eminence. One of the few colours we did not use at the camps. But the practical difficulties of sending down a diver with needle and thread and sufficient oxygen finally discouraged me. Besides, it would alert my employers to my true ambitions. Fortunately, there is no need for artificial branding. The lamps of the first submarine to chance on this particular chimney have already bleached the eyes of every shrimp a ghostly white. That will suffice for a badge. White. It is the mongrel of the spectrum, the idiot result of interbreeding among the other hues. Abysmally perfect! And there will be no price for this holocaust, unless there is also a Nuremberg in Atlantis.

From the side of my boat, a winch and cable suspend an object over the surface of the ocean. Slowly it is lowered into the waves. With luck it will plug the hydrothermal vent on the first attempt. The shrimp must be annihilated! They are cold and stupid. They cheat and crawl. Soon all the vents under my jurisdiction will be cleansed. My bomb was expensive. Only a little rubble from the ruins of Berlin has been stored in cellars by sentimentalists. They declined to trade directly with me. Obtaining a block of concrete from the bunker required a chain of contacts graded in colour from black to white. Somewhere in the centre must exist a man who is totally grey. Doubtless a bureaucrat. Enough! As I click my heels, my assistants erroneously conclude that I am shielding my face from the sun with an outstretched arm.

The Spoon

What seems to be the trouble?"

Dr Frazer regarded his new patient with only mild curiosity, although the fellow looked vaguely familiar and the dark gleam of anguish in his eyes promised a more intriguing case than usual. But Frazer was too tired for zeal; it had been a long day.

"I have a spoon in my mouth," came the answer.

Dr Frazer sighed. Was that supposed to be a riddle or a joke? If so, he didn't have the inclination to interpret it. "No, you don't," he replied with a cynical smile. "Your mouth is empty."

"Yes, I do. It comes and goes and there's nothing I can do about it. The damn thing seems to be scheduled."

"Is it there right now?" blinked Dr Frazer.

The patient nodded slowly. "And it's invisible. I look in the mirror but I can't see it. An invisible spoon."

Dr Frazer licked his lips and tugged his chin.

"Ah, you mean you have the *feeling* of a spoon in your mouth? That's more reasonable. My colleague, Dr Vaughan, would be interested in this phenomenon. I say he's my colleague, but actually he's my rival. He once treated a girl who thought her ears were spoons, serving spoons, ladles in fact, and her brains were broth."

The patient squinted. "Weren't they?"

"No, no, my dear fellow, they were merely the physical manifestations of an obsession, the inverse extrusions of psychosis. I know plenty about abnormal psychology, but it has never been my main area of expertise. As for Dr Vaughan, the reverse is true. He deals with madmen every day, but his empathy and erudition are lesser."

And Dr Frazer threw back his head, tightly squeezed his eyes shut, and chuckled softly to himself for a minute.

The patient said, "Yes. That's all very well. But I still have the feeling of the spoon in my mouth; and it's moving around in there, as if I'm being fed horrid meals by a dutiful ghost."

Dr Frazer suddenly leaned forward, his elbows on his desk. "What do *you* think the spoon signifies?"

"Well, I have been wondering about that a lot."

"And your conclusions are?"

The patient shifted uneasily on his chair. "Perhaps the ghost is real and not even a true ghost. That's what I fear the most. Let me explain, if I can. Did you ever visit a retirement home full of senile old people? Depressing places where subjective time no longer flows forward and where each day is a repeat of the one before. A favourite uncle of mine ended up in such a home, and I dreaded each visit. His senility was so severe I came to regard him as a sort of time traveller, for he was never in the present moment but always stuck firmly in the past."

"He didn't recognise you?" prompted Dr Frazer.

The patient sighed. "He often mistook me for someone else, a comrade from his distant youth, and sometimes he would refer to me by a selection of different names in the same disjointed sentence. On other occasions he thought I was an orderly or an intruder. Once he attacked me, feebly, with a bedpan. And all the other inmates of that institution were in an identical mental state. The present simply didn't exist in tangible form; on the other hand, the past was utterly palpable."

Dr Frazer nodded. "I comprehend everything you say, but what does it have to do with your illusory spoon?"

"The residents of the retirement home weren't able to feed themselves. Nurses came at each appointed hour with trolleys and trays; many nurses with numerous spoons, and the inmates were fed mush like infants. I asked myself: What do the wrinkled chrononauts feel now? Stuck in their own dim histories, are any of them truly aware of the spoon as it writhes itself between their shrivelled lips? How do they regard this interpolation of the modern moment into the endlessly looped past? Does it manifest itself merely as an uncomfortable sensation, as a mysterious lump in the throat, as a psychosomatic illness?"

"I like the tone of your words, for they have an academic ring, but not the ideas they invoke," said Dr Frazer.

The patient held out his empty hands and groaned. "Whenever I came away from visiting my uncle, I always congratulated myself on my good fortune—that I was young and fit in body and mind, an active participant in the present moment, that I possessed perfectly sound perception of the world, of time and reality. But then I realised that my uncle believed the same thing about himself. None of those residents appreciated the truth of their situation. It follows that one day, when I grow old, I too might turn senile and become like them, living in my own past, running the loop of my remembered life again and again."

"I see your point," mused Dr Frazer. "If one is senile, how would one know? But it's a pointless worry. When you are old, you may or may not face that affliction. Who knows?"

The patient leaned over the desk, his eyes fierce. "What if I'm *already* senile? What if I am living in the past now? What if you are in my past too, together with this meeting and your advice? It troubles me more each day that I may also be a resident of one of those retirement homes. That's my real concern. I worry that all *this* around me might be the illusion, the memory, and *this* here the truth."

He gestured first at the room, then at his mouth, and Dr Frazer realised that the first gesture stood for the entire world as it was, while the second represented the sensation of the spoon and a different world, the future. In the patient's strange delusion, the modern world was actually the past, and the spoon an artefact of the present.

"Really, my good man, this is a very arcane worry. I'm glad you came to consult me and not Dr Vaughan, my colleague. He would have laughed you out of his office, or persuaded you to subject yourself to irresponsible experiments; he's like that. As for myself, I will forego experimentation and simply smile you away instead."

"You don't believe me?" cried the patient.

Dr Frazer smiled blandly, just as he had promised. "There is no spoon in your mouth; I can see that for myself. You are a reasonably young man sitting on a chair across from me in a room in a respected clinic. You are not a senile old man in a retirement home that needs to be spoonfed. It is the oddest neurosis I've ever encountered! Please leave me now. I'll share this with Dr Vaughan otherwise."

The patient stood and stamped towards the door. Before he reached it, he turned and bellowed over his shoulder, "You fool, I *am* Dr Vaughan! I should have known you couldn't be trusted. You were always a cerebral coward, a charlatan, a quack!"

He slammed the door on his way out.

Dr Frazer kept his smile in place, but its quality slowly changed. "Yes, he was Dr Vaughan. Why didn't I recognise him the moment he came in? I must be tired, overworked. I should take a break. I'm due for a break at this time anyway. I think so, don't I?"

He lowered his hands to grip the arms of his chair, but to his surprise his fingers closed on the rims of large wheels instead. What were wheels doing on his chair? No matter.

He wheeled the chair back from the desk and frowned. Something was happening to his mouth. An invasion. He slumped and relaxed his facial muscles, allowing the spoon access, feeling it rattle on gums and tongue, as the drool poured down his chin.

Chameleons

I remembered that I was once a sailor shipwrecked off the coast of an uncharted island. I swam ashore and crawled up the beach and lay to rest and recover in the rising sun. Then I opened my eyes and saw figures clustered around me, and they all looked like shipwrecked sailors. In fact, they were all identical to me, and I wondered if I had become a castaway on an island of mirrors. So I stood and began heading inland and—

No. Something isn't quite right with this memory. I wasn't a sailor on oceans of water but a space explorer; and my ship was a spaceship. It had developed engine trouble, and so I landed on the nearest hospitable world. No man had ever set foot on this particular planet before, but when I opened the hatch and lowered the ramp and stepped onto the surface, I saw that my vessel was surrounded by other space explorers.

There were thousands of them, and they all looked like me, and I raised my binoculars to my eyes and saw a rippling effect in the crowd, a ripple that was rapidly expanding. This wave had spread out from me: I was the epicentre of the effect, of the transformation, and it was clear that the denizens of the planet hadn't looked like me before my arrival but had changed their appearance to copy mine the instant they first saw me.

So the members of the furthest reaches of the crowd beyond the ripple still retained their original outward forms, and I saw I had landed on a world overrun with chameleons. I was the first intrusion into their environment, the first new *thing* for many generations. They weren't chameleons quite like the ones we have on our own planet, but more highly evolved and sophisticated examples of the type. They were flawless living reflections.

And they were friendly, hospitable, charming. I spread my arms wide in the universal gesture of peace and said, "I come in a spirit of kindness and hope. I am here to foster an understanding between our civilisations and to encourage good relations between our solar systems."

"Thanks. We appreciate that," they said.

So I moved my right hand close to the holster that held my futuristic gun and spoke again, this time with a sneer. "On the contrary, the real reason I am here is to take over your planet and exploit its resources to your detriment. I will utilise force to accomplish this."

"We will defend ourselves with our own futuristic weaponry and mount a revenge attack on your world," they responded.

"But how can any kind of weapon truly be described as 'futuristic'? If it exists in the present then it is contemporary only."

"We agree," they answered.

I was satisfied. They were chameleons in every way, chameleons to the nth power, ultimate chameleons: they reflected not only appearances but attitudes and motivations. I threw back my head and laughed aloud in the most authentic and intense glee of my life; and innumerable copies of myself joined in with this demonstration of wild mirth, and the landscape vibrated with the rasping sawteeth of our blunt wit.

I was marooned and helpless and I let them know this and threw myself on their mercy. They had plenty of mercy, all of them an equal amount, but only after I showed my own, exhibited my compassion and forgiveness. Thus I became a member of their society and dwelt among them as a guest; and my presence grew less exotic and intrusive as time passed, until I began to forget that they were chameleons and not men.

After several weeks of a simple but pleasant existence in the vicinity of my spaceship, I decided to explore the planet and make maps of its main geographical features. It seemed a fruitful course of action to take, not so much for the sake of future expeditions from Earth but for the benefit of the chameleons themselves, who had no knowledge of cartography at all. On a misty morning I set off on foot with provisions.

During the emergency landing I had descended through thick cloud and had been unable to see what kinds of continents and oceans dappled this world. I was astonished and perhaps also a little dismayed to discover that I was on an island, a large island certainly, but one sufficiently isolated from other land masses to frustrate my attempts to learn if the chameleons were a species that dominated the entire planet or could be found only here.

Everywhere I went I met replicas of myself, but it was clear that the further my travels took me from the site of my landing the more recent was the fine-tuning of their features, almost as if my presence were adjusting a rougher approximation of my outer form and inner sentiments. And this indeed was the case: on one occasion I chanced upon a dead chameleon that retained the form he had possessed at the instant of his demise.

He had expired the previous day, and he looked more like my brother than me. And then I realised a simple truth. The ripple that spread out from my arrival had lost its transformative powers as its circumference widened: the chameleons nearest to me were able to model themselves exactly on my appearance, but those who were unable to see me had to borrow their reflections second-hand, as it were, and mimic what was already a copy.

But this ripple was constantly replenished, like a broadcast signal, and I remained at the epicentre of it, beaming information about my image out in every direction. And when I moved, the source of the transmission moved too, and those chameleons with good reception were always those I was currently among, while those at the limits of the transmission were oddly shaped, peculiar, and essentially wrong, and the more intriguing for it.

In the coastal communities of the island, at the furthest points from the location of my landing, the chameleons had barely resembled me at all until I neared them in person and they were able to make the necessary adjustments. Imperceptible errors in the copying process had magnified and distorted my features into a grotesque parody of the reality: a noteworthy and visceral example of information decay over distance.

I returned to my spaceship and found the same hasty readjustments taking place. Clearly the chameleons needed constant contact and reference to the image they mimicked to maintain an illusion of high quality. But soon they were perfect reflections again; while those on the coast, I knew, were already lapsing back into inexactitude. To study the imperfect copies in detail would be impossible: my presence changed the results.

It is true that I had access to dead chameleons in various stages of ludicrous approximation of my form, but it was the mimicking of my inner life, my thoughts, feelings, and sensations, that really interested me. I wanted to converse and dispute with a flawed *living* copy, and this could never be achieved due to the nature of the problem. I could only study those within range; and they were always depressingly my equals. And so I became lonely.

My loneliness was more acute than that of any stranded explorer who finds himself completely alone, for I was forced to confront and *mingle with* my lonely self, innumerable copies of that self, all identically and inescapably lonely, and the sheer psychological pressure of being surrounded by replicas of my loneliness was almost unbearable. Because I was lonely the chameleons were too; and because they were lonely and they were me, I was trapped.

This feedback loop was mortifying, and I even considered committing suicide by proxy, vaporising them all with my futuristic gun; but a guilty conscience was the last thing I needed, or one of the last things. Then I realised that if I was planning murder of them, they must be planning murder of me, and of one another, and once again I marvelled at the perfection of the reflection, the intricacy of the mimicry. They possessed my feelings, my thoughts, my identity.

So each chameleon believed itself to be the space explorer and assumed that everyone else was a chameleon. I frowned. Then how could I be sure that I was a real man and not merely the deluded reflection of one? What if I was a chameleon and not the original space explorer? This possibility disturbed me, and even though I attempted to dismiss the idea from my mind, a doubt remained. I had lost faith not only in appearances but also in souls.

While I was pondering this problem, I felt a ripple wash over me, a wave of transformation that passed and moved to engulf others. My body had changed. The bodies of all my companions had altered too;

and I watched as the ripple receded and worked its alchemical magic on distant individuals. I felt strange, as odd as I looked, and I knew that I was an imperfect copy of a new arrival, that a stranger had come to a distant part of the island.

Over the next few days my shape and feelings refined themselves: the new arrival was coming this way, heading inland. My tentacles became smoother, the eyes on the ends of their stalks bigger and brighter, my scales softer. I spoke in a high fluting voice. Then I saw him on the horizon striding rapidly towards me and remembered at last exactly who I was. Shipwrecked off the coast of this uncharted island, this island of perfect chameleons, I was a sailor.

Happiness Leasehold

The letterflap on the front door snapped like the jaws of a robotic crocodile, and something as wide and flat as a tongue fell onto the carpet. Harry put his mug of coffee down on the breakfast table and went into the hall to see what had happened. A letter. He scooped it up and took it back with him, slicing open the envelope with a knife already bloodied with jam. *A handwritten letter.*

His eyebrows rose in ironic astonishment. Nobody wrote letters in longhand these days. It was so archaic! He held the unfolded letter in his right hand and read it slowly while nibbling the triangular slice of toast raised aloft in his left. The script was clear and easy on the eye, flowing without actually being in a proper elegant style. It was a brief message but intriguing enough. Harry read it aloud.

"Meet me at noon by the war memorial overlooking the sea. My great-grandfather knew your great-grandfather. They were great to-gether! I have a tale to tell you of surpassing interest. Be there."

Harry winced. Why had he vocalised those clearly foolish words? It wasn't typical of him at all. He felt he had become a character in a rather stylised short story, if that conceit wasn't too pretentious, and yet how could he be blamed for reacting oddly to such an odd epistle? He would go to the specified location at the appointed time, of course, even if only to discover the agent responsible for this obscure practical joke.

For there was no doubt in his mind that it *was* a joke, a prank with no obvious purpose or merit. Or did someone wish to humiliate him for a solid reason? Possibly. He was rich, successful, lucky. It might even be said he was happy. But he knew of no enemies who might wish him any sort of harm at all, for he was also a friendly and modest person. The tone of the letter betrayed no hint of malice, only a baffling eccentricity.

Harry finished breakfast and spent most of the remainder of the morning doing what he usually did on a weekday. Two hours of leisurely but highly profitable work on his laptop, connecting with the managers of his various companies, issuing directives and agreeing to the initiation of new projects. Then a stroll in his garden while the wind chimes tinkled in the branches of the trees and the blossom scattered at his feet.

Half an hour before noon he went for a drive in his Bentley, following the old coast road to a small village where he planned to buy a cottage. After examining the building with a careful and appreciative eye from the outside, he climbed back into his car and drove to the war memorial at the very end of this sentence.

A character in a short story indeed!

It wasn't yet noon, but the stranger was already waiting for him, floppy-brimmed hat slouched dramatically over his features, hands in pockets as deep and incongruous as marsupial pouches. He didn't move a muscle as Harry parked and strode over to him, the sea holding its breath for the entire distance. Abruptly, as if his backbone were an electric eel, the stranger jerked, pushed his hat back, turned to face Harry's annoyance.

"What the devil are you playing at?"

The stranger winced at the cliché and said, "Mr Bingham? Harry Bingham? My name is Ricardo Gobie, and today is the final day of the pledge that binds together our fates. The contract expires now."

Harry sighed, then tried to grin, but couldn't conjure up enough mirth in this absurd situation, so he gazed at the sea and answered formally, "I'm not aware of any obligation towards you."

"That is irrelevant, I'm afraid."

Harry moved a step closer. The sharpened edge of the shadow of the war memorial hacked into his face like a crude axe blade, but he did not reel or scream. "If you'd care to explain without verbose digressions I may be willing to listen. I'm a tolerant man. I have a sense of humour, and even when that fails me I rarely take umbrage at japes.

This is a jape, Mr Gobie, isn't it? But I can't spend too much time here. I'm playing tennis later with the owner of a shipping company who wants me to invest in his fleet. Then I'm due for a siesta in a hammock in a hothouse. I have an appointment to drink many fine wines after *that*."

And he went on to list several other luxurious activities that formed a perfectly ordinary part of one of his normal days, but he didn't do this arrogantly. He did it naturally. If he really were just a character in a short story, he would be one of those protagonists who are hugely successful but lacking aggression and rancour. True, he had inherited wealth, but he had quadrupled the original legacy through his own efforts. How can any businessman without a mean streak be so spectacularly triumphant in his ventures? The author of the short story hadn't thought it through properly. Or was it all down to luck? Yes, that's right. Luck.

Ricardo Gobie licked his lips. "Your great-grandfather, George, was an infantryman in the First World War. During the Battle of Amiens in August 1918 he was caught in no man's land."

"I know this story. Go on," commented Harry.

Ricardo said, "I'm sure you don't know all the details. While he was pinned down by machine-gun fire, hiding in the blast crater of an artillery shell, a biplane belonging to his own side was shot down and crashed near him. The pilot was flung out of the cockpit into the steaming mud, badly injured but still alive. The wreckage started burning. The enemy aimed at the airman and tried to perforate him."

"Yes, they decided to set him a riddle," quipped Harry.

Ricardo missed the joke completely, just as the bullets had missed his great-grandfather that momentous day. "No, they were serious. It was against all the rules of war! He was doomed for sure. Suddenly your own ancestor, George, scurried out of his hole and ran across the anguished earth to the side of the airman. He stooped and flung the airman across his broad shoulders, but instead of lurching back to the crater, where they would be stuck without hope of receiving any medical attention for the injured pilot, George ran in the other direction."

"Towards the blazing biplane," nodded Harry.

"Brave to the point of madness," said Ricardo, "but he saved both their lives by doing so. He jumped into the cockpit of the smoking craft and wrenched the machine-gun from its mounting. Can you imagine the sheer physical strength required to do that? Without a spanner!"

"Just bare hands," intoned Harry, who knew the anecdote well.

Ricardo's eyes were shining like miniature cinema screens, but the film of the battle that was evidently playing in his mind didn't project itself onto those febrile orbs. It remained a private showing.

"Bare hands are hands without gloves or fur," prompted Harry.

Ricardo snapped back into the story. "Indeed. It was a Hotchkiss gun, very heavy, with a powerful recoil. George flung the airman into the mud, sat on him with crossed legs, and opened fire in the direction of the German trenches. Bullets zinged and zanged! Lubricated by his bleeding wounds, the airman slid over the slippery mud like a sledge, pushed by the recoil, with George on top. The longer George kept his finger on the trigger, the faster they went. A human sleigh!"

"And a human slayer too," punned Harry.

Ricardo nodded. "Rat-a-tat! Faster and faster towards their own side they went! The enemy lobbed a few mortar shells at them but missed, and the 'Tommies' who saw what was happening covered the insane retreat with rifle shots. Just as the Hotchkiss gave up, spitting out its final spent cartridge, George and the airman reached the lip of a British trench and plunged backward into it. Your great-grandfather was recognised as an authentic hero in the old style."

"I heard that tale when I was very small, and I heard it repeatedly in the years that followed," said Harry without resentment, "and doubtless I will tell it to my own children if I ever have any."

Ricardo stroked his chin, removed his hat, and ruffled his hair, making many of those stalling gestures that some authors force their characters to perform when they want to slow the action down for the duration of a short paragraph. Rather like this one. Then his manner changed. He became colder, less sympathetic, harder in tone, like a man who deliberately loses his patience.

"I doubt you know the *rest* of the story," he clipped, "and that's why I'm here now. I'm going to fill you in on the missing details. I promise you'll find them extremely pertinent to your life situation."

"I'm all ears," said Harry, who in fact had only two small ears, like you and me, but Ricardo didn't object to the figure of speech. He replaced his hat, grinned without humour, and said:

"George became friends with the airman, whose name was Ralph, but they came from very different backgrounds. My great-grandfather was a member of the landed gentry, the aristocracy, the son of an earl. Your great-grandfather was from the bottom of the lower classes, a painter and decorator. What could they possibly have in common? Nothing! And yet there was a bond between them. Part of that bond consisted of genuine comradeship, but part of it was also formed from obligation. My great-grandfather, an extremely influential man, was in debt to yours, who was a nobody."

"That's a nice way of putting it," scowled Harry.

Ricardo held up a silencing hand. "Nonetheless it's true. Anyway, Ralph the airman wanted to wipe out the obligation part of the relationship, and so he said to George the handyman, 'What can I do to repay you?' and George thought about this question for a full minute and then he answered, 'Everything'. And he meant it. And the friendship died from that moment and acquired the characteristics of a business contract. George had struggled all his life. Nothing had ever come easily to him, nothing good had ever dropped into his lap: he had been forced to struggle, grind, grasp, and fight for the tiniest morsel of happiness and success. He wanted Ralph to change that for him."

"To alter his luck for the better," mused Harry.

"Exactly. And my great-grandfather really was in a position to do that. His influence and power were strong enough. He was admired as an adventurer who hadn't needed to fight but did so anyway. He was respected and obeyed. To discharge his obligation to George, he pulled strings, whispered in ears, but the process left a sour taste in his mouth. He informed your great-grandfather that yes, he would give him what he wanted, but there had to be a time limit. They haggled over the exact span. Eventually they settled on a duration of one hundred years. My family would look after your family for precisely a century, not a day more or less. A contract was written up and signed by both parties. It is legally binding."

"Nobody ever helped me. I helped myself," said Harry with rising anger, "and the same was true for my father and *his* father too. We made it big by our own efforts."

"That's not true at all," snapped Ricardo.

"What do you mean exactly?"

Ricardo made an ugly face. "All the luck you thought was yours was *given* to you by us. When the war was over, George didn't go back to painting and decorating. He invested his war pension and bought shares in various companies. Ralph told him how to play the stock market properly. Before long your great-grandfather was a moderately rich man and he passed his wealth down to his son, who was helped by Ralph's son, and that's how the process continued, each son helping the other son as the generations passed, you included."

"Utter nonsense!" spat Harry.

"No, it's not. I'm afraid it's perfect sense. The one thing that George forgot to pass down was the secret of the pledge, the fact of the contract. All your success, every atom of it, was arranged for you. None of it is really yours. On behalf of my great-grandfather I have been pulling strings and whispering into ears for you. Do you understand? I am your only benefactor. Everything you have achieved only happened because of my influence. Without me, you are nothing. And—"

Harry interrupted him with a shout, "Sheer lunacy!"

Ricardo ignored him. "Today the contract expires."

"Liar! What rubbish!"

"I am reclaiming everything. The obligation has been fully and correctly discharged. You are no longer a successful entrepreneur. You no longer have savings in the bank or shares in any company. You own no property whatsoever. You have no job, no funds, no assets at all. And as for your beautiful wife—"

"She's on holiday! In the Caribbean!"

Ricardo winked. "Jamaica?"

"She went of her own accord!" yelled Harry.

"Not exactly," countered Ricardo. "She was a plant, one of ours, paid to be your 'wife.' All the beautiful women you have ever been involved with worked for me. They were hired. Your wife has been recalled. Give me your car keys. Come on, don't be difficult."

"Never! You won't steal my Bentley!" roared Harry.

Ricardo sighed, dipped into his pocket, and dangled a set of identical keys. "In that case, I'll use the spares."

Harry stepped forward, snarling. Ricardo suddenly held something in his other hand. A revolver. Harry froze.

"Best not, old chap, eh?" said Ricardo as he strolled over to the Bentley. Then he threw the gun to Harry, got in the car quickly, started the ignition with a fluid movement, and drove away, tyres squealing. Harry had caught the revolver. He aimed at the departing car and pressed the trigger five times. Every shot missed. Then the Bentley was gone.

Harry steadied himself against the war memorial. He had nowhere to go and no money to get there. But no money was just enough to get him to nowhere. A convenient fact. There was one bullet left in the chamber.

I'm the author of the story you have just read, and I'd like to say a few words about it now that it's done. I carried the basic idea of the tale in my head for more than eighteen years before I actually sat down and wrote it. That's quite normal for me: stories often ferment, or fester, in my mind for a long time before I seem able or willing to share them with readers. I don't know why this should be so. Maybe it's indolence or disorganisation. But I've finally taken the plunge with this particular piece, so the reason for the delay probably doesn't matter too much.

I'm not saying that "Happiness Leasehold" is a great story. I'm sure it's not important at all. Nor is the theme quite as original as I initially believed it to be. In fact, I doubt I ever really thought it was original. It's almost certain I'd read a tale by some other writer along the same lines that impressed me so much it encouraged me to make my own attempt. The conceit of an individual who abruptly discovers that nothing in his life is as real as he'd always assumed, that his own position in the world, and the world itself, have changed in an instant, is an immensely powerful literary device.

The master of this specialised theme was Philip K. Dick. His novels and stories are full of characters living in realities that are extremely unstable, that transform in the blink of an ego. Bubbles of illusion burst without warning. Memories of entire lives are found to be false, everything previously known and experienced has been simulated, personal histories have been retrospectively forged. The past was nothing but a mirage. Because Dick handled this subject matter so well, I felt there was little point in putting "Happiness Leasehold" down on paper. In its present form it would be nothing more than a very pale imitation of Dick's work. It needed something extra. But what?

Excuse me for a moment. The letterflap on my front door has just snapped. I think the postman has delivered something for me. Probably a new contract from a publisher. I am a successful author and nobody ever helped me achieve prominence in my career. I made it big by my own efforts. Yes, it's a letter. I'll just slice open the envelope. A handwritten page. How quaint! Some joker wants me to meet him by the war memorial at noon. Apparently his great-grandfather knew mine. Well, it's a nuisance, but I'll go anyway. There might be a story in it somewhere.

You are the reader. Yes, you! Don't look round, I'm talking to YOU. Sitting there in your chair, reading this story. It's almost over now. Consider your life and how well you have done for yourself. You have worked so hard and everything you have achieved is fully deserved. Nobody has ever helped you. By your own efforts you have made it big. You are a real person, not a character in a story. What's that noise? The letterflap on your front door has just snapped. I think there's a letter for you.

Life and the Plumbline

Lönnrot avoided Scharlach's eyes. He looked at the trees and the sky subdivided into murky red, green and yellow rhombuses. He felt a chill, and an impersonal, almost anonymous sadness. The night was dark now; from the dusty garden there rose the pointless cry of a bird. For the last time, Lönnrot considered the problem of the symmetrical, periodic murders.

"There are three lines too many in your labyrinth," he said at last. "I know of a Greek labyrinth that is but one straight line. So many philosophers have been lost upon that line that a mere detective might be pardoned if he became lost as well. When you hunt me down in another avatar of our lives, Scharlach, I suggest that you fake (or commit) one crime at A, a second crime at B, eight kilometres from A, then a third crime at C, four kilometres from A and B and halfway between them. Then wait for me at D, two kilometres from A and C, once again halfway between them. Kill me at D, as you are about to kill me at Triste-le-Roy."

"The next time I kill you," Scharlach replied, "I promise you the labyrinth that consists of a single straight line that is invisible and endless."

He stepped back a few steps. Then, very carefully, he fired.

—Jorge Luis Borges, "Death and the Compass"

To be literally reborn in the same city and into the same profession is a miracle behind which even the most devout adherents of reincarnation must suspect some artifice. The young writer from the *Yiddische Zeitung* was ambitious and disrespectful enough to engineer the transmigration of one especially renowned soul, that of the detective Erik Lönnrot, who had vanished at the beginning of March while investigating a series of murders with apparently mystical motives.

This writer decided, with the strange integrity of a journalist, to make his own enquiries into the crime, but not for the sake of truth. His real desire was to adopt the identity of Lönnrot and continue his work, partly as a way of sublimating his own shyness, for it would be simpler to live as another man than attempt to remedy his psychological ailment. He had met Lönnrot on numerous occasions and was his admirer, but first it was necessary to learn the fate of the detective. To this end he approached the most notorious criminal in the city, Red Scharlach, as the intelligence with the best contacts among the inhabitants of the darkest shadows of the urban landscape.

To ingratiate himself with Scharlach, the writer conducted a number of surprising robberies on banks and museums, always mumbling an apology and blushing as he made his profitable escapes. Within a short time he was recognised, and police commissioner Treviranus was on his trail; and so, a hunted man, dismissed in his absence from his job, his last remaining option was to hurl himself upon the mercy of an untouchable criminal. Fortunately, Scharlach approached him first with an offer of protection and employment. The writer was granted a personal interview and took the opportunity to make a request which amused Scharlach enough for him to grant it.

"So you want to know what befell Erik Lönnrot, and in the event his identity is free you wish to claim it? Yes, I defeated him, and his career ended at Triste-le-Roy, that house of confusion and despair. I set a trap and he walked into it alone, for his egotism was vast and not even his employers knew where he was going on that particular day. It might truthfully be said he outwitted himself. I will tell you about his last moments of existence."

The writer listened while Scharlach explained how Lönnrot followed the clues which he, the thug and dandy, had positioned with care around the city and which would be ignored or doubted by all others. Enticing Lönnrot to Triste-le-Roy was the culmination of a vow made by Scharlach to avenge his own sufferings at the hands of the police. By arranging and faking certain ritual murders at precise points on the map, he had compelled Lönnrot to study their geometric relation to one another and anticipate the location of the supposed *next* murder, which in fact was his own.

"How did he die?" enquired the young man.

"He found his way to the centre of the labyrinth I built for him, a labyrinth without walls, a labyrinth of clues, but it was the minotaur's turn to claim the victory. I was waiting for him here. He came to me and I caught him. He showed no fear, not even when my gun was aimed at his throat. He was still more interested in the symmetry of my revenge. Ever the perfectionist, he criticised the complexity of my maze and suggested an alternative and made me promise to kill him again in another life in his more elegant and simple labyrinth."

Scharlach outlined the labyrinth in question. It consisted of four points, A, B, C, and D, on a line. . . .

"All this suits my purpose," replied the writer, "and so henceforth I wish to be known as Erik Lönnrot."

Scharlach answered coolly, "Then I must kill you again."

"Only in the promised labyrinth, the straight line you mentioned. I will require funds to keep myself alive and avoid the police until you have designed this labyrinth."

"It is an extravagant suicide."

"What better solution to the tedium of life?"

Scharlach smirked. "You are thinking almost like Lönnrot, but your melancholy is too ironic and not sufficiently universal. He was a man of his word and so am I. Thus I will do what I can to keep the police away from you, but I will give you the money anyway. Treviranus may be a problem."

With disdain or respect, he opened his wallet and threw a wad of notes at the new Lönnrot.

Picking them up, the writer truly felt he had shed his old identity and was now the detective, reborn as an avatar with less reasoning power than his prior incarnation but an equal amount of curiosity and charm. Already he felt an impatient but resigned distrust of journalism. He grinned, but then noticed Scharlach's impassive gaze, which filled him with a need to justify his actions.

"I am not the first person to adopt the persona of a famous sleuth. Is the world not overrun with amateurs who claim to be Sherlock Holmes or Auguste Dupin?"

Scharlach snorted. "Those characters are fictional. Erik Lönnrot was real. Your symmetries are imperfect, but I forgive you, for perfect reflections are unsatisfying and inhuman."

"Will you allow me a week of mental preparation before committing your first crime at point A?"

"I am far too busy to play your game, but as you have assumed the identity of Lönnrot, so you can have no objection if I delegate my best man to act the part of myself. You *are* Lönnrot and he was reckless, so you will accept the challenge. My best man has the potential to be more dangerous than I am. He may be disposed to give you that week or possibly a little more."

"If he is clever enough to be your best man, naturally I accept him as Scharlach," agreed Lönnrot eagerly.

"Designing labyrinths is a pastime which no longer interests me. I have a new hobby: chemistry. My latest challenge involves the synthesis of variants of quinuclidinyl benzilate, a drug useful to criminals, but I may even legitimise this business."

"I wish you all the luck at my disposal."

Scharlach waved him away, and Lönnrot moved through the building which the dandy had made his latest headquarters. Two men sat on the packed earth of the patio, sipping from gourds. The smell of *yerba mate* was nothing to comment on, unless one wished to draw attention to local habits, something a genuine denizen of this city would never do. Out on the street the dusk was already thick and the pink walls of the low houses cooled with audible sighs beneath the rising moon. The silhouette of a horse grazed black grass, and elsewhere a guitar was played delicately out of tune. A man walked past, tossing a coin and whistling sadly. Far away, a woman laughed.

Lönnrot walked south, looking for a cheap hotel where he might take his meals in his room and read the newspapers, which he had forgotten he now despised, without attracting attention. The traditional feeling of being followed was strong. He decided that the outlines of a cloud which passed overhead were too precise. It seemed a bad omen, but he found his hotel in the Rue Menard, that new street which appears much older than any other, perhaps because it is so poor and more fully suffused with memories of the past. Certainly the immigrants who dwell there never discuss the future, preferring to talk about lost homelands. Lönnrot entered the lobby and declined to give his name when he paid for a room, but the issue was not pressed and he found himself climbing a dim stairway which terminated in a green door. Beyond was his bed.

He deluded himself for nine nights that he was flexing his cerebral muscles. He attempted every crossword.

On the tenth night he was kept awake by a series of explosions across the city. It was a carnival, and the blue, orange, and purple glare of bursting fireworks performed a simple but marvellous alchemy on the grime of his window, transforming it into a precious artistic substance; but he cared less that his room was illuminated, the stains on the damp wallpaper seeming to wink with each colourful detonation. Someone in a building further along the street dropped a firework into a mob of revellers. There was much cursing after the echo had faded and then more giggling as the crowd moved away.

The following morning, one and a half weeks after his meeting with Scharlach, the game commenced.

The owner of the hotel always slid the *Yiddische Zeitung* under his door, but on this occasion Lönnrot heard him loitering at the top of the stairs, muttering as he read the front page. Then he finished or grew bored, and Lönnrot received what he anticipated as his first clue—news of the crime committed at point A and the location of that point. He picked up the newspaper. With a shock he realised that Scharlach, or rather his actor, had already managed to outplay him.

The first three crimes, which were supposed to lead him gradually into the trap, had been committed simultaneously. The previous Lönnrot was faced with regularity in time as well as space, but this Lönnrot had no surfeit of dimensions. There was only space. He sat on the bed and clutched his head, wondering what Scharlach was intending. It was too late for regrets. A return to his past was impossible.

Calming himself with a great effort, he pondered deeply.

The crimes were listed in no special order, for the exact time of each one was not yet established.

The first murder (or accidental death) had taken place on the roof of the towering Hôtel du Nord. A figure was observed climbing over the railings by a watchman, who rushed to the top of the building and found not a potential suicide but a badly bruised naked corpse with a sooty bundle tied to its back, perhaps some sort of rolled-up sleeping mat. A different witness had tentatively identified the body as that of the respected mining engineer Adam Voynich.

The second fatality had occurred in a fountain, where a reveller was found drowned under the statue of a horse which dropped water from its mouth. This man was believed to be the thief and smuggler Donald "Maldonado" Yates (or Yeats). There was an empty *yerba mate* gourd in his deepest pocket.

The third crime was more similar to the first, for it involved soot, but this corpse was completely unrecognisable. A blaze had broken out in a fireworks factory. Amid the festive explosions of the night few people paid attention to this more sinister display. The factory was gutted and the roof had collapsed, but there was just one victim. Scraps of fabric (silk) had survived the inferno, but the only distinguishing features on the body were two items of jewellery, a ring and necklace both of green chalcedony.

Lönnrot knew that he was expected to wait for Scharlach at a point determined by these three felonies. His time of hiding was over. He went onto the street, found the nearest newspaper kiosk, and purchased a street map. Then he returned to his room and marked the points. They formed the promised straight line, but he could not decide which way the labyrinth pointed. The crime at the Hôtel du Nord was midway between the other two, so that was point C, but which of the others were A and B? Then he understood why Scharlach had arranged it like this. If there was a period of days or months between each crime, he would be able to force Scharlach to end the game early. For example, once he had points A and B he would automatically know the location of C and be able to wait there instead of at point D for his doom.

He needed to learn whether the drowning had preceded the fire or vice versa. This was crucial. Unable to bear waiting for the newspapers to give him this information, he checked out of his room and walked to the Hôtel du Nord, a prism as horribly magnificent as his own hotel was magnificently horrible. It was a warm day, but clouds of smoke had not yet dispersed from the pyrotechnics of the carnival. He noted how the estuary waters were less yellow than usual but withheld his judgment on the significance of this.

At the base of the Hôtel du Nord he came face to face with police commissioner Treviranus, who was holding a handkerchief over his mouth as if worried about catching or distributing an infection. For a moment Lönnrot's heart sank, but then Treviranus said something which filled him with an inexplicable sensation.

"So there you are, Lönnrot! Where have you been all this time? Most of us assumed you were dead, but not I. Too eccentric for that, I always said. Thanks for proving me right."

"I've been busy," stuttered Lönnrot, amazed that his oldest colleague, a master of scepticism, was fooled by his change of identity.

Treviranus was nonchalant or exhausted. He indicated the prismatic tower. "This is an unlucky building."

"What do you know about the victim?"

"He was attending a technical conference. Adam Voynich helped design the Wuddles mine in the Witwatersrand region of South Africa, the deepest in the world. That fact must be significant."

Lönnrot frowned. "Is it a gold mine?"

"Yes. Somebody was clearly after the samples he brought with him and chased him to the roof and beat him to death with a heavy flat object, perhaps an ingot of the stolen gold, which *must* have been stolen because we found none on him."

"That explains his bruising, but like all your hypotheses it is uninteresting. There must be more to it than robbery."

"Off on one of your wild tangents again?" sighed Treviranus. "I imagine you're interested in the shape the three crimes make? Well, I've already worked that out myself and can tell you that it's nothing more complex than a straight line."

"The crimes are spaced equidistantly?"

"Absolutely. We now think that the fire at the factory was started an hour before midnight and the drowning in the fountain took place an hour after, which probably means that Voynich was killed on the stroke of twelve. You like symmetry, don't you? An assassin could easily walk between those locations in the given time. From the factory to the hotel is four kilometres and from the hotel to the fountain is another four. It's feasible we'll find another body four kilometres beyond *that* point, which is in the marshes. Horrendous terrain. I'll have to get a man to fly above it to check it out."

Lönnrot rubbed his chin. "Did you say fly?"

"Yes, the police force recently acquired a balloon for surveillance purposes. We use it on the end of a tether. I wanted a helicopter, but they are too expensive."

"Scharlach owns one," countered Lönnrot.

"Exactly my point. He's good at making money, but we have to rely on what's left after the politicians have finished creaming off from the taxes. A balloon is good enough."

Lönnrot remembered the dark cloud with the sharp edges. "I must be moving on, there's much work to do."

He hurried away with a wave, leaving his colleague still breathing into his handkerchief and gazing up tiredly at the glass cliff of the building he so publicly despised.

Lönnrot was pleased that Treviranus lacked the insight to calculate the true location of the next crime. It was natural for the police commissioner to assume the murders, A, B, and C, had progressed in one direction along Scharlach's straight line, but Lönnrot, in his previous incarnation, had designed this labyrinth and knew better. The factory was point A and the fountain was point B. These two points were eight kilometres from each other. Voynich's killing at the Hôtel du Nord had *not* taken place at midnight, but after one in the morning, for it was the third crime and the hotel was point C. This meant that point D, where Scharlach was due to kill the detective a second time, was midway between the factory and hotel, a two-kilometre walk.

But as he strode along, Lönnrot began to wonder if he might be missing a subtle clue. Instead of proceeding directly to point D, he took a detour to the nearest public library, which according to his map was at the end of a nearby avenue, in order to think more carefully with the aid of wise and comforting books. Scharlach was extremely clever: the man who was acting his part could not be less devious. There had to be an extra element, something unexpected.

At a desk in the library, Lönnrot considered the map. He realised that he was looking at the straight line from *above*. What might it look like from the side? It might have a different shape. The roof of the Hôtel du Nord was exactly one kilometre above the ground, a fact he was able to check in an encyclopaedia. The next crime might not take place at ground level either, but up in the air. He doodled in the margins of the map and suddenly felt he had a good idea of what shape the straight line formed from the side.

It was necessary to mislead Treviranus before the police commissioner came to the same conclusion, or even better, to set a diversion in anticipation of his discovery that elevation might be involved.

He found a public telephone on the other side of the street from the library and made his call.

"This is Erik Lönnrot. Will you leave a message for Treviranus? Tell him that it was once believed there were only four elements in the universe. Voynich, the mining engineer, represents *earth*; the drowned man, Yates, stands for *water*; the unknown corpse in the factory is a symbol of *fire*. The next crime will have something to do with *air*. It might be that the force's balloon will be stolen and used to commit an assassination from above."

The voice replied, "This *is* Treviranus. Is that really you, Lönnrot? What are you talking about? The corpse is no longer 'unknown.' It belongs to Janez (or James) Irby, a former associate of Scharlach's. It was identified about an hour ago by Scharlach himself. He's not such a bad sort when you talk to him."

Lönnrot chewed his lip but did not deviate from his plan. "I want to ask you for a favour. It's a question of trust. I need to borrow your balloon to prevent it being used to commit a murder. If I am using it, the assassin won't be able to steal it, but you must listen carefully to my instructions. Moor the balloon at ground level but with a tether of a length which I'll shortly reveal to you."

"Your request is mad," snapped Treviranus.

"For old time's sake," cried Lönnrot.

There was a lengthy pause. "Very well, but only because I feared you were dead and am pleased to find this isn't the case. Whatever you're up to I'm sure I won't approve of it."

"Did you find a body in the marsh?"

"I can't imagine how you knew we were looking there, but no we found nothing. Maybe there were only three murders."

"Help me prevent a fourth," whispered Lönnrot.

"Fine. Just don't let me down."

Still feeling a thrill from speaking the word "prevent" when he meant "arrange," Lönnrot accepted the police commissioner's affirmative answer with gratitude and returned to the library, where he asked one of the assistants for a blank piece of paper, a ruler and a new pencil to replace his broken one. These items were brought from the basement, and the detective proceeded to draw a geometric diagram. He stared at it with a grimace and shook his head. Then he asked the assistant for a pair of compasses. Grumbling, she shuffled back into the basement and came up with the desired item. Once again Lönnrot applied himself to geometry. A second time he shook his head. He drew yet another diagram, and this time he sat back in profound satisfaction.

He stood and lurked among the bookshelves in the most obscure part of the building, wandering into the science section and flicking through a few textbooks on chemistry without reading them. He found a dusty corner and huddled down, thrusting as much of his body under a bookcase as he could manage. When closing time came, the librarian who had fetched his drawing equipment made a desultory search of the aisles and then turned off the lights and went home. Lönnrot was locked in for the night.

He slithered from his hiding place, annoyed that he had no pocket torch or candles to read by. Although the finest detective in the city, he could not be expected to think of everything. He wondered if there was someone else in the building, moving down a parallel aisle. It sounded like that, but he distrusted primeval fears and assumed instead that the spines of old books were creaking as they cooled in the stale night air.

When dawn came, he returned to his corner and waited for the library to open to the public before emerging. Then he casually strolled out and rang Treviranus to give him the exact measurement for the tether.

"When do you want the balloon moved to that location?" asked the police commissioner.

"I'll let you know just before I need it."

"You're making my life difficult. Don't ask me for a favour after this one. Can you guess where we buy the hydrogen for our balloon? From Scharlach! He's moved into chemicals, and the politicians take enough bribes off him to award him the contracts he seeks."

"That's the real world for you," sighed Lönnrot.

He returned to the library and resolved to make this building his permanent base. The one riddle left to solve concerned the time of the murder at point D. When would it happen? Then with a start he realised that this variable in the equation was entirely up to him. He was the victim, after all, and it was his responsibility to choose the day. It was not a question of working anything out, but it was essential that Scharlach commit the crime without getting caught, so the ideal time would be at night, a night with thick cloud cover. All that was necessary was to read the daily weather forecasts in the newspapers.

Lönnrot spent a further three nights sleeping secretly in the library. Then he walked out for the very last time and rang Treviranus, doing his best to feel a sense of finality. There was a perverse tenderness in his voice as he instructed the police commissioner to anchor the balloon as quickly as possible on the corner of Quain Street and Hladik Ulice. The length of the tether was to be 3400 metres. Treviranus grumbled but seemed dourly excited by this chance to make the maverick detective look foolish.

Lönnrot waited an hour and then walked slowly to the designated spot. The clouds were dense and the rain and dying light had herded most pedestrians indoors, but the area had also been cordoned off and a policeman stood at a discreet distance from the balloon, which bulged over the low buildings without touching them. Scharlach had chosen this location carefully. The air was still and the canopy did not sway as Lönnrot approached the basket which rested on the pavement.

He climbed inside and cast out the bags of ballast—lead shot or spoons or some such thing—and winced as they clattered on the street below. He rose rapidly and clutched the sides of the basket and gaped at the city with its white lights before he entered the clouds and felt cold. Wiping the rain from his face, he trembled for the first time since beginning his adventure. Visibility was almost zero. At last the balloon jerked and the line beneath twanged with a single, oddly musical note. He had reached his desired elevation.

This was the point at which Scharlach was going to destroy him for a second time. But how? A bullet was the obvious answer. He stood up straight to make himself an easier target, though he assumed it was the balloon itself which would be aimed at. To plummet to his death or burn . . . or both?

Something struck him a blow across the face.

He staggered. It struck him again.

The third time, he caught it. A small weight, the weight on a plumbline. He reeled it in. The end of a hose was attached to the line, a hose which snaked up into the clouds.

He held it close and a voice vibrated out of it.

"Delighted to meet you again, Lönnrot . . ."

"Scharlach? At last! Will you kill me now? This is the location of point D. This is where the crime must take place."

The faint voice chuckled. "Not quite. You almost got it right, but I've outwitted you again."

Lönnrot shut his eyes tight. "Tell me."

"As you wish. Confronted with the same problem I designed for you, an ordinary mind, such as the one possessed by Treviranus, would consider the labyrinth, in other words the straight line, to be perfectly flat. You saw past this childish assumption and realised that from the side it might have a different shape in another dimension, the dimension of height."

"Yes," said Lönnrot. "I had reasons to believe that the murder at point A was actually committed far above the ground, but the killing at point B was clearly committed at ground level, or to be more accurate fountain level. The crime at point C was committed on the roof of the Hôtel du Nord, at an elevation of one kilometre. I then thought that the shape of the labyrinth from the side was a simple incline. Extending this incline I worked out that the crime at point A occurred at an altitude of two kilometres. I surmised that you dropped the victim from your helicopter at that height strapped to a parachute onto the roof of the fireworks factory. Your expertise with chemicals permitted you to create an incendiary device which you attached to the victim's feet. When he landed on the roof it detonated and burned down the building, destroying most of the evidence except for a few scraps of silk, which is well known as parachute material. If this is really what happened, simple geometry suggested that point D was 1.5 kilometres above the ground, and this was the length of the tether I originally believed I required."

"But you changed your mind," pointed out Scharlach.

"Of course. I had second thoughts. I know how cunning you are, and I also realised you were pretending to be Treviranus when I met him outside the Hôtel du Nord. You kept your face covered by a handkerchief and fooled me, until I rang the real Treviranus later in his office. So then I tried to remember the exact words you had spoken to me outside the hotel. At one point you used the word 'tangent,' and I surmised that this was a clue. A tangent implies a curve, and I redrew my diagram in this fashion: the quadrant of a circle with the eight-kilometre distance between points A and B as the tangent line. This arc passed through point C, the roof of the hotel, and therefore gave a height of 2.7 kilometres for point D."

"But you rejected this solution too?"

"Yes, because it entails an altitude of 7.5 kilometres for the crime at point A, which is simply too high for your helicopter and too high to ensure that the victim's parachute doesn't drift off course. So I redrew my diagram again. This time I had the answer! The shape of the labyrinth from the side is a semicircle with a diameter of eight kilometres. Therefore both crimes at points A and B were committed at

ground level and the scraps of silk were a diversion, but the crime at
point C was the one committed in the helicopter. You pushed out
poor Adam Voynich *without* a parachute from a height of four kilometres. He landed on the roof of the Hôtel du Nord, which explains his
bruises and the motion which led the watchman to believe that he wit-
nessed a figure in the process of climbing over the railings, whereas
really he was simply dropping onto them from above. This third diagram gives an elevation of 3.4 kilometres for point D, which is where I
am now and where you will kill me. I'm ready."

There was a pause from Scharlach, then what sounded like a sigh,
followed by a giggle. "Sorry, wrong again."

Lönnrot spoke into the tube angrily. "Am I?"

Scharlach answered, "I'm currently in my helicopter, hovering directly above you, but my altitude is precisely five kilometres, and this is
the height at which the crime is going to take place. The real shape of
the labyrinth from the side is a sine-wave. The amplitude of this signal
is five kilometres and its wavelength is eight kilometres. You must see
that it connects with points A, B, and C at ground level. True, this
means that between points B and C it dips five kilometres *beneath the
earth,* but as no crimes had to take place there to fulfil the terms of the
labyrinth, the detail is irrelevant."

"This is unfair," protested Lönnrot. "The peaks and troughs of a
sine-wave may be of any height or depth according to whatever figure
you choose. There was no way I could calculate that!"

"In fact you do me a disservice," replied Scharlach, "because I
have gone out of my way to create a regular shape for the labyrinth.
Don't you realise that the line could be *any* shape from the side and
still appear straight from above? I was under no obligation to produce
something as regular as a sine-wave; it was merely an act of generosity
on my part. And in fact I did give you a clue. Adam Voynich was the
designer of the Wuddles mine, as I told you when I pretended to be
Treviranus. A little research in that library of yours and you would
have soon learned that the mine is question is five kilometres deep.
This was quite an obvious clue, really. Perhaps I felt pity for you, feeble detective that you are, though not for much longer."

"You will kill me now?" cried Lönnrot.

"I intend to do something much worse to you. I'm going to give you back your old life, the life of the young writer from the *Yiddische Zeitung*, with its painful shyness. That is the worst fate I can devise for you, Erik Lönnrot!"

"I refuse to give up my new identity."

"But it's not yours to keep. Didn't you wonder who Scharlach's 'best man' might be? I am the real Erik Lönnrot . . ."

"Impossible. He is dead. Scharlach shot him."

"But not with a bullet. It was a tranquilliser dart, a dart coated with quinuclidinyl benzilate, one of the most powerful hallucinogens known to science. Scharlach gave you a clue about this when he interviewed you. If you had read those chemistry textbooks when you were in the library you might have worked this out. It is a drug which makes a recipient highly suggestible and which can be administered in a number of ways—a solution into a vein or a spray into the lungs. After I entered the Villa Triste-le-Roy and was seized by Scharlach's accomplices, Scharlach himself told me about how he experienced a delirium which lasted for nine days and nine nights. He visited the same delirium upon me, his old enemy, and tormented me by suggesting more and more horrible visions. Under that onslaught I surrendered and gave my word to defect to his side, which is what he wanted all along. I am a man of honour and once I give my word I never break it, so now I work for him, so successfully that he has made me his successor."

"If you are telling the truth about the sine-wave pattern, then Voynich was also killed at ground level."

"Yes, I killed him at the base of the Hôtel du Nord, stripped him and strapped a rocket to his back. That propelled him to the roof. With the sounds of all the other fireworks, nobody noticed an extra rocket, even though it was much larger and powered by hydrogen. When it burned out, it looked just like a rolled-up sleeping mat."

"I don't know how I missed that," lamented Lönnrot.

"Shall I tell you something about the victims? Voynich was chosen because he was a mining engineer, no other reason, but Yates and Irby were Scharlach's accomplices, the very men who overpowered me when I entered Triste-le-Roy. They didn't like the fact that Scharlach had chosen me as his heir, and they were planning to go to Treviranus and tell him everything. They were the two men sipping *yerba mate* on the patio. I was there as well. I was the man who spun the coin in front of you. I followed you to the Rue Menard and to the library. I even heard the ridiculous story you spun to Treviranus about the earth, water, fire, and air connection of the murders."

"I don't know what to say."

"This is a game for real intellectuals. You just weren't up to the task. Now I'm going to cut you free and you will drift away. When you land you will be Lönnrot no longer but the young writer again. You will turn yourself in for the robberies you conducted."

"I refuse. I don't want my old life back."

"Did you hear that sigh I made a few minutes ago? It wasn't a sigh but an injection of quinuclidinyl benzilate in gaseous form into the basket of your balloon through this hose. I injected it at my present altitude, which explains how the crime at point D takes place at the peak of the sine-wave. You are already starting to feel its effects. You are becoming highly suggestible. My first suggestion is that we no longer share identities. I alone am Erik Lönnrot."

"The irony of this is unbearable."

"Yes, and there's another irony. There *was* an extra pattern to the crimes, not the four ancient elements, which are mere fancies, but the modern chemical truth of the states of matter."

Lönnrot frowned. "So Voynich represented *solid* (rather than earth) and the crime at the fountain was a symbol of *liquid*, and what you have just done to me must represent *gas*, but what about the crime at the factory? There are four elements, but only three states of matter."

"Not so, there are four of those too. The fourth state is *plasma*. Unfortunately I resorted to a trick in this case. Plasma is also a name for green chalcedony, the jewellery found on the charred body. This connection was a bonus, and I'm allowed a little wordgame in something that was surplus to the labyrinth."

"I suppose so," agreed the young writer, finding it difficult to oppose the will of Lönnrot above him.

"After you met Treviranus outside the hotel, you assumed it was Scharlach in disguise, but in fact it was me. Scharlach has adopted a more modest disguise. He is the policeman below. He is about to cut the tether. He's a busy man, so we don't have long."

"There are three points too many in this labyrinth. I can imagine a labyrinth that is but one point. When you hunt me down in a *third* avatar of our lives, I ask that you (or Scharlach) fake or commit a crime at point A, a second crime at point B, a certain number of hours later, then a third at point C, half that number of hours later. Then deliver the final stroke at point D, again half that specified time later. Whether you kill me or give me a life I don't want, make sure that all those points are at one location, not a location in any street or on any map. Locate all those points in my chest, just where the heart is."

"The labyrinth you have described is your responsibility to find," came the reply. "It is called unrequited love. Go out and meet girls and fall in love with them at shorter and shorter intervals. If you really want this labyrinth it will first be necessary for you to overcome your shyness."

"I feared that would be the case, but I will try. Goodbye," said the young writer. He dropped the plumbline, and it swung back into the clouds. He listened for the sound of the helicopter, but he heard nothing in that aerial soup. He was definitely moving; the line had been severed.

Life, hideous unwanted life, awaited him whenever and wherever he landed.

The Unsubtle Cages

Alone in a new city, the traveller decided to visit the zoo. It might be a place to find conversation, if not with people then with animals. He had not spoken for almost a week. He took a tram to the relevant suburb. The houses and factories were low and decayed. Dunes of rust drifted down the alleys, covering abandoned machinery. The wind was cold and constant. Newspapers from the previous century flapped across the wider streets, full of yellowing politics and adverts which could not be answered. They roosted with angry vibrations on the sagging telephone lines which conveyed static, sniggers and deep breathing from the hub of the metropolis to its rim. He had already come far, but this short journey seemed much greater. An adventure.

He was the only passenger who dismounted outside the gates. They were neither closed nor open, but broken just enough to provide a means of entry. He climbed through. The zookeeper introduced himself. His name was Rotpier. He was not a malformed dwarf, but he acted as if he ought to be. He led the traveller past the compounds of lizards and worms. A few withered birds stood in groups on the tin roofs. Even Rotpier could not say whether they were part of the display or not. They were indeterminate. At last, the final cage was reached. It contained many other cages, all of different sizes. They stood idle, stacked in corners or on top of one another. They were worn and dented but perfectly serviceable.

"What is the meaning of this?" asked the traveller.

Rotpier blinked. "They have to be kept locked up for their own good. If they escaped, they might start caging beasts and people at random or according to their own tastes. Then they would return to the zoo with their new charges. The result would be an undisciplined collection, arbitrary and unplanned. Spontaneous, possibly automatic."

The traveller stroked his chin. "I wish to buy one."

"This is a very unusual request. I must consult my memory. Yes, I believe there is a precedent. Many years ago, a man called Belperron purchased a cage and took it back to his apartment, where he experimented on it. There are no laws against that. They are not expensive."

The traveller removed his wallet and counted out the notes. Then the zookeeper hooked one out with a long pole. It was heavy but responsive. It could be dragged or strapped to a back with equal inconvenience. Perhaps it might be rolled, in the manner of dice, end over end. The traveller left the zoo and waited for the tram with sore hands. It came, and he paid a double fare. He sat opposite the cage, looking through its bars at the sombre view beyond the window. If the environment was trapped there, he must be free. The illusion comforted him to his destination. He pushed his new possession up the stairs of his hotel. He positioned it in the centre of the room. And this space which was not really his, this rented volume of continued existence, already resembled a new zoo. And he its keeper.

He waited for his first visitors.

It seemed an original method of defeating his isolation. His previous attempts to meet people had failed. The nightclubs were shut, the parks and subways deserted or unbearably strange. But now he had created a solution through the medium of business. Men and women would pay to tour his little zoo. They might bring children with them. Also laughter. It was almost feasible. He paced the floorboards for an hour before he realised that he needed a live exhibit to display in the cage. The answer was to lock himself inside. He would be fed and enjoyed until he achieved satisfaction. He did not swallow the key, but squatted over it. He removed his shoes and curled his toes. It was even more lonely in this simple cell, an outcome he had not anticipated. He licked his lips anxiously.

There was a rumbling from afar, as if a crowd were shuffling down the street towards his hotel. He imagined many outcomes. The authorities were coming to grant his zoo a licence or to close it down. The police were hurrying to arrest his prison and free him—a miscarriage of justice. He wondered why his cage did not return to the real zoo as Rotpier had predicted, with him as its trophy. The door of his room was closed. Possibly that was the reason. Or else it accepted the hotel as its home, validating the traveller's hopes. Then he imagined that the giant cage, the cage of cages, had detached itself from its location and was hunting its lost brother. He stood and gripped the bars facing the window. He was able to peer down onto the street. Rust dunes were shaken apart, settling evenly over the cobbles like the grains of a powdered sunset.

All his guesses were wrong. He saw rooms, dozens of them, sliding over this new desert, a caravan of cubes, misshapen, humped domiciles with grimy windows and flapping shutters like eyelids. Through each pane of glass, the unwashed outline of a traveller congealed. They were equally lonely, but the sum of all their feelings was still a single loneliness. One at a time, the rooms entered the hotel, passed through the lobby and up the stairs. He heard them in the corridor, squeezing between the walls. Now he felt the hotel swelling, an ego of brick and rotting joists and tattered curtains. The rooms were adding themselves to the collection. The symbolism was too obvious. He closed his eyes in the knowledge that each exhibit was its own visitor. And he experienced a relief so slight it bordered on monstrous despair.

Sigma Octantis

The southern night is brighter than the northern, for it is crowded with more constellations. When an explorer or other traveller first crosses the torrid equator from the upper into the lower hemisphere and glances up, he directs his attention towards the very centre of our galaxy and regards a highly sociable region of outer space.

Contrast such a person with the old fisherman vainly seeking refuge in an Alaskan Sound before the storms of the Bering Strait send icebergs to crush his ship and drown his crew; or the coal miner descending into a pit beyond the outskirts of a Spitsbergen camp, his skull jerking back as the cable on his cage snaps, turning the shaft into a fatal telescope which will finally focus on just one star; or the Inuit girl gliding over Nunavut snows on a sled made of caribou bones, traditional sealskin runners packed with frozen fish, in haste to reach the igloo of her lover, unaware that he has left it to intercept her and is now lost in a blizzard and will remain lost until she appears out of the white nothingness, knocking him down and accidentally crushing his lovesick head.

These events are already happening, and the lights which burn in the eyes that weep and glaze are the aloof jewels of the Milky Way's edge, the suns on the outer spiral arms, more lonely than the brows of feverish scholars in a library of nameless books.

Not an awkward simile for me: I once founded such an institution. The self-crowned King of Patagonia, a figure more familiar to his subjects as Giraldus Jones, had commissioned me to establish an archive in the dour gardens of his palace. My task was the careful editing of the literature of the aboriginals, four million pages in all, composed in hieroglyphs on the badly cured skins of giant sloths. Other authorities had announced them indecipherable, thus of scant interest; but Jones believed he had a key to their meaning. I applied his system with mixed results. Hints of a strange and perverted culture gradually emerged.

I had always treated with caution tales that the original inhabitants of this domain were ten feet tall. Sailors had spied them in the early days of rounding Cape Horn, and Magellan even hoped to trade with them, at least according to the log of his journey written by Antonio Pigafetta; but now the hieroglyphs seemed to confirm this. I was never a proper cynic, for I had seen enough wonders to warn me against dogmatic disbelief; neither was I gullible enough to perceive any evidence in these weird scribblings for some of the wilder racial theories of my employer, absurd prejudices too fashionable at that loathsome time.

Jones, I am sorry to say, was one of those men who spend inordinate amounts of time and energy trying to divide the human race into rigorous hierarchical orders. He took much of his cant from the German dissidents already settled in Paraguay, warty pioneers and bigots who had departed the fatherland in order to distance themselves from the Jews, but with one slant to his core belief: he thought it was the Celt, not the Aryan, that was the purest type of man. This contradicted Bismarck, who had insisted the Irish and Welsh were effete breeds; but like most extremists, the King of Patagonia did not care to resolve this discrepancy, preferring to ignore it, and the Iron Chancellor remained a hero in his scrubby domain, a bust of that successful brute looming at one end of the banqueting table that was the principal feature of his private quarters.

The skies above the grasslands of Jones's kingdom were nearly always free of cloud. It hardly ever seemed to rain down there, and after sunset the stars burned with minimal twinkle, hard and cold. Because there were so many constellations at this latitude, the classical stores of heroic names had been exhausted by astronomers, who fixed whimsical appellations to the arbitrary patterns. Thus it was possible for Giraldus to point out to me such signs as Tucana, Antlia, Volans, Apus, Telescopium, Pyxis, Circinus, and Pavo, a juxtaposition of tropical creatures and scientific instruments that would be deemed absurd among the elder Europeans. Then he jabbed a finger at a more mysterious zone of space.

"And there, my friend, we see the Octant, a most useful navigational instrument to insert into the heavens!"

I squinted miserably. "Exceedingly faint, is it not?"

"It is the southern equivalent to the northern Ursa Minor, the little bear that has guided safely home so many."

"I doubt anyone has been guided home by *this* collection of pinpricks. The name seems deliberate mockery."

"Indeed so," he sighed, "and the greatest irony is that the star closest to the South Celestial Pole is only the eighteenth brightest in an already dim constellation. Sigma Octantis is how it is designated, a counterpart to the sparkling northern Polaris but utterly useless to navigators. The jest is an excellent one, for in the glittering display that is the southern night sky, a void exists in the one important place."

"There are other methods of determining direction."

He flung a careless arm around my shoulder. "True enough, and yet all that dimness seems such a waste! Our planet turns on its axis, the stars go around that annoying faint glimmer, that pathetic distant sun that can only be seen properly through a lens. The Octant is a failure; we might as well admit the truth, and something ought to be done to change that fact. Axial precession is of no consequence here."

I turned my head and frowned. "I'm afraid I—"

He adopted the style of a lecturer, disengaging from my side, pacing the squares of his chessboard patio like a wandering bishop, always along the diagonals. "The world wobbles as it spins, but it's a very slow wobble, and in fact it takes twenty-six millennia for the Celestial Pole to make one revolution. Imagine what life was like back then! The evidence in the old scrolls you have already deciphered . . ."

"Myths and fables, surely?" I stammered.

He grinned and dismissed me with a wave; and he remained immobile in the centre of his patio, head craned back to drink the starlight with eyes the colour of parched soil, and I surmised he was performing calculations in his head, estimating angles, distances.

I had recently embarked on a thematic ordering of the ordinary books in his collection and already knew that one quarter of the grand total were devoted to astronomy and another quarter to astrology. I thought it rather peculiar that he blended those two disciplines so guilelessly, the rational with the far-fetched; but in truth this quirk was entirely in keeping with his character. Giraldus Jones had confessed to me that he was a believer and a sceptic, a man of faith and an atheist, that he encased contradictions like a volume that contains both arguments and their refutations, but although his skin was parchment-dry there was nothing bookish about him. He was too energetic, a bundle of prejudices and projects, a dominant scarecrow in a land of little owls and casual death.

I have so far neglected to give my own name. It is Owain Gower, and I am a linguist of superior aptitude. I record this remark not to demonstrate my vanity but to highlight the fact I am inept at nearly everything else. There is no false modesty here; my efforts at furthering myself in my homeland failed dismally. How I came into the service of the King of Patagonia is a muddled tale scarcely worth the telling, but you may safely assume it was because I had almost no other choice.

Although born and raised in Wales, in the little town of Rhossili, I was aware from an early age of the colony in distant Patagonia; my father had known men who sailed out there, who settled as farmers or miners, some growing rich in the process. Occasionally he would receive direct news, a letter filled with colourful accounts of skirmishes with gauchos, bandits, or aboriginals. The only colony our people have ever founded, Patagonia is still a source of pride to the Welsh.

And the flavour of those letters entered my blood, and I yearned to see the mountains and glaciers for myself.

And so I did, after failing in everything else.

I arrived in late 1928, the last year of world prosperity, a midpoint on the powdered bone path between the two great wars. I stepped from the rusty steamer onto the cracked quayside, and the last of my money jangled pitifully in my threadbare pockets. From Rawson I walked southwest and hitched rides with infrequent motorcars. At last I crossed into the isolated plain on the far side of Lago Musters.

Before the Welsh communities of the Chubut Valley and other remote tracts were finally absorbed into Argentina, the colony ran its own affairs with lonely precision, far from the gaze of international scrutiny. Abuses did flourish and minor tyrants rose by the dozen, and it was an unhappily frequent occurrence for megalomaniacs to be strung up high on telegraph poles or at least tarred and feathered. And when feathers were scarce, the scales of ugly strange fish were used.

Giraldus Jones was a luckier and shrewder example of the type. On the outer edge of the official territory, his regime was untroubled by punitive expeditions. And he had modest but vital funding from like-minded bigots in similar South American colonies who espoused the same philosophy of racial elitism. The German Paraguayans I have already mentioned, but the Confederates in Brazil were also a source of revenue; refusing to accept defeat in the American Civil War, they had fled into the *truly* deep south, into Rio Grande do Sul, grasslands almost as wild as those of Patagonia. I had entered a continent of lost dreams.

Jones at first used whatever money he raised to keep his subjects loyal. After a few years, they remained loyal through force of habit and he was able to divert some of his income to projects dear to his heart. His palace was a ramshackle old mansion connected to various outhouses by covered passages, the entire messy conglomeration painted a shade of yellow that resembled the petals of jaundice. I was given rooms in a structure that had once been a barn; with a token effort at conversion it became habitable if not luxurious. The library was located in the heart of the mansion itself. I began work every morning before dawn.

Surrounded by bundles of smelly scrolls, pinning each sloth skin to the table with a sneeze, I would methodically apply Jones's key to the texts. It had come to him in a dream, he said, but I had grave doubts about that. A rumour I heard from one of the cooks was far more plausible; namely that I wasn't his first archivist but merely a replacement for a scholar who had succeeded in breaking the code but had refused to proceed. In a corner of the chamber, bones lay scattered, and I began to assume they belonged to my poor colleague, now an archived soul.

I had no intention of disappointing my employer. . . .

And yet, even after translation, many of the scrolls remained gibberish, and I had orders to discard those and focus only on the sensible texts. So much exposure to an utterly alien mythology had a detrimental effect on my health; I dreamed of the gods, demons, and amorphous beings said to sleep lightly in the spaces between the stars. And I saw in my mind's eye with an astonishingly horrible clarity the obscure Patagonian civilisation of two hundred and sixty centuries ago, the cities of black bricks, blacker arts, and blackest laughter, a grim vision.

Jones often came to visit me while I was working.

His conversation was unpleasant.

"Religious texts include legends and lyrics, histories and codes of law, parables and moral instruction. I'm not interested in all that; I want you to separate the practical works from the chaff." And he would sit on the rim of my desk and press his hands together.

"Practical works?" I arched an eyebrow in confusion.

He leaned close, his breath like the bursting of an overripe fungus, and it took an immense effort on my part not to flinch. "The spells and figures of power, Mr Gower. The incantations."

And then to himself: "We must keep the weight down!"

"The weight?" I mumbled uneasily.

"The payload. The escape velocity of the Earth . . ." His sigh was deep and menacing, but he winked at me in its aftermath, and I realised that he wasn't angry or impatient but merely expressing hope in that unorthodox way of his. He stood and bowed ironically.

"Keep working, keep unlocking the secrets and segregating them. That is the law of nature. Categorisation . . ."

I licked my lips nervously and refused to agree.

Then he left with a choked laugh, and I returned to my studies. But his words continued to trouble me. Escape velocity? What could he mean by that? I abandoned my scrolls for a few minutes and went through the door that led into the part of the library where the normal books were kept. The rival astrological and astronomical tomes leaned on one another at drunken angles like weary revellers, and beyond them were the texts on rocketry, a relatively eccentric discipline back then. Bound collections of lectures and articles by Ganswindt, Tsiolkovsky, Esnault-Pelterie, Maul, Goddard, Oberth, and others greeted my roving eye.

One morning a few days later a muffled explosion awoke me, and I hauled myself out of bed and strode to the window. An outbuilding was smoking furiously but was still intact, and I saw the wooden door clatter open and a man stagger out. It was my moral duty to help, so I went down in unlaced boots. The man was kneeling at a trough.

He cupped his hands and lifted the water to his charred face again and again, but the grime was slow in coming off. I stood behind him, uncertain of what to say. "An accident?" was the opening gambit I eventually chose, and he turned to face me with a sardonic grin. The soot streaks on his face were as savagely artistic as tribal tattoos.

"No, a success. A success that was most unexpected."

I glanced at the burning outhouse. "You experiment with explosives in there?" My tone was prim, almost chiding.

"Not exactly." He climbed to his feet and dried his face on his shirt. A short man, his completely bald head gleamed in the early sunlight. "It's a propulsion system actually. A sort of pulse engine, but the fuel is new. I'm making progress every day, thank god!"

I scrutinized him carefully. "You are a monotheist?"

A crass question, and I had no motive for asking it, nor did I care what answer he gave, but he laughed. "Thank the *gods* then, if you prefer. The important thing is progress, always that."

"Progress." I rubbed my chin thoughtfully. "But—"

"But what exactly *is* progress?" He finished the question for me. "The facilities here are good, better than I ever expected, and that's enough for me. Back in Ruthenia the opportunities were thinner. So there's personal progress out here in the middle of nowhere." Then he leaned his head on the side and corrected himself. "Perhaps this is the middle of everywhere and the bleakness is just a cruel illusion."

"Are you suffering from concussion?" I asked him.

He waved a blistered hand. "I need a drink, a proper strong drink, and a chair to sit on while I enjoy it. I wonder how long it will be before Jones comes to inspect the damage? He won't be annoyed; the crucial thing for him is that I obtain results. And I have."

"Come back to my quarters," I said at once.

He accepted my offer and sat on my chair. I fetched him a gourd of steaming *yerba mate* from the kitchens, which he sipped with a smile and tightly closed eyes. "Most welcome!"

I introduced myself, adding, "I'm a translator."

"And I'm an engineer," he replied, then he thrust out his hand to shake mine; a firm grip. "Isaac Rajchman."

I was stupefied. "But Jones doesn't— Is he aware?"

"That I'm Jewish? Of course!"

"But I thought . . . He has peculiar ideas about racial groups, especially the Jews. When I first arrived he harangued me for hours about how the destiny of the Celts has been sabotaged by your people. Although I don't share his views, I listened meekly enough. I needed the work. His heroes are prophets of racial inequality."

Rajchman slurped his drink and shrugged.

"He's also a pragmatist. He'll use whatever help comes his way in this godforsaken outpost." He winked. "*Gods*forsaken, I mean, if that plural is grammatically acceptable to you."

I laughed. "I was impertinent earlier."

He held up his free hand. "No need to explain or apologise. I escaped Ruthenia on foot; the pogroms there were too regular and bloody for my liking. I went to Germany, then France and Spain, but I can't say the welcome in those countries was encouraging enough to make me want to stay. So I emigrated to Patagonia and here I am. Jones isn't the worst boss one might have in these dark times."

I cleared my throat. "Are they really so dark?"

"The darkness is coming, I'm certain of that. We're still groping in the twilight, the half-light of humanity." He placed down the empty gourd on the little table next to the chair and stretched his limbs. "Well, I must get back to work. It's a momentous day."

"But your equipment . . . Surely it was destroyed?"

"Indeed so. And doubtless Jones will have to send to Buenos Aires for more. But I must write up my notes. That's the real work now. I have just proved that a process hitherto only theoretical can be adapted for practical ends. It's a new energy source with phenomenal potential. The stars are a little nearer now, that's all I will say."

"Is Giraldus Jones a practical man or a dreamer?"

"He is both. Farewell, Mr Gower."

"I hope we might find time for further discussions before humanity's half-light turns to impenetrable dusk."

He waved a hand cheerfully. "Why not?"

And then he left my room. I paced to the window and stared out. Jones was standing before the smoking outbuilding, craning through the gaping doorway and calling anxiously for Rajchman. The contradictory nature of the self-proclaimed king was openly on display. He called to his peons to fetch buckets of water. Then Rajchman himself appeared and said something to Jones; the king wept, presumably with joy. This scene disturbed me, and I hurried to the cocoon of the library.

My work was completed after seven gruelling months. Of the four million pages, only thirty thousand consisted of spells, sigils, and magic formulae, and I had separated these in accordance with my instructions. Jones came to view the relevant scrolls and his humour was vast, typically Welsh and fulsome, almost whimsically aggressive.

"Excellent, Mr Gower! We must celebrate your achievement." And he told me that he intended to throw a dinner in my honour. "All parts of my grand scheme are coming along nicely!"

"Parts? I thought my work was complete in itself."

"No, no, it's just one more piece in a large project. I have blacksmiths and carpenters working on other parts; and Rajchman, my little engineer, you have met already. He's a genius . . ."

His eyes glazed over and he grinned; he had genuine affection for the Jew from Ruthenia. Here was paradox incorporated, a man bursting with racial bias violating his own ignorance.

I resisted the temptation to enquire further about his project, assuming he would resist revealing it to me; it was the first time he had mentioned a unity of purpose among the diverse commissions of his regime. This was a mistake, I later realised, for he was always happy to share the details of his integrated dream. To him it was obvious that a link existed between a collection of ancient scrolls and a new propulsion system, but for me they were the discrete eccentricities of an egotist. Jones, in my estimation, was no different from all previous autodidactic despots of this southern wedge—a simple adventurer like Julius Popper, Orélie-Antoine de Tounens, George Chaworth Musters, or Antonio Soto, a seeker of opportunity, not a creator or benefactor; certainly not an intellectual.

And in that judgement I was also partly wrong. . . .

He arranged the celebratory dinner for the following evening, and then with a final approving glance at the pile of scrolls, he said, "They will fit, all of them, I'm sure of it!" And departed.

I borrowed a horse and rode off into the wilderness to relax.

A few peons dug irrigation canals outside the grounds of the palace, a motley collection of sulky individuals, hired workers from the forests on the far side of the Andes, tough and silent; and they barely acknowledged my presence as I cantered past. Usually placid, they were known to burst suddenly with long repressed fury. The first overseer employed by Jones ended his last working day with his head on an improvised pike, nodding slowly to the saraband steps of his murderers.

Deep down I sympathised with these oppressed vassals.

But in those times, those callow and vicious days, open prejudice was regarded as normal behaviour and nobody else voiced support for natives, whether local or imported, and so I kept quiet. To rant *against* justice and fair play was considered good manners; Jones regarded it as the height of learning to quote Gobineau or Bismarck on the natural inequalities of the various races; but to whisper a word expressing approval of diversity was an offence that would earn instant exile.

And yet he doted on Rajchman. It was baffling.

I crested a rise and peered down into a crater below me. At once I was assailed by two visions, one internal, one external, and both affected me so strongly that I almost slipped from my saddle. The internal vision was another glimpse into the past of twenty-six millennia ago, the cruel cities and laughter, the temples studded with tiny crystals that sparkled with the extinct colours of that horrid age; and the external vision was an omen of the future, a static image, an inverted teardrop, silver and riveted, resting on broad fins, a celestial fish or torpedo.

I rubbed my eyes. The first mirage dissolved, but the second remained. No, it wasn't a delusion at all, not a psychic glimpse of days to come but a fact of the present, undeniable and solid.

The crater had been neatly scooped out of the earth by the impact of a meteorite in forgotten times, and now it hosted a machine that yearned for the stars, as if the blast of that vaporised space stone had congealed into a new form capable of leaping back into the void. I had devoured novels by Verne, Wells, Zamyatin, and others; I knew what I was staring at. It was a rocket ship, a space ark aimed at heaven.

Rajchman stood on a gantry with a metal cone pressed to his mouth, a megaphone, though he mainly directed operations with the gestures of his free hand. Peons obeyed without hesitation. They were loading boxes and crates. I rode down the steep inner wall of the crater, sending small stones rolling, but not a single glance was directed towards me. I called cheerily to the engineer, whom I regarded as a kindred spirit if not a true friend, but he behaved as if I were invisible and mute.

Nobody moved to obstruct me, but I had a strong feeling that I wasn't welcome, so I rode around the rocket once and then returned up the crater wall back to level ground. I had seen what cargo they were loading, and it left me in a state of very mild shock. The ship was being crammed, for no sane reason, with those scrolls I had separated from the dross, the magical works, the texts latticed with arcane spells.

I couldn't begin to guess Jones's intentions. He was thoroughly mad, I reassured myself; that was the only answer. In the evening I stood on the balcony outside my window with a pair of powerful binoculars. I scanned the glittering dome with an eagerness that astonished me, and there was an undeniable pull to the South Celestial Pole. I explored Octans star by star and drank the rays of each distant sun with an insatiable mental thirst, and then I finally resolved the pitiful spark of Sigma Octantis into a wan glow only slightly brighter and steadier than the evil gleam that might be found in the bulging eye of a dying man or horse.

I was both happy and unnerved when I learned that Rajchman was also a guest at my celebratory dinner the following night. The three of us sat on decaying chairs while a stooped servant shuffled to and from the kitchens and set down the dishes before us with toothless merriment, as if the joke were the food and the food of no consequence. The banqueting table was a warped monstrosity, dominating the largest chamber of the king's palace, covered with mysterious stains that often took the form of faces. Only the bust of Bismarck at the far end conferred a degree of normality, grotesque though his presence should have been.

Jones was already drunk, and he became effusive.

"You have no idea, Mr Gower, none at all, of what momentous events are about to take place in the world, and yet you are partly responsible for them! Imagine a guillotine, if you will. Every part must fit together neatly and operate smoothly, the frame, the rope and blade, even the neck that is to be sliced must interact with perfect precision. I regard your work as no speck inferior to that of dear Isaac here."

Rajchman shifted uneasily on his seat and blinked.

Jones called to his stooped servant for more wine; then he threw back his head and shouted at the ceiling, "Heroic is the word for us!" And he insisted on toasting me again and again.

"I merely did what I was hired to do," I said quietly, prodding the pale lump on the plate before me with a fork.

"You are a Celt, sir!" he boomed. "Just like me!"

"Well, those distinctions—"

He slammed his fist down on the table; the crockery jumped. "Listen! Why should all mankind share the same zodiac? Why should the Celt be limited to the same astrological influences as the dullards of other races? Would you share a soup spoon with a savage, Mr Gower? Of course not! And yet you are content to share Venus, Mars, and Saturn. This absurdity must not be allowed to endure longer!"

I laughed. "You propose to reorder the planets?"

He glowered, acutely disappointed at my obtuseness. "There is no call for whimsical idiocies, Mr Gower. Have you forgotten that the Celt is the best human being there is? Only he is comparable to the men who walked this planet before history began. On the ground around us are no remains of that magnificent race, no stone or glass, no shard of pottery or scrap of poetry; but in our blood they live still!"

I let go of my fork as if it were a nettle and turned my aching head with geological stiffness to stare directly into his face. "To prove what you are suggesting isn't feasible! You can't really believe the Welsh are the direct descendants of those lost Patagonians?"

"Yes indeed! Why not? There is a strong magnetism about this region that draws only our kind. Think about it. The only colony Wales has ever sought to establish. Here of all places! There must be a deeper connection to explain that. We are the scions, you and I, of those obscure, wondrous people, the heirs of their attitudes and faith. So it is time we started living again as they once did. Our birthright . . ."

I was at a loss for words. Nor could I expect help from Rajchman, who seemed engrossed in his deplorable feast.

Finally I spoke. "No amount of manipulation in the world will change the present lifestyle of the Welsh people. They are too thoroughly wedded to the culture that exists *now*. You will never be able to persuade or bribe them to abandon beer, rugby, and choral singing for the morbid delights of life in a city that reflects no light at all. Those simple pastimes are the true gods of the average modern Welshman."

I had meant this partly as a joke, to lighten the mood around the table, but Jones slammed his fist down again on the stained surface, making the crockery dance an encore. "Those pathetic idols of thin substance will be abandoned with haste once the deities of real power are accessible again! Adrift in the spaces between the worlds, they are now; but they can come together again and orbit our planet in a line. I have the power to make this happen, the ability to return them to us."

"I see," I said, not knowing how else to respond.

His voice dropped an octave. "There has always been only one zodiac, Mr Gower, just one that controls the destinies of all people. But that will never do. There must be another for the chosen race, for us alone, for the Celt. We are different, you see, and we should rule over the others in the same way those interplanetary gods will rule over us. Listen to me. I plan to send an artificial planet into space."

"I saw the rocket ship," I replied rather primly.

He drained his wine glass. "I commissioned Rajchman to design it for me, and he did so, most cunningly. My new planet, or satellite, will pass over the constellations, just as the ordinary planets do, but perpendicular to them, creating a new zodiac as it orbits our world, for what is a zodiac other than an apparent superimposition of planets on stars? Nothing. Our familiar zodiac is aligned east-west along the ecliptic; my new one will be aligned north-south, from pole to pole!"

I found it impossible not to protest at this juncture.

"With respect," I ventured, "astrology doesn't work. It's a superstition without any mechanism to enable it to—"

"Gravity, Mr Gower. That's the answer. The moon creates tides in the oceans; our brains are made of water. Gravity! The planets pull our ideas in different directions. It *does* work."

I shook my head vigorously. "The moon creates tides in the seas only because there is a very large surface area to act upon; have you ever seen tides in a wine glass?" And I lifted my own glass in derision. "Of course not! The amount of gravitational pull from each planet is tiny, about the same as that of a tram or bus passing in an adjacent street in any bustling city. This is nonsense. Your rocket ship will make a pretty light in the sky but nothing more than that. Forget it."

But Jones had an answer on his lips, and he let it expand until my ears throbbed painfully. "*Spiritual* gravity, Mr Gower. Not the ordinary kind. Shall I list the members of my new improved zodiac? Octans, Reticulum, Horologium, Eridanus, Taurus, Perseus, Camelopardalis, Ursa Minor, Draco, Hercules, Corona Borealis, Scorpius, Lupus, Triangulum Australe, and Apus. Fifteen signs in total." He summoned yet more wine from the stooped servant, drank it, and then frowned. "The two zodiacs intersect at two points. That should be interesting."

I filled my own throat with wine in desperation.

"And it's highly satisfying," he added blithely, "that both Polaris and Sigma Octantis are points on the route."

I felt the weight of his insanity crushing my mind.

"Your satellite will never achieve an orbit of such precision. How will you steer it from the ground?" I cried.

Jones's eyes bulged, but he wasn't angry. I saw that he was suppressing great horrible mirth, but not out of consideration for my feelings. He was building up the pressure to derive greater relief when it was released. But I scraped the leg of my chair, as if preparing to stand up and storm out of the chamber, so he spoke with alacrity:

"From the ground? I don't plan on steering it from the ground! No, the science of remote-control systems is insufficiently advanced for that. So it seems that little Isaac here must sit inside the capsule and pilot the vessel by hand. It will be dreadfully cramped, but there is just enough room. I'm confident he will be able to position it correctly once it passes outside the atmosphere. He's clever in many ways."

I sneered. "And how do you propose to get him back?"

"Get him back!" Jones was amazed.

"Well, I don't suppose you intend to leave him up there forever?" And I offered Rajchman a grotesque smile.

"I do intend that, Mr Gower. How insightful of you!" Jones rubbed his palms together like a demented djinn.

"Don't do it," I barked at Rajchman.

"I have no choice, no real choice," he whispered.

"What do you mean? Just ride away from this place. You can't be kept against your will, can you? Leave!"

Jones leaned forward and said softly, "There is a Jewish colony in the hinterlands of Paraguay. My allies there, the German settlers, don't enjoy the proximity very much; the reason they left the fatherland was to escape such neighbours. They think a modest pogrom might be worthwhile, but so far I have dissuaded them from taking such action. But if Isaac refused to help me with my schemes, well . . ."

It took a monumental effort not to choke; I hung my head as I realised that the relationship between the two was less paradoxical than it seemed. It was a simple case of coercion, blackmail. All I could think of to say in the circumstances was, "You'll kill him for no reason. Your zodiac won't work. Even if what you say about spiritual gravity is true, one satellite in orbit will have a negligible effect on the masses below. And how will you build others without Rajchman's aid?"

Jones was delighted. He jumped up and yelled:

"At last we reach the crux of the matter! As well as holding Isaac, the capsule will also take into space all the spells and sigils of our ancestors. Those spells are designed to call those gods. Unaffected by the distortions of atmosphere, the words chanted by Isaac will have real power: when the gods hearken to them they will come. They will detach themselves from the voids they occupy and drift towards our globe. Then they will follow the satellite around our world forever, in a pulsing line. And *they* will be the other planets in my new zodiac. Spheres of rock, ice, and gas will rule ordinary men, but authentic gods will govern the horoscopes of the Celts. Yes, gods! The gods of our ancestors!"

He paused for breath or perhaps for effect.

"Some men say that those gods are nameless. But I know the names of most of them. Would you like to hear?"

Then he threw back his head, opened his jaw so wide that I suspect he dislocated it, and bellowed a litany of awful sounds, so loathsome that my blood turned sluggish. I pressed my hands to my ears, but I couldn't keep out the words, the awful inhuman names, the appalling syllables that soon saturated my soul with black despair; and I screamed as loud as my lungs would permit, but my mind filled up nonetheless with fragmentary images suggested by those names, with disembodied claws, flabby jowls, haunted faces, tentacles, tendrils, and evil hearts.

I fell into a depression, and the following weeks were drab and vile. Only occasionally did I venture from my rooms and rarely did I speak to other residents. I did consider sabotaging the rocket ship, but some subtle force held me in a state of torpid inaction. Whether it was the cumulative effect of landscape, climate, and local culture, or whether Jones was somehow to blame, a vast apathy swallowed me up.

On the day of the proposed launch, I managed to rouse myself to make the journey to the crater; but as I neared the stables to choose a horse for that purpose, I was intercepted by Rajchman, who stepped from around a corner, as if he had been awaiting me. He was smiling, but beads of sweat studded his forehead, tiny rainbows appearing inside each drop as the sun rose over the roofs of nearby buildings.

"Glad you came this way," he said in a low voice.

"Rajchman, don't you think you ought to reconsider? I know that you are worried about your compatriots in—"

"If I don't do it, Jones will force some other Jew to take my place. He can find and compel them easily enough."

"Perhaps if we try speaking sense to him again?"

From the corner of his mouth, like a ventriloquist, Rajchman suddenly hissed at me, "Take a fast horse and ride in the opposite direction. Go as fast as you can. The rocket is a bomb."

I blinked foolishly at him and gaped. He added:

"What kind of man do you think I really am? I didn't design the craft to fly but to explode on the ground! A new kind of propulsion system. I told you this already. Atoms smash into other atoms. I don't have time to explain. Just be very far away by noon."

"Do you think the blast might kill Jones too?"

Rajchman gestured at the entire surroundings and nodded. There was something unarguable in his demeanour. An urgency gripped me; I ran to the stables, selected a horse, and settled myself into the saddle. "Goodbye, my friend!" I called as I rode out, but the engineer had gone. I never saw him again. I spurred my steed to the east.

The further I went from Jones's domain the more energised I felt, and I cursed myself for allowing the madman to attenuate my willpower. But it was pointless to fret about that now. I rode hard, propelled by Rajchman's warnings. Over the endless pampas I went. And then, when the sun was at its highest point and I cast no natural shadow on the ground, an unnatural shadow appeared ahead of me, a monstrously distended horse and man, a mutated burnt centaur on a frozen lake. . . .

A light so bright that it seemed to bleach the lush grass had caused this mirage. There was no lake, no ice; the whiteness was false. Had I looked back over my shoulder I would have turned blind, for this was obviously the glare of a bursting god's soul. And then the blast struck me; I tumbled and rolled on the ground and my clothes were lashed by a wind from hell and I screamed and cursed and thrashed.

When the blast had dissipated, I opened my eyes. In the western sky a cloud was rising, building higher, blossoming like a foetid jungle growth, a tower of vaporised debris, wood, stone, bones, blood, and thoughts. And it began to rain, particles as fine as soot.

A few scraps of annihilated scroll drifted down.

The ash of spells coated my face.

Nothing else that could be recognised survived.

And I wondered if anyone would even notice that Jones had vanished from history. In those open spaces, a self-crowned king might easily lose everything and the outside world care nothing. But if he had succeeded in his grandiose schemes, in reawakening that cosmic brutality and closing a dark circle twenty-six millennia old—

I didn't care to speculate on that. I still don't.

My horse had galloped away without me. I began the long walk over a series of undulating plains. When night fell I kept going. Sleeping under *those* stars was beyond my endurance.

I made my way to Rawson. I found a job and earned enough money to pay my passage back home. I could no longer tolerate the night sky of the southern hemisphere, its weight. When I crossed the equator my glee was intense; and yet my worries weren't resolved yet. In Rhossili I found the northern stars almost as disagreeable, for the empty spaces between them were alive with horrors, with gods my distant ancestors had feared, hated, and worshipped, a pantheon of madness.

My only escape was to move a place where bright lights drowned out all starlight. And now I dwell in London, alone in an attic, troubled only by notions of spiritual gravity and the possible astrological effect of each passing tram or bus in an adjacent street.

The Century Just Gone

New Year's Eve, 1999.

Two men in the attic of a tall house.

A failed party. Cheap whisky.

The shadows outside were drum membranes. The city boomed as dancers stamped another alleyway to death.

Rats fled and lonely talk turned strange.

Floyd wiped a thumbprint off his glass. He swirled its contents and said: "The twentieth century was a knife!"

Vance shook his head. "No, it was a gun!"

"That's not cruel enough. The metaphor has to be *nasty*. A gun's too fast and cold. Sure, there's something in it for the nose, but the smell of cordite doesn't make it a vintage weapon, not on its own. A gun can't get under the skin. There's no point licking it clean. You either use it or you don't. A digital tool. It's bang! or hush! Life or death, nothing between. No way of using it gradually or barely using it. It pulps parts of the brain which feel pain. Death without threat of torture. The knife peels a mind into segments of fear."

Vance dabbed his lips with a napkin as he smiled, so only his green eyes showed his amusement. "Introductions, do you mean? Whispers in ears as you deliver the fatal strike?" He folded the cloth and replaced it in a pocket. "I've never killed a man."

"How about a woman, baby, dog?"

"Not even a mouse, I'm afraid."

"Afraid? You'd be less of that if you *had* eliminated something. The more we destroy, the safer we grow."

"Are you confessing to murder?"

"I doubt it. A philosophical point, not a motto. We're the victims.

229

Our consciences are clear and thus we are vulnerable, a target for every pervert who is reminded of a shiny blade when he looks in a mirror. What is the only way for *us* to remain alive? Be like them, of course! In this attic, innocent and powerless, we're asking for a snuffing. What are the chances of an assassin dying in exactly the same way as he's killed? Too small to be calculated, I should imagine. The more nasty the murder, the better your insurance against fate."

"You've lost me now. I don't understand."

Floyd sighed and stood. He walked to the window and peered out, but saw little beyond the glow of the streetlamp which stood adjacent to the house, almost touching it. A bubble of drizzle, seemingly created by the hissing bulb from the general dark dampness, was the main feature. But a blend of sounds from below—laughter, shouting, and the drum city—proved there was existence outside this hermetic sphere of sick light. Clasping his hands behind his back, he nodded at this unseen life, jealous of the mirth. He muttered: "It's a policy."

And because his meaning was still opaque, he added: "I'm attempting to state something obvious in a mysterious way. Skin a man alive and get caught. Prison, yes, maybe a noose, depending on where in this world you dwell, but the chances of being skinned yourself are reduced. Almost for certain, you *won't* be skinned. No such guarantees for the innocent. That is the rub, or flay, if you prefer."

"I agree that no murderers I can recall ever died in the exact same way as their victims, but I don't accept there's any physical connection between a brutal act and a personal fate milder than it. The explanation is sociological, a quirk of the culture which apprehends the assassin, a specific taste in justice at that time. Very few modern moralities match the punishment to the crime because they prefer, or pretend, to advocate reason rather than symmetry. But that's not mathematical. To assert that *performing* evil somehow provides statistical protection from *enduring* it is fallacious causation. Seeing inappropriate connections is a myopia of the human inner eye."

Floyd lowered his voice. "I can't think of any other hypothesis for why this century, almost over at last, was so full of serial killers and sadists, sexual perverts and lethal parasites. The standard explanations just don't convince me. A better rate of detection? Absolutely. The doom of community spirit? Without doubt. The forsaking of religious morality? Beyond dispute. And yet, and yet. . . ."

"I know. It doesn't account for the madness."

"Not *truly*, not emotionally. I feel there's something else. Call it a malign spirit, if you like, a warped *Zeitgeist*. The twentieth century, as I announced before, was a knife."

"A sharp analogy. But not all monsters used one."

"Some probably unsheathed the loneliness, the confusion, the irony. Like us, they were just dislikable."

"Nobody has come to our party because we don't know anyone else. We haven't got any friends left to invite."

"Our own fault, or possibly our secret hope?"

"You're right. But what a way to spend the most precious New Year's Eve of our lives! Insulting the previous century. I speak like that with excessive confidence, for it's almost midnight and too late for anything wonderful to turn up and redeem it."

"Scorning its demons? Can't think of a more worthy thing to do. And there was a glut. So who was the worst?"

"No, who was the cleverest? A superior question."

"Maybe the same thing. Do we include figures from organisations and official ideals? If so, the task is boring, for the usual suspects march all over it, stamping on whatever it was they found inside themselves to abominate. I think Reinhard Heydrich would top my list, maybe Pol Pot or Bokassa or Bormann. No, on sickened thoughts I'll have Mao during one of his Leaps Forward. He hopped backward, of course, and that reminds me of Sports Day at my old school, when one of the games included throwing the symbolic cricket ball down a field. The girls always bowled underarm for some arcane reason, and half of them forgot to release it on the *forward* curve of their launch. How we sniggered to watch the ball fly over their heads and finally land *behind* them!"

Vance was astounded, but then he remembered that the truths of life are the same for all its subjects, according to species. He cried: "That happened in my school too. Even the girls I had a crush on did that, and I wasn't sure whether to celebrate or ignore the differences between us. In the end I opted to mock, perhaps more openly than you. They sobbed at my giggles, but I felt no guilt, still don't. Incompetence is funny, and ruination of beauty is educational."

"Yes, let's be satisfied with that metaphor. Mao hurled his country in the style of a girl. It flipped as it flew. There was a crush too, as in your case, but harder. Ponder on those words, dear friend. *Style of a girl!* I have a less precise idea of what they signify now than before. I wonder why we don't know any females? We don't happen to be misogynists, do we? I don't feel quite like one."

"You've never had a proper opportunity."

"We'll make a decision now to leave out monsters who were agents of systems. It doesn't have much to do with what I was saying. The bullying minions of Hitler and Stalin, the men themselves, were just variables in a dud equation. It's the individualists, the ones outside the local law, however unfair the context of justice, who should intrigue us. They spin the lottery of fate with axe, mallet, saw. They whip it round with silk scarf, thuggee style. They squat in their own brains at night, where it never stops raining, even indoors."

Vance said: "Poison is the way to do it. Remember that tea-boy with the penchant for thallium? Bitter case."

"A diabolical substance, but he only killed two. His name, I think, was Graham Young. Stir crazy before he was jailed. That could be a joke, but I'll have to check. Another go."

"David Berkowitz? Courting couples, New York, 1977."

"Only six victims for him, though I accept that romance took a back seat that summer due to his antics, or maybe not. So I'll play a pair of long Johns, Haigh and Christie, in chronothanatological order, to coin a word. And that's what once paid the official ferryman into hell: a coin, I mean, not a John, however long, and that pair were certainly extended after they swung for it. Haigh sucked blood, dissolved victims in acid. Christie walled them up, other stuff."

"The worst? Albert Fish, painter and decorator and cannibal. Boiled girls with carrots and potatoes. Indulged in self-mutilation when alone. Happy to be electrocuted in 1936, shorted his chair, so it was said. Too many needles jangling about in his scrotum. Been pushing them in most of his life. Polymorphic pervert. Rusty old man!"

"Fifteen victims at least. But Carl Panzram didn't molest the weak. He went for the strong, more than twenty of them. Hanged in 1930, his last words revealed a gruff wit: 'While you're fooling around, I could hang a dozen men.' I wonder if he really could? And who might they be? Would he hang other killers? Fritz Haarmann?"

"Ah, yes, the butcher of Hanover. Panzram was stronger but Haarmann was more devious. Killed men by biting their throats, sold them as meat, disposed of bones in the River Leine. Depressed economy, dark stairwells full of fluttering newspaper. Strings of sausages from human guts. Clean them out first? I doubt it. The wurst!"

"Either of them stand a chance against Bela Kiss? Who knows if his total was higher than Haarmann's? Picked up girls in Budapest, pickled them in oil-drums at home. His secret was discovered, but he swapped his identity with a soldier killed in May 1916. Never caught. Spotted three years later crossing a city bridge."

"Too far? Or not far enough? Peter Kürten *wanted* to get caught. And more than that, he lusted after his execution. The Vampire of Düsseldorf was decapitated on 1 July 1932. Final question: 'Will I still be able to hear, at least for a moment, the sound of my own blood gushing from the stump of my neck?' And what's the right answer? Poor Peter's hopes were cut short by his head rolling out of range of the spurt. Or maybe it was kicked there? Both options will do."

"No subtlety in that lunacy. And hardly any fun. John Wayne Gacy is my next candidate. The killer clown. Strangle, stab! No, I can think of another from the 1970s. Theodore Bundy. Club, stab, strangle! That's an extra outrage, plus three more corpses. Official tally, thirty-six. Actually, it doesn't sound so many when spoken like that. I'll pass over to you while I search my memory for someone new."

"Dr Marcel Petiot. Guillotined in 1946. Befriended Jewish refugees, stole their money, incinerated them. Oily slick on his clothes and hair. Gestapo turned a blind eye and file. A freelance Nazi in the basics, but the women adored him. That Gallic brutality works like a charm. Stubble, garlic, handsome shrugs, hot death."

"The Nazi era? Thanks for reminding me. Bruno Ludke. Simple rob and stab. But I bet you can't trump him. Grey, slippery. Eighty-five victims minimum. Captured by the SS and reserved for medical experiments. I can't imagine what they tested on him. A cure for the common cold? Or a remedy for the human condition? Strange to think they wanted to *give* him something with a scalpel. It normally takes. But he's a high mark in this sickness, for he was surely the most prolific, the most promiscuous, and his very last moment, his nemesis, was also evil."

"Wrong again! Haven't you heard of Pedro Lopez? Nothing left in the pack now. Three hundred innocents, though perhaps some of them had guilty secrets, but I mustn't argue with the wording of conventional sympathy. He wasn't even executed after his capture. There isn't a death penalty in Ecuador. Too bad for the hills, the equator."

Floyd grinned and exhaled in bitter acknowledgement. "Well, you win *that* game. You surprise me, dear friend. I had thought my morbidity more developed than yours. Unhappily, lists of these sort prove nothing. What I need to learn is who would come out on top if they were pitted against one another, the century's dirtiest, the hundred worst, whoever they are, under controlled conditions. A special environment or arena. What a gift to the memories of their victims! A gladiatorial battle, using their own weapons and tricks. In an arena."

Vance chuckled. "What's this? A righteous revenge fantasy? I've had them too. Why stop at a hundred?"

"Pure logistics. The arena can't be too big or cramped. Best not to lump our top athletes in with minor criminals. Loners need room to move, duck, run, hide, and strike. And the names soon get dull further down the list. There's quality as well as quantity, and many kinds of luck inside different men. Just because Lopez killed more than Haarmann doesn't mean he's got ten times as much horror in his soul. If they don't meet, fight, and die, we'll never know. The jury will remain out. I like the sound of that legal phrase. It dilutes the depravity of our curiosity. If only we had the power to make it happen!"

"Yes, if only. The arena. If only."

"A desperate way to cross the threshold of a new millennium? But we have a social conscience, that's clear."

"The arena. We're not so weak, after all."

They nodded to themselves as a substitute for silent contemplation, bones clicking and grinding in their necks. Stiff and tense from knowing what was right and from impotence, they affirmed their own courage, safe in an awareness it vindicated their faults, the loneliness and mistrust. If only. The arena. And the little bones continued to click, the keys of a gutted piano, mandibles of an invisible insect. If only. And the dream of the ultimate contest cooled slowly, like a cuffed lip or smoking gun, but the twentieth century couldn't be that. It was a knife and needed to be tested, a final test, each tooth of its serrated blade at war against the others. A slow cool, glowing.

"If only we had a single guest!"

The doorbell didn't ring, but the party livened up.

The visitor was probably an angel.

But Floyd and Vance thought: *maggot!* It was the filthy white colour and segmented body which deceived them. Also how it rippled and writhed. Still it stood upright, and its compound eyes were full of points of hard intelligence, all glittering in complex patterns, as if it were computing data connected with its sudden arrival, such as the shapes of the eddies in the disturbed atmosphere of this room, a series of calculations which in fact it could do. It folded one pair of arms and touched the palms of a second, as if praying to itself.

Floyd poured himself a drink. He didn't spill a drop. "What's this? The end of the world for real? Good timing!"

Vance was more rational but equally incorrect. "An extraterrestrial being? We are not our leaders. Can't even take you to them. Why not rest here and tell us about your home world?"

"He might want us for a zoo."

"Better than this attic nonsense. Imagine it! A cage on some planet on the far side of the galaxy. Endangered species and all that. They may want us to breed, fetch us girls."

The angelic maggot spoke: "I'm quite human."

"Come now," laughed Floyd. "We're not falling for that old trick. A typical *real* person doesn't materialise from thin air. At least never in my experience, which despite its manifold frustrations is *wide*. So knock that joke on its slightly slimy head and remove your costume. Three at a party is a merely pathetic quantity."

"Whereas two is no party at all," added Vance.

The visitor considered the situation and shuffled a step forward. A titanic burst of will enabled Floyd to hold his position, but he refused to look at the moving feet, or whatever stood in for them. He tapped the bottle on the table. "Help yourself."

"I can't drink. I'm a sort of projection."

"From our sick minds, you mean?"

"Not there. From your coherent futures," the creature lisped, as it rocked unsteadily on the carpet. "Thousands of millennia beyond. Note my careful research. I speak. And now I pause for you to understand. I have an offer. You let me in. I am ready."

"Suit yourself," said Floyd. "Don't mind me."

He drank from the bottle while Vance blurted: "How did we do that? Let you in, I mean. Can't recall issuing invitations to any future. Know what a gatecrasher is? A freeloader?"

The maggot bowed. "I talk fluent colloquial."

"Do you now?" scoffed Floyd. "Isn't that rich? Try us with some, to confirm the claim. Or is it a bluff?"

The visitor licked its lips, helping its tongue complete the motion by guiding it with finger and thumb. It mumbled: "You're a creep, a pair of creeps. You are suckers, also a pair."

All Vance could think to say was: "Not bad."

"I shall try to obey you," it added, "but you must help me first. A point of principle. Give me permission."

"To do what exactly? Don't ask me. Ask Floyd."

"Cosmic truth. I am from a moral race, a moral humanity. Your ideas are right. I can implement them now."

Floyd hurled his bottle, aiming at the creature's head. It was more than an impulse, but he was at a loss to understand why he had thrown it so soon, and why he had just missed.

He said: "I won't humour you. That last and first men stuff doesn't inspire me. I have enough problems with the middle kind. Go back to your sense of wonder, the Rings of Saturn, wherever. The century's as good as over. It was packed with incident, more than enough. There's a minute or so left. Don't burst it at this late stage. The detonation might concuss something in the next. We're tired."

"Me too," said the creature, yawning, displaying crystalline teeth, arranged in rows in stratified gums.

"Tired of what? Are we so simple to you?"

"Of waiting. Not for your answer but my question. Now I give it. If all has proceeded to plan, we are what mankind will become. The rules of morality have been perfected for us. We have few cities, but many roads. Where they all meet there is an iridium tower on which is carved all our laws. We are harsh, sublime. Your remote descendants will appreciate and comply. We are flooded with justice, and now it overflows into old worlds such as yours. I am a missionary."

Floyd rubbed his hand, aching from where he had clenched the bottle too hard. "So that's your position? You have scientific powers? An envoy from the shape of things to come? Back to clean up our act. That's nice, truly it is. I'm happy for you." He continued to clench again, on air, a packet of cigarettes, reflexively.

"I may not adjust without permission."

"Do what you like, mister. I look forward to watching a maggot work a few miracles. How many millions of years separate your kind from ours? Almost glad I can't find a girlfriend now, if there's any chance I might be your ancestor. But carry on. You have my full consent to interfere in the running of our society, anyhow, anyway. I don't see fit to disagree. The future must know what's best."

"Slowly," said Vance. "We don't know what he means. Don't sign away our rights just yet. Not so fast."

"It's safe. He doesn't look too well."

The visitor seemed to throb, a convulsion as if something large were hatching inside. A rub of damp wings, pressure pushing the pale segments apart, thin membranes expanding into windows, trapezoidal portholes into its internal mechanics. There *was* another creature within, glutinous and gossamer, and very big, curled up tight. One leg only was fully free and it probed the inner walls of its dungeon, entered the

translucent veins, tickled the heart, pushed but lost its grip on the pulsing organ, shared the vibration, ached and withdrew.

"My apologies. I haven't set properly."

Vance fought back his rising gorge. "A parasite? It's hideous. Like
a giant wasp. Also a moth. Fused."

"Merely another projection. A double exposure, if you will. Nothing fatal. I am here, primed. The focus back through time is difficult.
Many lenses are required. Don't trouble yourselves. The pain is mild.
Life is less diverse among the old stars. Different phyla combine at-
tributes and structures. And the sun is dying above our cities. But we
have morality. Plenty for our needs and surplus."

"Tell him to get to the point," snapped Floyd.

Vance said: "What can you do for us?"

"Your idea called me. It opened the door to my signal. We watch
and wait for such opportunities. You already believe in our justice.
Thus we favour you. In that sense you work for us. The arena, its
combat, is our faith also. We applaud its idealism, the balance. The selected deviants will be deposited at random coordinates within it. That
process is pure. Then they will turn upon one another, precisely as you
have posited. Only one may be preserved. They will know immediately. They must kill and die until a single loneliness remains."

"You have the fantasy too? The hundred worst?"

The creature began to deflate as its parasite was digested. And for
an instant Floyd thought he was watching a concertina ready to be
placed in its box and forgotten under a chair. But then it winked in a
new way, using the flap of skin between the sixth and seventh fingers
of one hand as an eyelid, and the musical resemblance was destroyed.
Its total aspect was glacial and disgusting, a combination close to paradoxical, until it puffed out its cheeks and warmed with the strain. Its
edges, lost behind perspective, turned crisp, charred.

Vance breathed sharply. "You're *not* human."

"Long mutations. Evolution. The men won, remember that. Remember it and rejoice. Despite the ice, the comets, we endured. And
when the world was sealed and frosted with bars of new elements,
massive atoms numbered as far above unnilhexium as gold is above

hydrogen, we retreated into our silk cocoons. Our rivals then were cosmic freaks. The men won because of morality. We emerged when they had decayed. We migrated to other planets and back. Morality saved us. We have utopia at last and it is empty, too bare of detail to shelter deviance."

"How will you set up our arena? With machines?"

The visitor nodded. "For us, that is easy. But we have a code. When we locate a time with a suitable idea, we act only after permission. Now I am ready. I await your decision."

"Will we be allowed to watch the contest?"

For the first time, the maggot seemed confused. "If you prefer. The screen here may be adapted. Behold."

Floyd was delighted. "The television?"

"A live show. With players abducted only from the twentieth century, as you specified. The men won, and now we can export our justice to other epochs. We share the ideal."

"The decent men, you mean? The good people."

"Most people are good, deep inside. We have confirmed this. We have arranged it. Describe your arena. Is it a city? A city of moderate size. An industrial city with sprawling suburbs. Such cities generate gravity, physical and hypnotic. The chosen hundred will converge. The patterns of death may be complex and fluid."

And now Floyd found the situation ironic rather than grotesque. The notion that this inhuman thing could provide belated justice for inhuman crimes was hilarious, awful, invigorating. Snatched back from graves and moulded from grease in crematory chimneys, the butchers and perverts of the sickest century would face themselves at last. And no innocents this time. The taste of their own medicine, surgical instruments, whatever it took. A comforting if somewhat bland thought that futuristic retribution was as compulsively consistent as ancient. Eye for eye, gut for gut. The cutting of the cutters. Perfect.

He nodded. "It's a city. Where else?"

Vance added: "An urban environment is correct for this contest, the narrow alleys, broken lamps, concrete tunnels and overpasses. That's the natural hunting ground of those predators. Slum, dosshouse, and sewer. No green spaces. All brown and black."

The visitor leaned forward, an angle impossible for it to maintain, but it seemed more secure in this position, stable, as if another ground pulled on its body from a different direction. It leaned until Vance saw Floyd's grinning lips, a thousand rubber grins, reflected in its faceted eyes. "But do you give permission?"

Floyd nodded. "Yes, you have it."

A clock struck twelve. It was midnight. The year 2000. There should have been fireworks outside, loud music, and perhaps there were, but the room seemed dipped in heavy light. It muffled all sounds, made the walls and furniture swim out of focus. The adjusting of unseen lenses, away in unknown ages, smooth and sharp.

The creature folded its arms, shimmered, snapped. It faded. Maggot, angel, man, it was gone. Stale air rushed to fill the vacant space, wind tinged with the odours of its body. There was a faint pop. Neither Floyd nor Vance smelled the future now, for the vacuum had also sucked the air from their nostrils. A reverse sniff. The absence was curious. It stank, symbolically. The silence was gone. The future was open. Unlike a bottle of champagne there was no cork.

Floyd rubbed his hands in glee. "So the party's only just started after all! We'll watch this together."

"Pull up a seat," said Vance, frowning.

He turned the set on. A picture appeared on the screen. A street in a city, lonely, silent, and damp.

No rats fled. Floyd stared at the hiss.

He jabbed at the remote control. A different street appeared. "Hey, it works. I can switch viewpoints by changing channels. We must be using surveillance cameras mounted at points all over the arena. And it's like a real city! Garbage, graffiti."

"Where are the contestants? The gladiators?"

"Give them time. Probably dazed, trying to reason out their sudden return to existence. Shall we make it a betting game? Spice up our wait until they emerge? And our little debate will be settled now, so one of us might as well make a profit."

"Chalk up the odds. What will you give me for Haarmann? 8–1? Think of a fair price for Ludke. 3–1?"

"Graham Young? 100–1. Little poisoner doesn't stand a chance. Lopez will snap him up for supper, if Kürten doesn't. Blow a kiss to Kiss when you see him! He'll be crossing a bridge, I shouldn't wonder. I fancy the Boston Strangler, Albert DeSalvo. No, his case was never proved. 45–1 at best. He may have been a patsy."

"I see nothing. It's dark. No lights."

"Well, it's an empty city. Empty except for our players. They could be in any of those houses. Who knows where they were deposited? Random, the maggot said. Petiot at 30–1. He hasn't got time to erect a furnace. Panzram and Lopez at 2–1, joint favourites. Brawn and rope, always good in a shopping precinct. No fooling around."

"What's behind that shadow? That one!"

Floyd squinted. "Another shadow. Sure it's moving. That's what all shadows do, fast or slow. It's not Berkowitz or Bundy. Keep changing to different cameras. There must be something. Seventy channels. That's an awful lot of cameras. No hurry."

"To hell with this. I'm going out for a walk. Follow the maggot's example, try to gatecrash a party. This is boring. It doesn't work. We must be imbeciles, sick idiots."

"You have no sense of history, Vance!"

Floyd continued to jab at the buttons of the remote control, and on the screen the roads came and went faster and faster. Vance's last sight of the television before he fled the attic showed him a moving image of one archetypal street, spinning, rotating, growing shadows, losing them. No mouths open for talk to turn strange. Just the geometry of the single street, its monochrome atmosphere.

He left the door ajar as he clattered down the stairs, throwing his jacket around his shoulders, feeling the slap of a pocket full of change against a kidney. He didn't wince. He decreased his pace, his left hand groping the banister like a girl's thigh, but going down, not up, as if he had developed a new fetish.

At the base of the stairwell, he kicked through the old newspapers, reached the front door. He was out. The night air was chill and pure.

No smoke, no sulphur. No fireworks? It wasn't right. He pushed on, hunching his shoulders along the pavement to the end of the street. He turned the corner, listened for sounds of revelry. There were none, and no lamps in any window. The city had become its own negative. He wasn't even sure if there were any colours left. And there was a perpetual hiss in his head—not traffic but the segmented sky.

He wandered deeper into the anomaly. He passed dead shops and blank pubs. Shadows and slithers always beyond, congealing. There was no sense of menace, and that in itself was extremely disturbing, for it suggested he had been stupefied by something worse. He didn't turn on his heel and run back, because of this awful immunity to horror. But he permitted his reason to lead him in a wide circle, a loop that brought him outside his front door again. He paused to glance up. And there was the blue flicker in the highest window, an aurora boreal-is captured and caged in a single pane. Silent, but a visual scream.

When he returned to the attic, he was surprised to find the cynical Floyd dancing among the furniture.

"Excellent joke. How did you manage it?"

"What do you mean? I didn't."

Floyd gestured at the screen, even though it still showed an empty road. "Famous now. On television!"

Vance rubbed his jaw. "You saw me? Doing what?"

"Walking down that street, looking shifty. I underestimated you, it seems. You're a little tinker. But how did you get inside? Pretending to be one of the players! Brilliant!"

Vance said: "I've got a very bad feeling. Listen carefully. Suppose the arena is *this* city. Our city."

"Why should that be the case? It's a game."

"Because we belong in it. Not as we were, but now. Look, we've made a dubious assumption. We thought the gladiators would be fa-miliar to us. From books and films. Ludke, Haarmann, Kürten, and the others. We thought we knew the worst. But they were the ones for whom there was evidence. A charter of *named* killers. Even when they were never caught, their crimes finally exposed them. Our list . . ."

"Was wrong? You mean we lacked the right data? Perhaps we did.

What does that mean? That the worst criminals of the twentieth century remain anonymous? That they were too slippery for the law? So all bets are off? Is that why you're depressed? Because the players are unknown? But it'll be educational to learn who they were."

Vance trembled. "Incapable of being known."

"Incapable? That's nonsense."

"Shadows. Not human. Why did we assume the worst were human? You've finished us, Floyd! Think of all those missing people, the violations we weren't even aware of. Deeds in the spaces between our blinks, behind or beneath our senses. Unrecognised."

Floyd turned, the side of his knee knocking over a chair. "You mean creatures? Like the maggot or wasp?"

"No, those were men. Future men. Something else. What did he say to us? The men won. We share our planet with a different genus of evil. Not human. Maybe not shadows. They can't be seen. That's why there's nothing on the screen except empty streets."

Floyd spat. "We can't bet on intangibles!"

"No, but what are the odds for us? Don't you see? By inventing this contest in this arena, we've arranged the deaths of all but one of those things. That's big. It means we're eligible too. We've both scraped onto the list. We're part of the game."

"The hundred worst of the *twentieth* century, remember? Midnight has gone. This is the twenty-first . . ."

"You gave your permission just prior to midnight, Floyd. You signed their death warrants inside the specified century. Perhaps to the maggot that counts as murder. A strict, sublime law. Yes, it's true. It must be right. The real list includes us."

"Must be a way out of this. A technical loophole. There was never a year zero. Doesn't the next century really start in 2001? We'll use that as the basis of an appeal. There's still a year to go before the change. Somebody or something might outdo us in time. They can't begin the game yet. It's not fair. Not balanced."

"People don't think like that. It's accepted that the year 2000 is the start of the twenty-first century. And that maggot was a person. The future must have sanctioned our standards, our error. Indeed, if it *is* a standard, then it's not an error."

"But midnight hasn't come everywhere. The world has to complete its axial spin first. What if somebody in the west, say America,
sneaks in a last atrocity or two? Pushes us off the list, I mean. Then
we're sure to be swapped, removed from the arena."

"A slim hope. You may keep it."

Floyd said quietly: "Lock the door, will you?"

Vance did so. It was probably his imagination that made him hear
a sound on the stairs outside.

They sat on chairs with their knees touching. They waited. They
had passed into another century not in a time machine but in a lonely
party. Not unique enough to mark them out as sufficiently different
from other men. But there *was* a special fact about them. Alone among
the humans of this city, the old century had made false promises about
its successor. The sum of its decades, not a gun, but not a knife, was a
liar. Because something else was true for them.

The new century was already over.

Acknowledgements

"The Swinger," first published in *Dark World*, edited by Timothy Parker Russell (Tartarus Press, 2013).

"Bitter in Sour," first published in *Dark Doorways*, edited by Eric Beebe (Prufrock Press, 2006).

"The Old House Under the Snow," first published in *Postscripts* #2 (2004).

"Rediffusion," first published in *Never Again*, edited by Joel Lane and Allyson Bird (Gray Friar Press, 2010).

"Casimir the Converter," first published in *The Brothel Creeper* by Rhys Hughes (Gray Friar Press, 2011).

"The Hydrothermal Reich," first published in *Bernie Herrmann's Manic Sextet*, edited by Gary Fry (Gray Friar Press, 2005).

"Life and the Plumbline," first published in the limited-edition issue of *A New Universal History of Infamy* by Rhys Hughes (Night Shade Books, 2004).

"The Unsubtle Cages," first published in *A New Universal History of Infamy* (Night Shade Books, 2004) (falsely attributed to Thomas Ligotti).

"The Century Just Gone," first published in *Darkness Rising* #2 (2001).

All other stories are previously unpublished.

www.ingramcontent.com/pod-product-compliance
Lightning Source LLC
Chambersburg PA
CBHW061438030726
47503CB00005B/1464